When the Light Fades

KATHY
RODGERS

POOLBEG

Also by Kathy Rodgers

It Started with a Wish

Afterglow

Misbehaving

About the Author

Kathy Rodgers lives in Longford with her two sons. Her novels *Misbehaving, Afterglow* and *It Started with a Wish* were national bestsellers. Currently she is working on her next novel. She has also written the final chapter of *Goldsmith's Ghost*, a novel which involved ten writers from three different counties in Ireland (Longford, Westmeath and Roscommon) and was published in 2002.

Published 2006
by Poolbeg Press Ltd.
123 Grange Hill, Baldoyle,
Dublin 13, Ireland
Email: poolbeg@poolbeg.com

© Kathy Rodgers 2006

The moral right of the author has been asserted.

Copyright for typesetting, layout, design
© Poolbeg Press Ltd.

1 3 5 7 9 10 8 6 4 2

A catalogue record for this book is available from the British Library.

ISBN 1-84223-247-9
ISBN 978 1-84223-247-7 (From January 2007)

Typeset by Type Design in Berling 10.3/14.3
Printed by Litografia Rosés S.A., Spain

www.poolbeg.com

Acknowledgements

Once again I have to thank my editor Gaye Shortland for all her help and for giving me a laugh along the way. Thanks to Paula Campbell and her great team in Poolbeg for all their hard work. Thanks to my agent Dorothy Lumley for all her help. Thanks to all the booksellers who put *It Started with a Wish* on their shelves. A very special thank you to all those who bought a copy. I hope you enjoyed it.

Thanks to Eamonn for the title and to my family for all their help and encouragement.

Mary Carelton-Reynolds and all the staff at Longford Library have given me immense support and encouragement in my writing. Thank you for a terrific book launch and thanks to all the people that turned up! Thanks to Audrey who is always eager to meet for a coffee and discuss progress!

This book is for my sister Ann and her family – my way of saying thank you!

Last but not least, I couldn't forget two wonderful boys who brighten up every day: Shane and Kevin.

For Ann, Maeve, Áine, Kate and Thomas

Chapter One

September 2004

"Good morning, Castletown Arms Hotel, Laura speaking, how can I help you? Let me see . . . Yes, we do have rooms available on Friday and Saturday next . . . That is the 17th and 18th of September . . . Yes, there is a leisure centre, opening at seven . . . Breakfast is served until eleven . . . Can I put you on hold for a moment, sir?" A slight pause. "Mr Goodman – I have called Mrs Joyce – she'll be with you shortly to deal with your complaint . . . Look, maybe you'd like to wait in her office? Just go on in."

"Very well. I just hope she's not much longer . . ."

"*Mrs Joyce to reception, please, Mrs Joyce to reception . . .*"

In this case, the intercom was unnecessary. Mrs Joyce (that is, myself) was taking a deep breath and straightening her skirt just off reception, prior to entering, and had in fact overheard the closing part of the exchange between Laura and Mr Goodman.

Yes, Laura, yes, I found myself growling silently.

Already this morning I'd had to speak with Gina, a fiery redhead in self-service. She had blown a fuse with an irascible old lady who was part of a religious excursion to Knock which had suddenly descended on the hotel for tea, coffee, scones and whatever else took their fancy.

"Gina, you cannot be rude to customers. If this happens again," I braced myself for her inevitable reply, "I'm going to have to switch you to kitchen or bedroom duties."

"That's not fair, Mrs Joyce! You haven't even asked me about the abuse *she* dished out to *me*! Two busloads of Blessed Virgin fanatics drop in without any notice and they all expect to be served and seated instantly! And there's only me and Kevin on self-service this morning!" Gina tugged roughly at the strings of her apron. "It's not fair – I'm *leaving*!"

"Really, Gina, there's no need for that. She might be an old cow but it's not her fault that the bus company didn't let us know. I'll talk to them and ask them for their schedule, make sure we're better prepared next time."

"I can tell you their schedule! We'll be plagued with surprise visits till the end of September, when these old fanatics go to ground. Catch them with their rosary beads at Knock or climbing Croagh Patrick in November? No way! They'll be waiting for the end of Mass in their heated churches so they can gather and gossip about the latest unmarried mother in their neck of the woods, the bitches!"

"Okay, okay, Gina, you've made your point – there's no need to leave. We need you here – you're doing a great job. Look, we'll talk later, if you want."

God, I found myself thinking, is this where I imagined myself when I was in my teens? Hannah Joyce, hotel owner, groveller to hotel staff and customers alike. Well, not quite owner . . .

Now I walked towards the reception desk and Laura, with the phone pressed against her ear, pointed towards my office. She looked tired and I guessed her two-year-old son had her up half the night again. We exchanged knowing looks. Another difficult one. Best get the loud ones to a quiet place as quickly as possible or you'll get the domino effect: other people within earshot will decide you've spoiled their day too, and the merry-go-round will begin. A wink from Laura told me this one was male – goodness, how we had perfected the sign language over the years! However, I already knew who it was, thanks to my little bit of eavesdropping.

I went through the door of my office.

Murdoch Goodman stood with his back to me, apparently oblivious to my entrance. Six foot five, an orthopaedic double bed was his only requirement. Give him that and he would cope with anything else the unpredictable hotel trade could bring: rowdy rugby parties, singsongs – he would even get involved on rare occasions. Just that bed, though . . . what could have gone wrong?

"Ah, Mrs Joyce, Hannah," smiled Murdoch, turning suddenly. "I was just looking at your photos. I see David is still whacking the golf-balls. I'll have to try and get over early some day soon, win back that bet he won last time."

"Now, Murdoch, you know I'm not going to spend the morning talking golf to you." I found myself stiffening with resentment at the thought of *that* game. "Laura says you're upset about something – what can I do for you?"

Murdoch Goodman seemed like part of the hotel itself. Stayed two nights a week on average. In sales, he'd tell you.

Never said what precisely. No wedding ring and always alone. Always sober-suited with plain ties. Typical loyal company man, dependable, perhaps uninspiring.

"What can you do for me?" said Murdoch, his face and voice hardening suddenly. "It's a bit late for that. I pre-paid as usual for Room 50 earlier this week. Didn't get it, though. Room 48, single bed, it's not on, Hannah." He winced and rubbed his back vigorously.

"God, I'm sorry, Murdoch." I stifled a laugh at a sudden picture of this giant man with legs dangling from the end of a single bed.

"Yeah, so am I. It was even less fun when I heard giggling and squealing in Room 50 for half the night and me having paid for it!"

"Murdoch, I'm truly sorry. I can't imagine how that happened."

"The receptionist seemed a bit confused about the matter – could see my booking on the computer and seemed to think Room 50 should be free. However, there was no doubt but that it was very much occupied."

"Look, Murdoch, I'll look into the matter. And I promise you it won't happen again. Are you staying tonight?"

"No, I'm not – fortunately perhaps."

"Well, we won't charge you for your next stay. Unless you'd prefer a refund?"

"No, no, next time will be fine," said Murdoch, softening to a smile once more. "You don't have anything for a sore back in the meantime, though?"

"Actually, I do. I can ring Helen in the gym. She does hot-stone, Indian massages . . . you name it." I felt proud at my sudden inspiration. "The treatments usually cost between fifty and eighty-five euros. We'll arrange this one free of

4

charge – our apology, sort of, for spoiling your night's sleep."

"I won't take you up on that today – time beckons. I'll have to suffer on until the next time round. Yes, I suppose that's fair enough. Free bed next time around and my wounds healed free of charge. That should keep us out of court. Thank you."

With a smile, he left – off to flog something undesirable to some poor unsuspecting individual. Getting up each morning and heading off somewhere new – the idea really appealed to me. Instead I was trapped here in "the dungeon", which was what Sammi and Timothy called my office. David had agreed to convert an old storeroom for me when the penny eventually dropped that we were spending most of our time trying to out-shout each other over the phone in his little nest.

So, there you had it if you stood at reception and viewed the adjacent offices in the background: three solid oak doors, one labelled in gold plating *Mr David Joyce, Hotel Owner/Manager*, the others *Mr Desmond Feeney, Assistant Hotel Manager* and *Mrs Hannah Joyce*. No title for Hannah. In a fit of pique at this slight, I had hired an interior-design consultant to maximise space, light and comfort in my miserable little cubby-hole. "Isn't the master's piece of crumpet entitled to some comfort in her anonymity?" I retorted, pointing fixedly at my door as David hyperventilated over the cost of the oak furnishings, recessed lighting and state-of-the-art equipment.

My computer hummed in the background and I reviewed the morning's events so far. Who put a guest in Room 50 last night? Nobody, according to the computer on my desk. For later investigation. Whoever was responsible would pay dearly.

I looked around the office, and my eyes paused momentarily at the painting of the Castletown Arms. The artist's signature was invisible from where I sat but her aura and presence continued to hang powerfully in my little room. Eunice Jones. God, yeah, I had sat beside her all those years ago, fascinated at the emerging tapestry of colour and light and shade while she worked. She'd be past ninety now – went up west to live with a niece. I felt a sudden pang of guilt. It was Eunice who gave me a feel for art. Without her, my own modest paintings would never have made it to the atrium of our local theatre. I had the niece's phone number, somewhere. How long was it since I had painted? Maybe ten, fifteen years?

"Don't get sentimental, Hannah," I whispered to myself.

At least I'd won the battles with David over the years to preserve the exterior of the hotel – it was still exactly as Eunice had painted it. Bringing in the conservationists was a bit mean but there comes a time to make a stand. The inside was all changed and I closed my eyes to imagine a past vision of the cosy open fires, the nice formality of dining-room service only. Thoughts of playing hide and seek in the old bedrooms with Cormac brought me suddenly back to the present.

My brother Cormac, drunk and boisterous in the bar again last night. His usual insulting self once you put a glass in his hand.

Dad, you should have seen it coming – you didn't think of the trouble you'd cause when you made that will.

The phone rang suddenly.

"Hi," I said.

"Hi, how's it going down there? Nothing out of control that needs a man's hand, is there?"

"Nothing that I can't handle. How did your golf outing go?"

"Fine, stopped off at the club bar for a few pints after. Did you not hear me come in? Listen, I'll be down there in an hour. See you then."

The phone went dead.

That was David. David Joyce. My husband and father to my stepdaughter Sammi, now twenty-seven, and my son Timothy, nineteen. I felt a resentment starting to rise when I remembered how, all too easily, he'd persuaded me to do the Sunday morning shift. Sunday was the day after the night before when David donned his lads-only hat. Eighteen holes of golf in the afternoon, and the round got replayed endlessly in the bar afterwards, with different results imagined.

Sunday is also the day when customers have loads of time to complain, I reflected acidly. Stop yourself right there, Hannah – David works bloody hard, he really does.

I looked at our wedding photo on the wall and closed my eyes to draw down the past . . .

Chapter Two

October 1981

"Hannah, come over here, meet David Joyce." My mother was perched regally at reception. Her blonde hair was newly styled as usual; she was dressed elegantly and was wearing her hostess smile. "Welcome home, dear!" She greeted me with her usual hug. "David is our new manager – he started last Monday."

Immediately, I sensed that something significant had changed. I did a quick mental inventory of past managers, reaching deep into my childhood. Dad always went for solid, obedient types that would not challenge him and would allow him to continue ruling the roost. Caretaker was a better description for what he usually hired: someone who would mind the house safely while he was away and not have too much changed when he came back. Mr O'Boyle, Mr Flanagan – middle-aged men winding down from more hectic establishments or nearly-made-its who had resigned

8

themselves to accepting that their big chance had passed them by. This one was clearly different, I thought, suddenly conscious that I was a walking advertisement of my student status – wet – rucksack in place – dishevelled. Your timing, Mammy – you could've at least collected me at the station . . .

"Hello, I'm pleased to meet you, Hannah."

"Pleased to meet you, David," I said, feeling the firm warmth of his handshake and the directness of his gaze. Five eleven. What was this with me always guessing men's heights? David Joyce looked mid-twenties with the naturally curly black hair that some women pay fortunes to acquire in hair salons. His twinkling brown eyes compensated for a jaw that was firm and hard-set. Ambition, I thought automatically. That's what that is. Yeah, nice . . . I blushed suddenly, aware that he was waiting patiently for me to give him back his hand.

"Hannah is in St Pat's in Dublin, studying to be a primary school teacher," my mother volunteered. "Look at you, Hannah, I bet you've been living on coffee and crisps all week. Off to the kitchen with you now – Pascal will give you something to fatten you up."

Dismissed. As usual. Sometimes I wished my parents had nine-to-five jobs. The hotel was their gem, the children being the add-on trinkets. Cormac and me. I wondered what Cormac thought about the new manager, but that would have to wait. Nine o'clock Friday night – no self-respecting hellraiser would wait around until now for sister's monthly visit. I'd bring him breakfast in bed tomorrow – he'd fill me in then.

Five minutes later I was in the little staff dining room just off the kitchen, munching away on the roast beef dinner Pascal had expertly conjured up for me. Good old Pascal. Never let me down.

What's with Dad and this young fellow? I wondered. He

9

doesn't look like he'll be anybody's caretaker. Was Dad going to ease off at last, like Dr Breslin recommended years ago after his heart attack? But Dad of course knew more than the doctors.

Roast beef consumed, I went to the staff fridge to check out the dessert situation. Bowl of fresh fruit salad in hand, I swung around – and let the bowl go crashing to the ground, startled by the sight of a little girl, right there, staring up at me.

"Look what you made me do!" I yelled somewhat childishly. "Children are not allowed in the kitchen! What are you doing here?"

I grabbed her by the arm and ushered her hastily towards reception.

"Let me go, let me go, you're hurting my arm! Daddy, Daddy!"

My mother and David Joyce came rushing out from the bar.

"Ouch . . . you little bitch!" I yelled as she sank her teeth into my wrist. "I found her prowling around the –" I broke off.

She was now nestling in David's embrace, staring outwards at me with ferocity. Her glossy dark curls bobbed as she started to sob.

"It's alright, Sammi, it's alright," he was saying. "Have you been creeping up on people again?"

"His daughter," mouthed Moira silently from the reception desk.

David continued whispering softly to the child, wiping her tears and smoothing back her curls. "Could you excuse me, Mrs Duignan? I'll take Sammi back to the house. She's had her share of excitement for today."

"I'm sorry, I didn't realise, if I had known," I gabbled. Little vixen, I thought, rubbing my tender wrist.

I was surprised to find myself suppressing a feeling of disappointment that David Joyce was "spoken for".

Chapter Three

I woke up the following morning and opened the curtains to look out at the gardens where I had spent most of my childhood years. My parents had pumped all of their energies into building up the hotel but that didn't stop my mother from being intensely house-proud when it came to our private dwelling. Jimmy O'Reilly, a keen local gardener, had arrived religiously every Wednesday morning for years to tend to these gardens with love and care.

I took some breadcrumbs outside to feed the birds. I looked up at the vast expanse of blue sky and was momentarily lost as I watched wispy white clouds sail by. The garden path wound down towards the area that myself and Cormac always liked to call "the woods". School holidays were long and uneventful and this was our secret hiding place. Mammy seldom came into "the woods" – she would just holler from the garden path, fearing the grubby soil would ruin her shoes. One summer we decided that we were going to make a tree-house. One that was big enough for us to live in. We had great plans until Cormac cut his hand with the saw and ended up having to go to Casualty. He was forbidden from continuing with the tree-house project. We rounded up a few friends to finish it off. Jimmy helped and only for him it would never have amounted to anything. Once it was completed, Cormac wanted to take it over – I fought my corner and told him that the tree-house was mine. Threatened to tell Mammy that he was using it for secret smokes. Thankfully, he tired of it quickly and it became a haven for my reading and drawing.

Now, "the woods" looked small – the tree-house had been blown down in a storm a few years before. A bird was nibbling on a cooking apple. Goodness knows the number of pies that were made in the hotel from the same trees. I cried when we had to cut down some of the bigger ones but we had little choice. The architect had pointed out the cracks in the house foundations and the only solution was to uproot my beautiful trees. Apart from my mother, the rest of the household seemed impervious to the charms of the garden and it was thus that I came to call it "mine" – my home from home.

Back inside, I filled a vase with freshly cut flowers. At least they didn't take these away, I thought. Jimmy would turn in his grave if he were to witness the ruthless culling of nature.

Movement upstairs suddenly interrupted my thoughts. Twelve noon. That would be Cormac. My parents were well into work at the hotel by now. Couldn't Dad at least have dropped into my bedroom to say hello? Couldn't my mother come home and make enquires as to how my studies were progressing?

"We're doing this to secure your futures," Dad had said from behind a washing machine at the hotel laundry when I complained that other children were having more fun than us.

The toilet flushed and the door of Cormac's bedroom slammed loudly.

He's not coming down, I mused. I'd better go up or I'll be back in Dublin without meeting any of my family.

"Coffee," I said to the heap beneath the blankets.

Cormac sat up, his long dark hair momentarily covering his eyes. He had a Hugh Grant sort of look about him. Smug, good-looking, charming and I had known women to call him sexy but goodness knows how they could say that about him. He smelt of stale alcohol and tobacco. Well, what did I expect?

Cormac was the major disappointment of my dad's otherwise carefully constructed world.

"Twenty-four years old!" Dad raged to Mammy on my last visit. "Twenty-four and his sole possessions are his Yamaha 750 bike and a blonde hussy from a County Council housing estate. He'll be out of this house as well as the hotel someday soon!"

"Don't go getting worked up," Mammy replied. "You know what Dr Breslin told you."

Now Cormac peered blearily at me. "Hiya, sis . . . what's new? Did you bring up any toast?"

"No, I'll do some in a minute. Here, take this."

He took the mug and grimaced as he sipped.

"Tell me," I said without any preamble, "I see we've got a new manager at the hotel. A David Joyce. In his mid-twenties, I'd say?"

"He's more than that. Thirty, I think. Dad's surrogate son. Came with good references. Dad hasn't stopped drooling about him since he came. It's enough to make you puke. You'd think you needed something special to run their precious hotel – sure it pretty much runs itself."

"Where's your bike?"

"Oh, I dropped by at the hotel on my way home last night – and the Ayatollah insisted that I leave it there. He wasn't going to bail me out of a police station. As if." Cormac was in full flow by now, really enjoying feeling sorry for himself. "Your man, the new manager, he's a widower with a brat of a girl tagged on. Dad is paying him two thousand pounds a year more than the last man *and* has given him the house behind the hotel rent-free. Never gave a minute's thought to the fact that the house was my crashing-out spot after I cleared the stragglers from the after-hours functions. Typical of Dad to show no appreciation. I'm through with busting my butt for that man."

That was as much as I would get out of Cormac over the weekend. An account of his woes. I had to side with Dad on this one, but a younger sister lecturing her brother was not the cure. Besides, soon I would be back in Dublin, completing assignments for the coming week.

"I'll get you that toast," I said, rising from the corner of the bed.

Chapter Four

In secondary school, Mrs Smith had said that I had the qualities that made a good teacher: a love of children along with a sense of fairness. These arbitrary judgments were career guidance in its infancy at secondary schools and swayed many an impressionable young person towards the wrong road. I was lucky – I absolutely loved my time at the Drumcondra college.

I had studied hard in secondary school and got enough points to get into college. Of course my parents objected – they wanted me to study hotel management. I refused and was mildly surprised that my parents didn't persist with it. I went to St Pat's, slightly anxious but pleased to get away and forge my own way in the world.

On the second or third day I got talking to Brenda on the way to the canteen. Brenda was a petite girl with short curly brown hair and a mischievous giggle that I had heard swell into something more boisterous while she was in conversation with other students. I knew she'd be good fun to be around. She lived within walking distance of St Pat's and the only thing that tinged her otherwise happy life was the fact that she still lived at *home*. Brenda loved Irish, my weakest subject. "I'll give you a hand with it," she offered the first day we met. In our second year, we got a flat together just across the road from the college. Our flat became popular with a constant flow of human traffic to and from it.

We spent many a late night together both partying and studying.

I started to keep a journal the week after I had met David, when Brenda bemoaned the fact that all we'd have in years to come was fading memories of these halcyon days. Well, I was going to keep them alive and a trip to Eason's the following day marked the birth of a ritual for Hannah Duignan. In a state of drunken melancholia the following night, I surveyed my first entry in the famous book.

24/10/1981

Dear Journal ~

I hope we are going to be friends and that I can trust you. You see, I'm going to be telling you lots of things from now on and I want them to be our secrets. I'm in my bedroom ~ I had to get away from the shower downstairs ~ why is it always our house that has these parties? Ray ~ whatsisname? ~ Wheatley was knocking on my door just there now ~ thinks he can get into my drawers just because he bought me a pint of Harp in Foley's tonight. I saw the Durex among his loose change as he fumbled at the bar. Prick. Too stupid to see that nobody gives a shit

16

*about his "expertise" in "matters genetic" ~ "everyone should
check their family history for longevity, baldness, sagging boobs"
~ crap! Ray, knock as loudly as you like, you're not getting in!*

*Brenda thinks it's very funny me writing to you. She wrote
on your cover: The Chronicles of Hannah Duignan ~ The Story
of the Country Virgin Who Came to Dublin. Thinks she's
funny just because I won't let these juvenile mammys' boys into
my pants. She won't laugh when my biography, no, my
autobiography is a bestseller.*

*Now, David Joyce wouldn't be puking his guts up outside
Foley's, would he? Pity he has that spoiled brat of a daughter ~
not a word to her when she nearly bit my hand off. Fuck you,
Mr Joyce! It's just that I'm tipsy and again there's no talent
about ~ I wouldn't be thinking about you if there was something
decent downstairs.*

Bye for now,
Hannah

I'm going to write down the place and the day each time
I write in the journal again, I thought drunkenly. Then, I'll
know, be able to track back . . . this one is in Drumcondra
and it's a Thursday.

* * *

My thoughts returned to Castletown frequently that
week. Mostly, my visits were just token ones, as my parents
were too busy and Cormac, well, was just Cormac.
Generally, though, I returned from my visits with my purse
a little heavier through Dad's generosity. Two weeks in a
row, though . . . I wondered what it was like to be a young
widower with a daughter . . .

Chapter Five

"Hannah!" boomed a loud voice from the hotel bar. "Come over here, will ya? I want you to meet Councillor Nugent. He's helping me with my planning appeal. What has you home again this week, girl? Run out of money? Ha ha!"

Frank Duignan. Standing at the bar counter, silver hair oiled back. He wore a tailored dark suit, white shirt and conventional tie, with a tiepin. He never wore casual clothes, always dressed for business.

Frank had gone to London penniless, worked on the building-sites for years and came back to buy the local hotel in his hometown. Businessman, entrepreneur, friend of all people political. My dad.

"I know Councillor Nugent, Dad – and you shouldn't be drinking brandy. Look at the colour of your face –"

"Ah, away with ya! I've a woman at home who does enough of that scolding. Anyway, I am taking *some* of your advice, lightening the load. Did you see our new manager – great lad, I can feel the weight lifting already."

"Eh . . . yeah, I met him last week . . . Is he on duty tonight?"

"That's the great thing, he's *always* on duty. Lives on the grounds. Has a young daughter. I was doubtful about that at first, but it turns out to be a bonus. Never leaves her alone at night and is always at hand if there's a problem."

I made my excuses and left as I didn't want to hear it all again. Same conversation. Different politician. The County Council. An Bord Pleanála. The local begrudgers. How he'd never vote Fianna Fáil again after Pat Mulcahy let him down – the free drinks and meals – the crook! Dad had applied for planning permission to extend the hotel and it seemed to be dragging on since I entered secondary school. At one point, in a fit of pique after losing his latest battle, he bought a local Bed & Breakfast establishment to handle the occasional overflow of guests from the hotel. Quite simply, he did not want anyone else to have it. It was the job of the Duignans to cater for your accommodation needs in Castletown. Once bought, he passed the responsibility of running it to Mary Drake, who had come as breakfast cook to the hotel before I was born. A pang of guilt rose within me. Mary was more than that. My baby-sitter, protector from Cormac's wanton teasing, confidante and comforter during troubled teenage years. I really must visit –

"Hello, there. Home again?"

I turned to face David Joyce. The square lines of his jaw seemed to have relaxed slightly. Immaculately presented, lean frame. A subtle hint of a recently showered man as he stood a little closer. He must be settling in.

"Well, yeah – Dad hasn't been well lately, must keep an

19

eye on him. How is Sammi?"

"She's fine – you just got off to a bad start last week. Forgotten about it already."

An uneasy silence descended. David stood there in his well-pressed navy suit, white shirt and sharp maroon tie. Did his wife ever wear a T-shirt and faded jeans, I wondered while pausing to consider my own attire. How did she die?

"Would you like me to tell Pascal to fix something for you to eat?"

"Thanks, but I can go and ask him myself . . . It's no problem."

Reluctantly I left him.

* * *

After eating, I wandered outside, taking in the surrounds of the hotel for the umpteenth time. The light was on in David's house and the sounds of children's nursery rhymes wafted through an open window. I peered through an opening in the curtains. A little girl. A Barbie doll. Must be lonely, I thought. I knew the feeling well . . . even when your mammy *is* alive . . .

I retraced my steps to the hotel.

"You staying the night, then?"

I jolted in alarm, jettisoned from my private thoughts.

David again.

He laughed apologetically. "It's not just Sammi – it's a family trait – creeping up on people."

"It must be. No, I'm waiting on Mammy to come in and drive me home – Dad's drinking, so she'll be collecting him."

"Your dad's not going home tonight, Hannah. He's

entertaining the politicians and has reserved a room for himself. I don't think your mother is coming in. Come on, I'll take you."

"Ah, no – it's okay, I'll get reception to ring me a taxi –"

"No, you don't need to."

"What about Sammi?"

"Mary Drake from the B&B is with her right now. She'll stay with her until I get back."

David eased his car out into the night at the edge of town. I wondered to myself what he thought of Castletown. The name no longer applied, really, as the old castle in the town centre lay in ruins. It was a listed building, however, and the conservationists often spoke of restoring it to its former glory. Talk, but no money.

"I believe you're a good tennis player." He smiled at my suspicious face. "Don't worry, I'm not spying on you. Your mother told me. You know, proud parents and all that."

"You'll probably know the name I took for Confirmation so."

"Not quite, but she was getting there . . ."

I grimaced as I imagined my mother's outpourings. Always talking about her children but rarely to them. Maybe she should pin my story of achievement on the hotel notice board. Then everybody would know, save her vocal chords . . .

"Is this a Ford Granada?" I asked, anxious to divert the spotlight from myself.

"Yes. I didn't buy it though. The last place I worked gave it to me in lieu of money owed. Partly why I left, free house, free food, free car, nanny for Sammi and nothing but excuses when my bonuses were due."

"You're probably passing through here, too. You'll have

21

your sights on a big city hotel, your own place maybe?"

"Well, yeah . . . at least I had until . . . " his voice trailed away. "Tennis," he said suddenly. "I'm not so bad myself. How about tomorrow afternoon? I'll give you a game?"

"Okay." God, where's your resistance, Hannah Duignan?

"I'll book us for three o'clock, then. Now here's your stop."

Impressive, knows where I live and familiar with the local clubs already.

He pirouetted the Granada to face outward from the house.

"Thanks for the lift," I said.

"You're welcome." We locked eyes momentarily in the dark of the car. "See you tomorrow, then. Bye."

I got out.

"Bye, David," I whispered softly as the lights of his car disappeared into the distance. The only sound I heard was the crunch of my feet on the gravel as I walked up the drive. I opened the front door with my key. The house seemed eerily quiet.

"Is that you, Cormac?" My mother's shrill voice came down the stairs to greet me.

"No, it's me, Hannah!" I shouted up.

I felt a private tingle of excitement. I was meeting David tomorrow. Was this a date? I wanted to talk to someone about it but years of keeping my own counsel stopped me from rushing up the stairs and into my mother's bedroom to share my news.

* * *

"Aagh, dammit," David groaned as another point went sailing by his despairing dive.

I walked back towards the serving area with a grin of

quiet satisfaction on my face. Mammy had probably done her share of boasting, but she didn't need to exaggerate my tennis. I was an international competitor for my secondary school and losing finalist at the National Community Games in Mosney and you had to be very good to get that far.

David had arrived in polo shirt and shorts – he looked boyish, almost younger than my original estimate.

I wasn't prepared for the surprise in the rear seat. Sammi. Silent. Glowering.

"Mary has guests at the B&B. Couldn't oblige," said David.

Momentarily, I felt anger that I wasn't asked if I minded. This was quickly replaced by self-admonishment for my selfishness and admiration for David. He was not going to apologise for having his daughter along. They were a package deal. You took both or else . . .

"Six-two, six-one . . . you thrashed me!" he moaned. "I should have listened to your mother."

His tennis gear was bathed in sweat. His competitiveness was no match for a schools international competitor.

"Nice legs, though," I taunted.

"Whose?"

"Yours."

"Eh . . . okay . . . will you be coming down next weekend?"

"I will."

"Sure we'll pack up, then. I'll meet you at the car in ten minutes – after a shower."

"See you then. I'll take care of Sammi."

Sitting in the car, I felt somewhat hot and uncomfortable. Hurry up, David. It's not nice when you feel someone's eyes boring a hole in your back.

"You're not my mammy," she said to break the still silence in the car.

23

Chapter Six

"You're going back to Castletown again, this weekend!" exclaimed Brenda. "What's got into you, girl? There was a time you couldn't wait to get out of the place!"

"It's Dad . . . he hasn't been well lately, since his heart attack."

"Uh huh, okay. It's just that you're missing the gig in Wexford Street. Scope are playing – don't you remember them from the last time?"

"I do . . . you and the drummer, then trying to match me off with the bass guitarist. You'll have to count me out on this one."

"Your loss, I've given up on you – you're wasting the best years of your life."

* * *

24

"Hello, Hannah, dear," said Mammy from the manager's chair in the office. "Your dad and David have joined up with the Castle Restoration Committee. They're at a meeting in the community centre right now. They always run late."

"I see. I think I'll run on home, Mammy. Is Cormac out there?"

"I haven't seen Cormac since Tuesday. Another bust-up with your dad. Will we ever see an end to it?"

"Can't answer that, Mammy . . ."

* * *

Saturday passed uneventfully. I loitered around the town, popping into the hotel on several occasions. Eventually, Moira at reception spoke up: "Mr Joyce was called away suddenly this morning, Hannah. He's gone for the weekend."

My face went beetroot red with embarrassment and annoyance – at Moira for her keen observation and David for spoiling my weekend.

* * *

"Will you get that knock on the door, Brenda? I'm up to my neck in assignments. It's probably for you anyway."

Brenda had been wafting on air since Saturday – "got it on" with the drummer were her words. I wasn't going to ask for a detailed explanation of what that meant. Force of habit made me warn her to be careful but there was no need – she was on the pill. She didn't consider herself promiscuous – her definition of that was someone who gave in on the first night – but hell, she was a woman and she was going to use what God gave her while she was young enough. Occasionally she mocked me for my morals but never in a really belittling way.

I heard voices in the hallway.

Then Brenda at the sitting-room door.

"It's someone for you, Hannah. Says his name is David – David Joyce."

There was nothing I could do but look up from my textbooks and gape at the door. I really would have appreciated a phone call to say he was in Dublin. My hair was greasy and I was wearing my worst pair of jeans. I met his direct gaze as he sauntered in.

"Would you like to sit down?" Brenda asked, clearing some stuff off the single armchair.

With a quick glance David surveyed our shabby sitting room. "I thought I might take you two girls out for a drink?"

"Oh, thanks, but count me out," said Brenda. "I've had more than my share of late nights – but Hannah here, she could do with a break from all this studying. Couldn't you, Hannah?"

* * *

"Gin and tonic, please."

David went to the bar of the Gresham Hotel, while I struggled to control my emotions in a quiet corner booth. What neck! And I hadn't the guts to turn him away.

What's got into you, Hannah Duignan? I said feebly to myself. He's a widower, at least nine years older than me if Cormac's got it right, and with a child from Hell who's made her feelings clear . . .

David returned. I tried to sound normal, detached. "So you're up for a meeting of the Irish Federation of Hoteliers tomorrow? Dad is surely letting go – he wouldn't miss those meetings for love nor money until now."

"Your dad has the vision and dreams of a young man, Hannah. Says he needs a young 'suit' to talk up these officials in Bord Fáilte and that. He feels more comfortable topping up the glasses of your TDs and councillors."

"Don't I know it?" I felt angry with Cormac immediately. How often had Dad laid his plans out on our kitchen table while Cormac eyed them disinterestedly? "Are you listening to me, son?" he'd shout, his face red with frustration. Occasionally, he would thump the table and sometimes Mammy had to separate them when Dad just lost it completely. Now, here I was in the company of a stranger who would push the dream forward, with Cormac on the outside.

Where did I fit in?

But I found myself forgetting Cormac over gin and tonics, with Guinness for David and easy conversation as the night progressed. His eyes lit up especially when Sammi's name came up.

"She misses her mum, Hannah," he said suddenly.

"What happened to her, David?" I asked with some trepidation. "I mean, if you don't want to talk about it . . ."

"No, it's okay. Claire was her name. It happened nearly three years ago. Car crash – she hit a tree."

I could see that he was struggling so it was time for a change of subject. "Gosh, it's midnight. I really fancy some fish and chips. How about you? My treat."

"You're on – I could do with something to eat."

We collected our food from a takeaway on the

Drumcondra Road and made our way back to the flat.

In the quiet of the sitting room, I suddenly felt David's fingers toying with the blonde curls that hung round my neck. It was so calm, spontaneous. I found myself kissing him urgently as he lay back on the couch. My bra was unhooked expertly and I felt warm hands, then lips, caress and tingle my breasts.

"David, aahh, David, please don't go any farther . . . You're driving me mad . . . We've just met, I . . ."

"It's okay, Hannah, it's okay."

We lay there for about an hour just wrapped in each other's arms.

Suddenly, David got up.

"Time to go, Hannah. I took a room in the Gresham for tonight . . . earlier I was tempted to ask you to stay over, but I thought it might be . . ."

"You'd have been right, David Joyce." I wondered if he picked up on the lack of certainty in my voice.

"You'll be down at the weekend, then?"

"Yes."

Chapter Seven

My parents appeared not to notice my weekly returns to Castletown or if they did they were not letting on. Cormac was oblivious to it all: – he was spending most of his nights with Louise – the "hussy from the County Council housing estate" – to the continued disgust of our father.

"That blonde hussy is dragging him down to her level," Dad would say.

Mammy would sit there silently, neither protesting nor agreeing.

Christmas and New Year arrived and David was intensely busy. It was hard for us to snatch some time alone together and most of that was in his spacious Ford Granada. Our petting was becoming more intense and David always had to wipe the steamed-up windows of his car after our sessions.

"You can't keep me out much longer, Hannah Duignan," David gasped on Valentine's Night as I brought a halt to a particularly sweaty session in a laneway near our house.

"I can. I'm not doing it for the first time in your car and I'm certainly not doing it down at my parents' hotel. You're going to have to wait."

What David didn't know was that I also was aching for the day when it would happen for us.

But still I held out.

The days lengthened and we were moving into summer.

It was time to have a serious talk with Brenda.

"Geez, Hannah, he's a fine thing! I wouldn't kick him out of bed for eating crisps!"

My cheeks were hot with embarrassment, the result of a convent education. "Well, as I said, we haven't done it yet – and he's frantic – and I don't know how much longer *I'll* last before I explode. Now, about these condoms –"

"Ahh, don't go for rubbers, Hannah! They take most of the joy out of it. I can give you the name of my doctor and she'll put you on the pill. About time, too – I began to think you were one of those boring girls that want to wait until the wedding night. You need to be on them a few weeks, though, so you'd need to make an appointment immediately."

"Okay. And thanks."

* * *

"Surprise!"

David jumped suddenly when I came up behind him in the hotel bar. It was Thursday and I had come home a day earlier than usual as we had no lectures on the Friday. David had turned up unannounced the previous week at my Drumcondra flat, armed with condoms and desperate. But, remembering Brenda's words, I sent the poor lad away unfulfilled once more. Cue some unmerciful teasing from

Brenda. She seemed to have an endless supply of tunes and songs about a girl's first night. Most recently, it was one by Kiki Dee.

"Hannah," he said somewhat formally, "great to see you. Look, I need to talk to you when I finish work. Will you stay around?"

God, this fucking hotel, I thought as I hung around waiting obediently. My parents were always consumed by it, Cormac resented it and David was reluctant to display his affection until he was a safe distance from the place. Coming up to Dublin with a hard-on was fine . . . Damn him, he won't be unhooking or unbuckling anything belonging to me this weekend . . .

"Great to see you," said David, wrapping his arms around me in the safe privacy of the hotel office.

My resentments ebbed, then melted away. "What was it you wanted to talk about?"

David shifted a little uncomfortably. "Look, Hannah, your dad asked me only yesterday to represent him at a Bord Fáilte conference in Donegal. It runs over the weekend – Saturday and Sunday. I'm going up tomorrow night . . . I was about to ring you, to, eh, ask you to come with me . . ."

"Gosh, David, I'd like to . . . I'd love to . . . but a hotel conference . . . Dad's colleagues in the trade . . . I don't know."

"Your dad knows about us, Hannah. Tackled me about it. I told him quite clearly that I worked for him but I'd be out of the place in no time if he made any attempt to control my love life. He seemed to back off hastily."

He would, I thought silently. I could imagine Dad admiring David's directness. "*Love life*" . . . those were David's words . . .

I conjured up mental pictures of some of Dad's trade colleagues leering and groping me in the past while under the influence of their favourite tipple. "Ah, pay no heed to him, love," Dad had said when I told him of Billy Grennan's lunge at me in the hotel bar. "The wife's just died – he's harmless behind it all. Kick him in the groin if he tries it again."

"Okay then – only, one thing: I'd prefer not to stay at the conference hotel."

"Thought you wouldn't," David replied. "I've made a booking at the Ostan Gweedore. It's outside Bunbeg and only a few miles from the conference centre. I'll be leaving at five o'clock tomorrow evening . . . It's a long journey, bad roads."

"I'd need to be getting home then, wouldn't I? A girl needs time to consider her wardrobe, doesn't she?"

"You won't . . . eh, come on, I'll take you home."

Chapter Eight

Bunbeg. Friday evening. The journey had passed quickly, David's Ford Granada cruising effortlessly along the roads. I looked over at him occasionally during our journey, wondering if he sensed the electricity I was feeling.

We arrived at the Ostan Gweedore with its spectacular view of the sea. This close to midsummer, the evening was still bright.

David completed the formalities of checking in while I surveyed the hotel interior. I followed the sign towards the Library Bar and immersed myself in examining the various titles on offer. This would be ideal to while away the time while the "suits" pontificated elsewhere about the state of the Irish hospitality trade.

David was back suddenly. "I've left our stuff in the room upstairs, ordered us smoked salmon and prawn salads and a bottle of wine. Had to act quickly as they were about to stop serving."

"That's perfect, but no wine for me – I just don't feel like it tonight."

"Eh, that's fine. I'll cancel it then – no alcohol for me either."

We ate our food quietly in the bar, looking out at the glittering sea.

Ignoring the barman's call for last orders we then made our way to the bedroom. Instinctively, I knew that two single beds would not greet me and I was right. A giant bed lay waiting in the dim lights that David had obviously activated when he had come up earlier.

There were few words. I was amazed at how calm I felt. Brenda had offered me a book – the *Kama Sutra* she called it. Every position possible, the only limits were your imagination and your upbringing, she said jokingly.

"No, Brenda," I had said firmly. "Thanks, but no thanks. When it happens, I want it to be *our* night – no place for gurus or gymnasts – it'll just be us: me and David."

That first night met all the idealistic dreams I'd had since I first became aware of my body as a teenager. I did not want my senses and memories of this night to be affected in any way – that was why even my favourite glass of white wine had been put on hold. Okay, I was not totally innocent but the adolescent fumblings in fields and darkened cinemas and sofas in student flats were all incidental as I waited for my time to come. This was it and I engaged on equal terms with David Joyce, man of the world, young widower, that night. God, I both took and gave! I found I could accommodate him easily while delirious with excitement at the feel of every inch inside. "Horse-riding and tennis – you'll be fine," Brenda had said when we discussed my fears earlier. She was right. There was no discomfort. It was as if my whole being was lit up and the apex of this burning inferno was where David was probing, thrusting, then thrashing until he eventually came to a shuddering halt.

"God bless us, Hannah Duignan, God bless us!" moaned David as he lay back in exhaustion.

"My first time, David . . . my first time . . ."

* * *

"What are you going to do today?" asked David as he fixed his tie in front of the wardrobe mirror.

I was lying on the bed, having woken David at half six for a repeat of the previous night. I wasn't letting him sleep while I lay awake, yearning for him to take me once more. This time slower, more tender but the lights burned brightly nonetheless. I smiled to myself as I remembered David's reaction last night when I threw his offered condom across the bedroom.

"I'm taking *you* in tonight, David Joyce, and nothing else!"

I must remember to pick up that condom, I thought suddenly.

"Are you not going to answer me?" he said.

"Sorry – you'll be at your conference until four o'clock. I'll have lots to do – explore, go down to the village. Give me a minute and I'll go down with you to see you off with breakfast."

* * *

I looked out at the clear blue expanse of Gweedore Bay stretching out towards the Atlantic from the hotel dining room. The sky was almost cloudless and I squinted to identify the merging point of water and heaven in the distance. The wreck of an old fisherman's boat stood at a tilt on the strand, somewhat like the Leaning Tower of Pisa. There was a haunting beauty to the place that attracted tourists in their droves. The families of local fishermen, however, would see the Atlantic in a different light – a dangerous beast their loved ones faced on a daily basis as they sought to eke out a living, sourcing fish from its waters. These waters had claimed the lives of many with a crushing all-powerful finality once the storms began to blow.

"Beautiful, but unpredictable, savage," said the breakfast waiter, noticing my focus on the vista in front of me. "My grandfather was lost to it when Dad was only five years old. Eight hundred lives were lost during the Second World War when a boat was torpedoed, right out there."

"I'm sorry. I guess it's more difficult to appreciate its beauty when it has snatched lives at will from so many. It looks so serene, so calm right now."

"Indeed. Do a week on Tory Island though, nine miles out, and you'll quickly accept you've never faced a storm before. As an alternative, you could catch the ferry from Burtonport to Arranmore Island if you're tempted. Not as wild and only twenty-five minutes by boat."

David was talking to the assistant manager at reception. I murmured in mock disapproval on his return: "You're not going to treat *all* of this as a working weekend, Mr Joyce? A girl might take offence and withdraw her favours . . ."

"This one's down to you, my little sex kitten. He's offered us a better room for tonight at no extra charge, looks out onto the sea." David gestured towards an elderly couple. "Our next-door neighbours last night. I think they complained about the noise . . ."

I noticed the old lady directing her gaze towards my hands, probably looking for something in the shape of a gold band that would enable her God to forgive me for my licentious sexual abandon.

Chapter Nine

I retreated to the Library Bar once David had departed to the conference in Dungloe. I was intrigued to come across *Christmas Eve*, a book of short stories by the Irish-American author Maeve Brennan who might have been the inspiration for Holly Golightly in Truman Capote's *Breakfast at Tiffany's*. I ordered myself the chilled glass of white wine that I'd deprived myself of the previous night. I felt a warm, reassuring glow within when I reflected back on my sexual initiation with David. The barman placed a small complimentary plate of cheeses before me and I nibbled away while thumbing through the book – my mind more consumed by the author's troubled life than the stories themselves.

By noon, I had finished off my second glass of white wine and I decided to phone Brenda from my hotel bedroom.

"Hello, Brenda, what's it doing up there?"

"Is that all you have to say? We all know what goes on in

Dublin, it never changes. You sound like the cat that got the cream. I want to hear it all, start to finish."

"None of your business, you nosey cow! I'm as virtuous as ever," I replied, giggling helplessly.

"I don't think! Jesus, you sound drunk as well and it's just gone midday. I'm telling you, you're a harlot, a jezebel and a lush as well!"

"Ah, I'm not really a lush – though I will be if I keep at it until David comes back. I think he's the special one for me, Brenda – pity about this Sammi though – she's a real pain – no, I'm being selfish, she's just a baby – I'll crack it with her yet. Listen, I'd better let you go, there's a knock on my door . . . see you Sunday night."

A young man in the trademark hotel uniform was at the door. He coughed apologetically. "I was sent up by the assistant manager to help you move to your new room, madam . . . Is it convenient right now?"

"No time like the present, Caoimhín," I said, eying his name badge. "It won't take long – we've travelled light."

Back in the foyer of the hotel, the receptionist provided me with details and phone numbers for various leisure activities. "Most people swear by a simple cycle up the coast road. You plan your own itinerary and are not dictated to by anyone as to how and when you get back. You can hire out a bike in the village."

* * *

Bunbeg
Saturday 19/06/82

Dear Journal ~

I'm here in the Ostan Gweedore waiting for David to return from his conference. I wasn't talking to you yesterday but I know you won't blame me. I've had the most wonderful experience: my first time to commit my body fully to a man's desires and it was fantastic. Perfect. Everything I could have wished it to be.

David is a wonderful lover. Funny the crazy unrelated thoughts that enter your head at the height of passion. Last night the western Shane flashed across my brain when we consummated our love. Alan Ladd, the gunslinger, is explaining to the disapproving mother: "A gun is merely a tool ~ only as good or as bad as the man that is holding it." I think you'll get my drift . . .

I was so euphoric this morning that I was kind of drunk by noon, but I've blown away the cobwebs since. I cycled down the coast road to Burtonport earlier and saw the ferry head off for Arranmore Island. Then cycled back past here through Falcarragh and up to Dunfanaghy as far as Horn Head ~ what a name and what a view! I had lunch at Arnold's Hotel in Dunfanaghy and another glass of white wine, my third for the day. Poor old Father Dempsey would consider me a "fallen woman" at this stage ~ with all this sex and alcohol he'd have me shipped off to the Magdalene Laundries.

There is so much beauty and yet sadness in this place. Almost every little village has been subject to some major disaster at the hands of the cruel sea. Imagine, Arranmore Island is only three miles from Burtonport, yet nineteen people making the crossing in 1935 ~ mostly young migrant workers returning from Scotland ~ lost their lives to a gigantic wave that smashed them to eternity against the rocks. I found myself staring at the old people down there today, wondering if some of them might be the brothers and sisters, even the parents, of those who perished, so young were some of the victims. I saw sadness in some eyes . . . I don't know, I'm rambling on like a historian but it's about me too, thanking God for what I've got right now.

I'm going to make love with David as soon as he gets back, I don't care what the catechisms say . . . I deserve my happiness . . . we do . . .

Bye for now,

Hannah

* * *

"Mmm, now, now, David Joyce, it is only gentlemanly to ask a lady if she wants to partake before taking advantage of her vulnerable situation."

Slowly, I had come awake to the sensation of fingers running up my knees under my dressing-gown, caressing me between my thighs.

Back from my cycle, I had undressed, showered and set about recording my memories until a deep sleep took hold.

"And does the lady wish to partake? I mean, I could shower first if you want me all Brut and deodorants."

"You'll do fine. I like your natural male smell . . . Come up here and show me what you've got for me . . . We can shower together afterwards."

* * *

"Table for two," the waiter in the Ocean Restaurant recited as he ceremoniously led us to our seats at a window looking out to the sea. I shuddered momentarily as I imagined once vibrant lives on the "leaning boat" that was now part-submerged in the rising tide.

"This is a five-course menu," groaned David aloud. "It's a

shame – there are some lovely dishes on it, but they stuffed us down at Dungloe today – I don't know if I'll be able."

"Why not have an aperitif, whet the appetite?"

"Good idea and I won't feel guilty about it seeing that the curfew on alcohol is broken."

"You noticed it . . . tasted it, I bet. Now are we going to order?"

Later we sat in the terrace outside the Silver Fox Bar watching the sunset.

David cleared his throat a few times before talking. "Hannah, I don't think I'll go down to Dungloe to the conference tomorrow. It's a right drag. Maybe we could do something here, go horse-riding, maybe scuba diving – I think you can do it out on Arranmore. What do you think? Have you dived before?"

"Yeah, in Majorca. Me and a few of the girls in college went there last year. Did two dives. I have a certificate somewhere."

"Good, that's what we'll do then. It'll wrap up the break and then we have to make tracks for home – that's a fairly hefty journey. Now, I don't know about you but I'm off to bed. Knackered . . . need to get the head down . . . you'll know the feeling," he said in a voice feigning disinterest.

"Sure if you're that bad, I'll just sit here and watch the sun disappear completely."

* * *

Drumcondra
Monday 21/06/82

Dear Journal ~

I'm back to talk with you again. David has just left. It's five in the morning. I should be trying to get some sleep but it's impossible ~ I can't do it, my head's in a spin. David has asked me to be his wife ~ I'm in shock ~ I want to be so much. I've said yes ~ sort of. I should be happy. I have no doubts but that it's the right thing for me but it's the fears, you see ~ the spectre of Claire has always hung in the background for me. I've tried to put his silence about her down to the fact that he's merely closed the book and moved on but I find myself rescuing complexity, intrigue, from this simple explanation.

We'll tell Sammi together, that's what we decided ~ I'll have to face that stare again ~ accusing, threatening.

We went on the boat to Arranmore yesterday ~ did our dives. It was something special, travelling among the fishes with someone you know. Not talking, but communicating nonetheless, occasionally touching.

God, his timing is strange. There I was afterwards, stumbling out of the sea in gigantic flippers and not so flattering bodysuit and he up and asks me. I didn't know what to say, tried to make light of it ~ "Help me off with this stuff first, for God's sake!"

I'm going to buy some packets of "sticky stars" in Eason's right away ~ maybe gold, red, green and black. I'll rate my days ~ brilliant, good, ordinary, bad ~ I'll be stamping my feelings as to how my day went. You don't mind, do you? I'll start with a gold for our weekend in Bunbeg.

I have to go now, get some sleep or I'll never be able for class today.

Bye for now,
Hannah

Chapter Ten

Over a year had slid by. I sat in David's car on the road back to Castletown, fingering my engagement ring resentfully. Sammi was playing with her dolls in the back. Mammy and Dad had organised a big do at the hotel. I couldn't really refuse as they had given me every support during my three years at St. Patrick's. All of Castletown needed to know that their daughter had graduated – there was simply no way out of that. For once, I found myself envying Brenda back in Dublin – her family would attend the formalities, okay, but this was going to be a night on the town with her co-graduates. God knows who would have her pants down later on but at least she was doing exactly as she wanted. It almost seemed purer.

"All right back there, Sammi?" I enquired softly.

"Yes, thanks, Hannah. Are you going to be a teacher at my school?"

"I doubt it. All the jobs are filled right now." I shuddered at the thought that I might end up teaching the offspring of childhood friends at St Emer's, mixing with teachers who'd taught me.

"I heard Mrs and Mr Duignan talking in the kitchen last night. She said he was to talk to Councillor Nugent immediately. He's on something . . . a committee . . . I didn't hear everything that was said . . . Daddy said it's bad manners to be listening in like that . . ." Sammi's small voice trailed away.

David smiled silently.

"The Board of Management of the school," I remarked bitterly. Damn my parents. Could they just not leave it? My future husband working for them, the site for a house that suddenly materialised once the engagement ring appeared. In their eyes, it was a foregone conclusion that I would be ensconced in the teacher's chair at St Emer's any day soon. When were they going to stop treating me like a trophy child – did I have to paint *"human being"* on my forehead? At least I'd won the battle over our wedding. David and I were having a private wedding in Mauritius. Just the two of us. Nobody else.

Cormac and Louise were huddled in an alcove of the hotel bar when I came in. He was drinking a pint of Guinness and there were, what, four empty pint glasses at the table. I sat down beside them in a show of solidarity – I knew he would be hurting today despite his bravado – he'd be thinking, this bitch is showing me up again. His scruffy jeans and Jimi Hendrix T-shirt were his protest at his own compromise in gracing us with his presence today. Cormac was very bright but he was paralysed into laziness by his conflict with Dad.

"Things don't just happen in life – you've got to make them happen": another of Dad's catchphrases that sailed past Cormac's ears as Dad continued his futile, fated struggle to mould his only son in his own image.

"Well, sis, congratulations," Cormac said, slurring slightly.

What would he be like later on?

"What a day for you, what a day – teacher's job nearly in the bag, soon to be married to Ireland's next PV Doyle, instant family, wow, I'm so glad for you!"

Louise giggled apologetically. "Congratulations, Hannah! Don't mind him, he's delighted for you – *we* are. Your engagement ring is lovely – let me make a wish on it."

"Go ahead."

She took my ring and made her wish.

I wondered what she wished precisely.

"So when are you getting married?" she asked.

"October the fourteenth, in Mauritius."

Sometimes I felt that Dad had got it all wrong. Louise's parents were decent, inoffensive people who'd got very few breaks in life and she mirrored them both. If only she could be more assertive with Cormac, the self-centred brat. If not, she would spend the rest of her life balancing the chips on his broad shoulders.

Dad was talking to Seán McGonigle, the school principal. "Hannah, come on out here, I want you to meet some of our guests. You know Seán from your own schooldays." Dad's face was flushed and he was holding a brandy glass in his hand. I had overheard Mammy offering to do the driving on the way back home from Dublin so he could go ahead and have "a few drinks" – but, no, he brushed her suggestion away – he had it all under control. Anyway, if something untoward were to happen, he knew people who could get him off the hook. Vaguely unpleasant memories of my early childhood filtered back . . . what were they . . . loud voices in the kitchen . . . something more . . . no, it wouldn't surface . . .

The voice of my old school principal interrupted my thoughts. "You were always going to make it, Hannah – you had that application, something your brother lacked. Congratulations."

I glanced at my watch. Eight thirty.

I'll have to last a little longer if only for Mammy's sake. Bring down the darkness, God, bring down the darkness.

* * *

I went home alone at midnight that night. David just could not escape Dad's attentions down at the hotel. Cormac had disappeared for a while – most likely to the Europa Tavern up the street where he could play pool and darts with fellow bikers – but only after accidentally dropping a tray of drinks upon poor Mrs McGonigle's head. He returned just as I was leaving. Briefly I flirted with the notion of getting him to come home to avoid any more fractious exchanges with Dad or anybody else that took his fancy. However, the one thing he and Dad had in common was their stubbornness so I let it go.

In my bed, I pondered my imminent marriage, so early in life, and the unrelenting suction of my home place that had already vacuumed up my dreams of travel, exotic faraway places and experiences that are meant for the young . . .

Castletown
Sunday 26/09/83

Dear Journal ~
Me again. What a day ~ what a fucking day. My graduation and it's been hijacked by my parents. First I get a call from Mammy not to hire a cap and gown ~ she's bought them for me. I mean, who in their right mind would buy those yokes? Is she going to a fancy-dress ball soon or something? I'm so pissed off. It was my day. I should be painting the town red with Brenda and the gang in Dublin. Fuck you, David, for fading into the background when I fought it out with Dad. "The invitations are out, Hannah, we can't turn back now ~ we'll have a quick drink with your friends, but then we've got to get back to the hotel."

Here I am tucked up in bed and they're all down at the hotel, probably toasting themselves right now ~ having forgotten what the day is all about.

It's about time I had a word with David ~ he's sure to be puzzled when he gets an application form in the post that he never looked for. Deputy Manager at the Gresham Hotel. He's got to go for it ~ we could have much more fun together in Dublin ~ David, Sammi and me, away from the stifling oppression of the Castletown Arms.

Bye for now,
Hannah

The phone rang shrilly in the dead of the night, interrupting my restless sleep.

"Hannah, you'd better get down here quickly," my mother said urgently. "It's your dad – Dr Breslin is with him – it looks bad."

I got to the hotel at three thirty. It was too late. Frank Duignan had been pronounced dead ten minutes earlier. In the foyer of the Castletown Arms Hotel, the pride and joy of his life.

"It's how he would have wanted it," Billy Grennan drunkenly pontificated while getting too close in offering his condolences.

Somehow Dad's suggestion of a kick in the groin seemed off the mark tonight . . . .

"Go home, Billy," I whispered softly through my tears.

* * *

The next few days went by in a daze. David took the lead in the making of funeral arrangements as I groped around for explanations as to what happened after I went home that night. I felt ashamed of my resentments – it wasn't fair – Dad had put on a "do" for me and I was the only one not with him when he died. Tentative rumours were circulating around Castletown – talk of Dad engaging in verbals with Pat Mulcahy, the councillor who "betrayed" him, in Dad's opinion – and Pascal heard loud noises from the kitchen at two in the morning, minutes after Dad and Cormac had gone in there together.

My mother appeared stoic and composed throughout – maybe she could piece together the jigsaw for me?

"I spoke with Dr Breslin, dear. He was constantly at him to lighten up on the work and the drink. He worked hard, your father, but even on a quiet day he'd get through half a bottle of Hennessy. He had a lot more than that yesterday . . . his heart just gave up."

"I know, Mammy, but he was only sixty-four! There's talk going round about Cormac and – "

"It is as Dr Breslin says, Hannah. My Frank was arguing with people from the day I met him, probably long before that. It was part and parcel of the life he led. No. It was his second heart attack, a massive one this time, that took him from us."

"Where *did* you meet him, Mammy?"

"What? God, surely I've told you that before?"

"No."

"It was at a ballroom dance in Tarmonbarry. Twenty-seventh of August, nineteen fifty-eight."

"What brought you together?"

"I've been with your father for almost twenty-six years, dear. It hasn't been easy, sometimes. When you're married long enough, some of the earlier memories will inevitably dim. It's just life. Come on now. We need to find Cormac – he needs us right now."

* * *

The day after the funeral Declan Burke, the family solicitor, phoned. We were to attend a reading of Dad's last will the following day. Dad's instructions, not his, he replied evenly, when I called him insensitive and tactless. Mammy just took it in her stride, merely asking that I help her keep tabs on Cormac to make sure he attended the reading of the will. Cormac had hardly spoken since the night Dad died except to throw a tantrum about wearing a black tie for the removal and funeral. Selfish bastard, always in protest at the world and its formalities – couldn't see the pain he was causing. Dad was one of seven himself, four boys and three girls. All except Uncle Eugene were there. I recalled him dropping in religiously with presents at Christmas but that stopped quite suddenly when I was ten. Never saw him since and his name was never mentioned.

After the funeral Cormac had disappeared – presumably to Louise's flat. I didn't know the address but I did know Louise's mother's house, so I called there that evening. She gave me the address of her daughter's flat. "Cormac doesn't come to our house any more – had a falling-out with Louise's dad," she said in a low voice.

The following morning saw me ringing the bell at Louise's flat. Louise answered the door and invited me in with a nod of her head. She looked pale and drawn, working her fingers through her blonde, dishevelled hair to put some order on it.

"I'll get him up," she said, embarrassed, looking around at the untidy mess. "Cormac had a few friends back last night, drowning his sorrows and all that. I can't stay too long myself – I've got to get to work." Louise worked at Belmullen Electronics factory in the accounts department.

"How is he, Louise? I mean, he never tells me and Mammy anything."

"Cormac seems to be falling out with almost everybody these days, Hannah. Except me, that is." She smiled wistfully. "Living in the shadow of Frank Duignan has not been easy for him. Constantly humiliating him in front of other people. I shouldn't be saying it to you but I won't pretend that I liked Frank. Christ, he could make you feel like you were nothing with one lash of his tongue!"

"Could you rouse that brother of mine?" I said acidly, stifling a hurtful response that was making its way from my brain to my tongue. God, hadn't she some sense of timing to bring all this up now? It was just that Dad didn't suffer fools gladly. I wanted to keep my fond memories.

I stood looking around as I waited for Cormac. Better not sit on that knobbly tweed sofa, I thought, visualising the stains, maybe even fleas, that my formal black suit would carry away from it. Only the legs of the coffee table were visible beneath the clutter on its surface: an ashtray full of cigarettes-butts, empty beer cans, a brandy bottle and the remnants of a Chinese takeaway. A familiar smoky smell hung in the air, one that seemed to follow Cormac around wherever he went – his bedroom at home, the house at the back of the hotel. The once beige carpet was threadbare, the floral wallpaper torn in places.

Eventually, Cormac came into the room and dropped nonchalantly on to the sofa.

"Hiya, sis."

"Is that your only line, Cormac? Dad's will is being read in less than three hours. Could you not have stayed at home these past few days, if only for Mammy's sake?"

"She told me she was fine, so I left it at that . . ."

"Aagh, you're hopeless! Could you put your shoes on and clean yourself up so we can go in to the solicitor's looking like a half-respectable family?"

"Anything to make you happy, sis. But I could tell you what's in it right now, save us all the bother," grunted Cormac as he reached for his shoes.

* * *

Hannah Duignan, aged twenty-one. Graduation ceremony 26th of September 1983. Owner of the

Castletown Arms Hotel the following day. Well, almost. Cormac had got a ten per cent interest in it, the Bed & Breakfast and another site that Mammy seemed to know nothing about. There were other minor considerations but that was the gist of it. Declan Burke had read out the will in a blunt, dispassionate way – the only preamble was to offer his formal condolences.

It was that day that I took to face-watching as a hobby when I needed to be diverted from my own feelings. The thunderous looks that Cormac was directing at me, the stiff composure of my mother's face as she formally signed a waiver of any overriding rights she might have had. I sought to check in with myself – what was my reality at that moment? Embarrassed? Yes . . . But that's not a feeling . . . That's a situation driven by a circumstance. Proud. No, doesn't qualify, it's a vice. Confused? No. Ninety per cent is measurable. Elated. Yes, that's it. Elated. And I didn't know why.

"Was it as you expected, Cormac?" I asked as we walked out onto the street.

"No."

Chapter Eleven

September 2004

I returned my daily journal to the bag on the office floor.
These journals had been part of my personal space for so
long and I guarded their privacy with zeal. I turned to my
computer.

Laura from reception looked round the door.

"Your friend Lily is out in the foyer. Wants to see you.
Shall I send her in?"

"Oh, yeah, I suppose. I hope we're not facing another
row about *her* Erin and *my* Timothy," I said resignedly. Such
arguments between mothers never provide winners, just loss
– lost sleep, lost friendships. All the girls in the world and
my son went and picked my best friend's daughter to hop
between the sheets with.

Laura interrupted my thoughts. "Mrs Joyce, I think you
should –"

"Hannah, can we talk? It's important." Lily Meagher

stood at the open door. Trust her not to wait for confirmation that I was available. Never give a man time to make an excuse, she used to say. Now she was applying it to her friend of fifteen years.

I met Lily Meagher for the first time when bringing Timothy to his first day at playschool. Well, "met" is not really the right word. "Collided with" would be more accurate. I clipped the wing-mirror of her car as I was navigating my way up the narrow driveway of Mulligans' Montessori school. She was out of her car in a jiffy. Small, blonde, bespectacled. Furious – hopping mad in the driveway.

"Look what you've done! Were you not watching where you were going?"

"Listen, I'm really sorry, I'll get it fixed . . ."

Lily did not appear to hear me. "What will Vincent say?" she said aloud, seemingly to herself, while scratching her head frantically.

Fred Mulligan had come out of the house at that stage. He walked directly to Lily's car. *Snap!* The distorted wing-mirror had regained its original shape.

"Ladies, you can relax – there's no damage done. They make them very pliable these days – can withstand impacts at low speeds."

Lily went over to look at her car and then looked back at me. Suddenly we were both laughing, with Lily pausing to have the first say: "Talk about first-day blues! I'm a bag of nerves myself."

"Add me to that, especially after this. Have you time for a coffee? I'd like to make this up to you."

She looked at her watch. "Yes, I'd love one. It would help me chill out, I hope."

Minutes later we were sipping at steaming mugs of coffee at the Coffee Dock, the only one of its kind in Castletown at the time. Quickly, I became acquainted with Lily's CV to date. She was married to Vincent and he worked as an architect with the County Council. One daughter, Erin, aged three. Thankfully deposited for her first day in the playschool before Mammy's tantrum on the driveway, was how Lily put it. Came to town in the summer when Vincent was transferred on promotion. Not working herself, but looking. Mortgage interest rates were so high right now . . .

My turn.

"The Castletown Arms," Lily repeated when I finished. "Me and Vincent had a drink there once. Tell us, though, if you were a qualified teacher, why would you bother with the Montessori for Timothy? Couldn't you do it yourself?"

I reddened with embarrassment and annoyance but reined in. It wasn't Lily's fault – she wouldn't understand the irony of her question.

"Wish I had the time, Lily, I really do."

I didn't keep records, but I'd say Lily and I never went more than three days without meeting up for coffee since that first meeting. Until recently, that is. Until Timothy . . . and Erin . . . where it all began.

Jerking myself back to the present, I braced myself for Lily's tirade.

"Laura, could you excuse us, please?"

Laura evaporated.

"Lily, we've been over this ground before. There's nothing you and I can do. We'll just have to get on with it, accept –"

"Are you with it at all, Hannah Joyce? I'm not here about them. I'm here about Vincent. He's left me. He's staying at your fucking hotel since Friday –" She ran out of words abruptly, choking in a flood of tears. "Her name is Sinéad – twenty-seven, works with him on the County Council. Apparently, it's being going on for quite some time and they were about to be 'outed' or squealed upon, whichever you prefer. They decided to come out into the open – 'Be honourable about it,' Vincent said. Hypocritical bastard!" Lily's tearful helplessness was now replaced by a cold anger.

My head raced as I got to grips with this. Vincent Meagher, studious, academic, meticulous attention to small detail, nice man, reliable – boring – I couldn't place him with *any* other woman, never mind one twenty years his junior . . .

I spoke my thoughts aloud: "But what's he doing in our hotel? I don't get it . . . wouldn't he be with –"

"With her, that's what you were about to say, wasn't it? He should be with *me* and it's about time that you kicked yourself awake, Hannah, so you can talk some sense about this. How should I know why he's staying here? But I want you to put him out. Straight away." Lily's cold anger was about to dissolve again. "What are you doing now?"

Vincent Meagher's name was flashing out at me on computer as a resident at our hotel since Friday. Room 73. A single room. I'd half-expected Room 50. Might have explained the noise described by Murdoch Goodman.

"You're right, Lily, he *is* here," was all I could muster at that moment.

"Great. We're really up and running now. Haven't I been telling you just that for the last ten minutes? What medication are you on, woman?"

"But it's a single room, Lily –"

"So what? You mean he can't have sex in a single room?"

I got to grips quite suddenly. "He won't be staying here tonight, Lily," I said with firm assurance. "I knew nothing about it and would have sent him packing had I been on Reception on Friday. I'm sorry about this, sorry about it all. Look, I'll call round to see you and –"

"Just get him out, Hannah."

The pain and exhaustion in her voice were palpable. I thought I understood. Renewal of our friendship was not a priority to Lily right now.

Laura looked back around the door when Lily was gone and I knew by her expression that there was something else wrong.

"What is it, Laura?"

She stepped inside. "It's Timothy and Erin. They spent last night in Room 50 – the night porter saw them creeping out about six in the morning or thereabouts."

Good on ya, Timothy! No point trying to make good of a bad thing. Throw more of that oil on the fire! Father and daughter – fornicating under the same roof, each not knowing the other is there. So what if a wife and mother who also happens to be my best friend is devastated by it all? Find yourself some new friends, Hannah – do you really need someone who is upset by trivia like that? Sure, wouldn't it be worse if it was something serious, like?

Twenty minutes until David came on duty. I wrote down his first and second tasks of the day on a Post-it note and settled down to wait.

1 Throw Vincent out.

2 Ground Timothy.

Chapter Twelve

"David, Vincent has to go, he cannot stay here. Why didn't you at least tell me?"

David had arrived spot on time at one o'clock. Immaculate in a black pinstripe suit, red tie and the customary white shirt. The curls were diminishing and there were sprinklings of grey starting to appear. But the strides across the foyer remained the same . . . Twenty-three years on, David Joyce had subsumed the vision and drive of Frank Duignan and brought it to a level that not even Dad had dared to dream. Right now, though, he was making things very difficult for me.

"Hannah, Vincent came to reception and booked a room just as thousands do throughout the year. A *single* room. This is a ninety-bedroom hotel with one hundred and fifty beds. I didn't know either until I met him in the bar Friday night. But it wouldn't have made any difference had I known – I would have let him in."

"God, how can you say that? Lily is my friend. Did he tell you anything?"

"Look, at an estimate, how many people with marital problems pass through these doors? Some mightn't have problems at all but are just getting their end off with someone else. And are you fooling yourself that we don't have gays and lesbians here on a regular basis? Ask Dennis the porter how many single beds he has to prise apart over a week. And you want me to put Vincent Meagher out on the street? Forget it."

"Right. Well, I'm going up to tell him that he can't stay. But you didn't answer me – did he tell you anything?"

"I'll take the second part of that first. Vincent booked in because Sinéad is out looking for an apartment. She is 'on notice' at her parents' home, as they know about Vincent. But, whatever the situation, you can't go up and throw him out. Even if I agreed with you, and I don't, we still couldn't show him the door. It's against the law. Discrimination. You've seen it with the travellers, getting large awards from the Equality Authority just because someone looked the wrong way at them. It's the same law for separated men *and* women. Their cases just don't get the same publicity. Now can we close the door on this subject? I came in here to do some work."

"Will you tell Lily, David?" I pleaded, annoyed at the feeble resonance to my voice.

"No, I won't – you gave her a promise you could never keep. You're going to have to tell her yourself, or not tell her. It's your choice."

"You seem to know Vincent's fancy lady . . . Sinéad, you called her."

"I've partnered her in golf competitions occasionally. Is that a sin?"

* * *

I drove through the open gates of our house, Cedar Woods, two miles from Castletown. Inside, I seethed angrily at David's determined stand about Vincent – knowing that he was right didn't make things any better. I had also meant to talk to him about Timothy but his abrupt dismissal of my concerns meant that we never got to that. I should have ordered my priorities better: Timothy first, Vincent second. Too late, now.

Our home stood resplendent in the evening sun on its grounds. The space . . . that was the outstanding feature, inside and out. Three thousand square feet, excluding the garage – surrounded by matured trees that gave privacy but, being a safe distance from the house, did not interfere with the natural light. Dad always claimed that every man should have his one acre on which to set down his family roots – endless green fields lying idle and they continue cramming people into sardine boxes, he would say. I couldn't fault him on that one as I relived the fun Timothy and Sammi got from our sprawling house and grounds. Swings and slides, trees to be climbed, five-a-side matches on the back lawns. A path wound its way round the back of the house and joined up at the front – I would go dizzy peeling vegetables at the back window as the kids flew past repeatedly on bikes, trying to win the Castletown Grand Prix. The builders started on the house as soon as we announced our engagement and we moved in on Christmas Eve, ten weeks after our wedding. That was our goal and we were happy to endure the overwhelming smell of paint so we could start our first Christmas as a family on the right note. The click of Sammi's shoes as she ran up the bare stairs to pick out her bedroom.

At that stage she had come to accept me in her life, though it had taken some serious bribery. Timothy was born the following autumn and this was the cue for Sammi to relapse into the child from Hell once more. I was puzzled at the little bruises that appeared on his body from time to time until I caught Sammi pinching him one day. I smacked her and sent her to her room but she sneaked out to phone David.

He was parked in the driveway in minutes and we had our first serious disagreement.

"She's only a little girl, Hannah – you know it hasn't been easy for her. How could you? We're right back where we started now, the day you first met her."

"No, we're not. We've moved on – we have a son and you're his father. Do you not want to look at his bruises?"

While I walked in the garden with a sobbing Timothy, David was in the kitchen, his daughter sitting on his knee as he talked to her. I saw her curly head nodding and David kissing her forehead. Father and daughter walked into the garden hand in hand.

"Sammi has something to say to you."

I was still annoyed with her but one look at her little hurt face made me realise how much I had come to love her.

"I'm sorry, Hannah, I won't pinch Timothy again."

I handed Timothy over to David and bent down to her level. Her little body trembled as I wrapped my arms around her.

"It's okay."

Minutes later the whole incident was "forgotten" but David's reaction stayed with me. A moment in time, cut out and pasted into my memory.

Over the years, David and I became lord and lady of different manors. He ruled the roost at the hotel and I made the big decisions on our house. I was taken aback when he put his foot down on my proposals for a redesign of our kitchen – Neff appliances and hand-carved kitchen units. I had just run it by him as a courtesy.

"Really, Hannah, this is way over the top. The conservatory, okay – the patio and decking fine, although I don't know when *I'll* get time to sit out in it. But the kitchen, changing it for the sake of it – it makes no sense."

"Don't be such a skinflint, David. You'll be able to write most of the cost off by coding it as an expense to the business. What's got into you?"

"But you don't *cook*. I'm not having tradesmen stuck in my face every morning for the next month just because you want to change something that doesn't need changing. Sure you hardly even use the one we're standing in right now."

"Ah, but all that will change when I get my new kitchen!"

"Look, you can go ahead and do it if you want but you're stretching it if you expect me to give you a blessing on this one. I'll just keep slaving on at the hotel while you and your lady friends drool over your new showroom with your cappuccinos and pastries!"

It was lovely to see David's handsome face so animated. Usually he wore a bored, resigned expression and I often felt the urge to slap him just to see if I could rid him of that particular look. He glared at me, his seductive brown eyes growing bigger in his head. Privately, I thought we should argue more often. I had got my way, won the battle – more important, though, I had for once stirred the dormant spirit my man kept hidden beneath his perfunctory efficiency.

Chapter Thirteen

Our twenty-first wedding anniversary was only weeks away. Twenty-one years since we took our wedding vows at Port St Louis on the beautiful island of Mauritius. Looking at our wedding photos, I felt tears suddenly stinging my eyes. "Let them all out," my friend Alison would say. "They're part of life's tapestry, the bigger picture. I wouldn't let anybody take my maudlin moments away from me."

"Mauritius, nineteen eighty-three," I whispered to myself while retrieving an old journal from the locked cabinet in our bedroom.

Port St Louis, Mauritius
Wednesday 26/11/83

Dear Journal ~
I know I've been neglecting you lately but you just have to

forgive me. David and I are going home tomorrow. We've had a lovely two weeks. I really should have written it all down as it happened but some things had to be set aside for our special time. I've sent David out to buy me some underwear as punishment for all the pairs he's lost me on the beach – running down there together in the dark of night, bras and pants washed out to sea or so full of sand that any amount of showering won't remove the traces. David is sure nobody saw us – so that means only he, you and me know our secret! Not that all those episodes stopped him using our bed. He gave me flowers last night. I gave him a small statue of Lothario, the seducer from The Fair Penitent.

Mauritius is so beautiful, it's –

I snapped my book shut suddenly at the sound of a voice downstairs.

"Anybody home?"

Alison. Alison Byrne. The third part of the coffee-drinking triangle.

"I'll be down in a minute, Alison!" I shouted and went to make sure my secrets were safely locked away first.

There are small towns like Castletown in almost every county. What was it at the last population census . . . five thousand four hundred people? Yeah, something around that. This number swelled considerably between April and September when the tourists took over the place.

Tourists – who would have believed it? It's not like we're beside the sea or anything. We've always had our lakes, okay, and a hardcore of fishermen escaping their wives for long, idyllic days angling on the waters. No, it was the restoration of the castle and the development of what was generally agreed to be one of the country's best golf courses that really sparked the boom. Previously redundant historical sites were restored carefully and marketed energetically both at home and abroad. Yes, Castletown had its attractions these days, I reflected, and sometimes it was taken for granted by people who did not see or appreciate the work needed to get it there. It needed leadership, enthusiasm and an almost insatiable drive. These had come from David Joyce, my husband, and a surge of resentment flooded through me as I silently acknowledged the impact he had made on my hometown since he first arrived with a mop of black curly hair and a little girl in tow.

Over the years, we had settled into our marriage and adapted as best we could as the lights of those famous nights in Bunbeg and Mauritius started to wane.

"It's just life, dear," Mammy would say as she brought swift closure to one of my "maudlin moments". "Look at all you've got and it all began with your poor father's hard work, God rest him," she'd say while starting to list the material comforts in my life that had not come at the right time for her.

But I was bored.

And that's where my female friends come in, I thought as I trotted down to Alison – they are essential to my survival in the repetitive drudge that Castletown serves up. Do I sound disaffected, I wondered. Well, that's how it was, at least today . . .

"The kettle is boiled!" Alison's voice came from the kitchen.

Female friends. Yes. "Circle of Friends" was the title of some song but, Alison, Lily and I didn't need a circle – we had our triangle and it was unbreakable. It might be soured with Lily right now, but sure that was the fault of my men, Timothy and David. We'd bounce back, we'd show them . . .

"Alison, look at you, you look great!" I exclaimed as we broke from our customary hug. "What is it – almost a week? We're slipping up – let's catch up, I have the whole day." I wiped out a mental to-do list with one swift blow to the brain.

Taking a look at Alison's life, one could consider that she was smug. She had the doting husband, the lavish lifestyle, the golden Labrador and not forgetting the two high-achieving sons in university. Her life looked like a fine tapestry yet if one turned it around there was the other weaved and worried side. It had been ten years ago – there we were sitting at Alison's kitchen table, our children playing together in the garden. It was then she told Lily and myself that she had breast cancer. "I'm begging God to let me live to rear my sons," she had said. It had all seemed a little surreal. There we were sitting at her kitchen table, a pile of empty Tayto bags and half-eaten cookies around us, the occasional fly hovering over the lemonade glasses. I knew I should start to clear the table but I sat there numbed by her revelation.

"Oh, Alison, this is awful . . . I'm so sorry . . ."

"We will help you through it," Lily interjected, frowning furiously at me for my despair. She took Alison's hand and squeezed it reassuringly. "I know lots of people that came through this and you're going to be another one."

"Don't they look adorable?" Alison said, her eyes brimming with tears. She was looking out at her two sons playing soccer with Timothy. She had called them "bastards" a few days earlier after her darlings had engraved their names on the dining-room table. It was the first and last time I heard her swear.

Her illness made little of all that had gone before. Alison

made a deal with God. All she wanted was to live to raise her sons. All through her chemotherapy and check-ups, her faith never wavered. She believed that she was going to get better and she did. From that time on we became closer, Alison, Lily and myself.

Alison was a good few years older than us two but she didn't look it. She sat at my kitchen table, her auburn hair swept back and tied up behind, her face make-up free – thankfully she looked the picture of health.

"Well, where do we start?" she said mischievously. "Vincent and Lily or Timothy and Erin?"

"There's no dodging it with you, is there? I think I'll take Vincent and Lily – I seem to know more about them than I do about my own son."

"She's furious with you, Hannah. Giving him a bed in your hotel to facilitate his fornications with that – Sinéad, I think that's her name –"

"Ah, no, that part's not right. He's booked into a single room."

"When did that ever stop anybody? Wasn't Sinéad in the bar at half past one Friday night with Vincent and your David? She's got history, this one. Vincent's not the first. Her specialty is getting her knickers off for older men." She sounded bitter.

Ironic, I thought. Alison never lost out on information because she was a dedicated home-bird and had all the local gossip. Here she was telling me what was going on under my nose . . . Why doesn't David tell me things these days? He's humiliating me in front of my friends. Why keep so quiet about it . . . this Sinéad who liked older men . . . surely not? I composed myself, banishing the thought. Communication, isn't that the key word? Don't companies have seminars in our hotel to encourage their staff not to hoard information, especially when it can be vital to running a successful business?

"David won't put him out and he won't let me do it. It's against the law, he says. End of story. Case closed. There's nothing I can do, Alison," I said helplessly.

"Probably not, but David shouldn't be so self-righteous. Lily reckons it's more to do with David keeping his inside track to the Council. He's always had a hotline to Vincent and this Sinéad."

"That's ridiculous," I said, anger rising in my voice. "You can't come in here saying things like that about David!"

"I'm not saying anything bad about David," Alison replied evenly. "I'd react exactly the same way myself in your situation, Hannah, but the dogs in the street in Castletown know that David's favourite route for planning applications and all that stuff is Council officials."

"Who would have thought Vincent had it in him?" I said, anxious to divert the conversation. "He's as dull as ditchwater."

"Eddie said exactly the same to me in bed last night. Was joking that he needed to spice his own life up a bit, have an affair maybe. I took firm hold of his prized asset and told him there were wonderful carving knives on the market these days."

"Is there anything we can do – to help Lily, I mean?"

"Not a lot. I suppose David is right – putting him out of your hotel is neither here nor there. If Vincent is determined to have it off with this one, he'll always find somewhere. I had a dream last night . . . Vincent coming back to pick up his clothes . . . walks in on Lily . . . she's taking it from Maurice Greene . . . you should have seen the look on

Vincent's face!"

Coffee mornings with Alison were never boring. I burst out laughing. "Maurice Greene? The county footballer? Sure he's about the same age as this Sinéad – so what has you dreaming about him?"

"Wouldn't it be perfect, Vincent getting a dose of his own medicine? As for me, a girl is entitled to her dreams. Sure, isn't he the only hunk in Castletown?"

"You've given me an idea, though, Alison. It won't be Maurice Greene, but I'm sure there's many a man would be interested in Lily."

"Eh . . . it was a dream, Hannah, that's all. We couldn't go interfering like that. Sure we don't even know if she would want a man. Even if she did, knowing Lily, she'd go out and get him herself. Stay out of it."

"We're already in it, at least in Lily's eyes, but you're right," I said, my mind continuing however in its state of promiscuous imagination.

"I notice you've baked no scones for me this morning."

I laughed, recalling the last time I had invited Lily and Alison over. I had made scones and bought a jar of strawberry jam from the country market. It took Lily all her strength to prise the lid off the jar. Then once she had bitten into the scone she made a face. "Is it me or do these taste funny?"

"You're right Lily they do taste – stale," I remarked, getting up to get the bag of flour. It was past its sell-by date.

Now I could only laugh at my first attempt at being a domestic goddess. "Well, it hasn't put you off coming back to me for coffee, Alison!"

"Goodness no – and I could do with another."

Two hours and several coffees later, Alison departed

down the driveway. What would I do now? There were the minutes of the Tidy Towns' last committee meeting to be prepared. Instead, I rummaged through my CD collection. Soon, the music of Andrea Bocelli was wafting lyrically through the house. Closing my eyes, I smiled at the memory of our girls' night out at The Point. God, he was fabulous, I thought, and David missed out on it all . . . He had first option but business and all that. Rich, beyond even Frank Duignan's dreams. Cash-wealthy, time-poor, the relentless cycle of the Castletown Arms continued onwards.

My daytime reverie was interrupted by the sound of a key turning in the front door.

"Is that you, Timothy? Come in here, I need to talk with you."

Silence, except for the quiet rustle of feet on the thick hallway carpet. He's not getting away that easy, I said to myself, moving swiftly towards the hallway.

"Sammi! God, this is a surprise! And you've brought Baby Dan!"

I hugged Sammi – she smelled of baby vomit and shower gel. "Mmm, you smell just like a young mother should. David will be delighted –"

"He already is. I dropped in at the hotel first. Says he'll be down later."

Of course, she would. He's her natural father after all.

Chapter Fourteen

"Well, to what do we owe this surprise?" I called from the kitchen, while rustling up a salad for Sammi.

"Ah, nothing in particular, just a brainwave. I think I'll stay until morning, if that's okay, Hannah?"

"As long as you want, as long as you want."

Sammi was now a mother herself. She left home for college nine years ago but did not complete her degree. David was furious. She flitted between a number of clerical jobs over the next few years: insurance companies, telesales, temporary work with the Department of the Environment. Then Alan came on the scene and, with Baby Dan, paid employment was not high on her list of priorities right now. There was always David if she was badly stuck but, while generous, her father was not the type to lavish cash upon his children.

The relatively small age difference between Sammi and

me ensured that I'd have to settle for Hannah instead of Mum. If only that was all, I grimaced. If I were to review my journal reflections of Sammi across the years, I'd probably take her key back right now. Thoughts of her turbulent teenage years came to the surface.

"My mother is *Claire* Joyce, the *first* Mrs Joyce. Have you got that? *You'll* never replace her!"

I closed my eyes to the expletives that followed. Forgive and forget, they say. There was a price to be paid for falling in love with her father. For that memorable night in Bunbeg when we first made love. Sammi was the price . . . part of it, anyway.

She was dressed in a white T-shirt and cropped jeans – it looked like she had slept in them too. She looked pale and drawn. Her hair was tied up in a ponytail, her childhood curls still evident, and motherhood had done no harm to her trim, svelte figure. David had often harangued me to bring her to the more exclusive boutiques, buy her some "real" clothes, he'd say.

"I'm going to visit Lorraine in Galway tomorrow, so I'll be out of your hair come morning, Hannah."

"Come on now, we got past that stage years ago! Though I'd have driven you to Galway myself if you had made that offer at fourteen, I have to admit!"

"God, I was such a cow back then and you took it all in your stride. The support you gave me when Dad tried to bully me into returning to finish my studies!" Nuzzling Baby Dan's ear, she said, "Think, I wouldn't have you . . . What'll you call her when you start talking – Gran – Nana?"

I stiffened a little as the thought of Timothy working on the real thing with Erin surfaced.

She gave me a watery smile. Then she turned away and I

got the feeling that she was holding something back from me.

"Is everything alright?" I asked as we went upstairs to her old bedroom.

She didn't answer.

In her room, she dropped the baby bag on her single bed.

"Oh, you smelly baby!" she said, nuzzling Baby Dan's stomach with her face.

He laughed gleefully at her and kicked his chubby legs in the air.

I found my chest tighten as a mental picture flashed in front of me. What if Sammi broke up with Alan? She might come back home permanently. I inhaled slowly and then breathed out again. Could I stand David's continual fussing over her?

"Oh, pooh!" she said, as she took off his jeans. "You're a messy, messy baby!"

Sammi got him changed quickly and then we returned to the kitchen. Already my pristine kitchen was filling up. Bottles, a push-chair, a cuddly teddy bear, a play mat. On the kitchen table was another baby bag, his blanket thrown across a chair. She still had to unload the car. I felt a rush of shame. Why were resentments surfacing then ebbing? Where was the balance? Shouldn't I just be pleased to see her? I longed to backtrack to find that place in my life where I took the wrong turn and found myself in this resentful place. There was a time I just loved this entire commotion and having people around. Now, I felt like I was overdrawn; I had nothing more left to give.

"Dan never sleeps day or night," Sammi said as she placed her son in my arms.

He looked so adorable I couldn't help but laugh at him.

I had to kiss his button nose and he gave me a gummy smile that just melted my heart. Seven-twelve at birth, exactly the same as Timothy. I had hoped to have more children after Timothy, but it just didn't happen. Having Sammi around distracted me from my own maternal instincts – compensated in some way despite our turbulent relationship.

"I can see he's got you under his spell, Hannah."

"She wants you to call me Gran," I whispered to him. Dan continued with his facial contortions. "Can I feed him his bottle?"

"Thanks, Hannah, that would be great. I'll make us some fresh coffee."

Yes, I thought to myself as I held my grandson, he'll make me feel young again. Baby Dan will remind me of my own child. He'll take me back to that time when I was happy, contented with my life.

Sammi came back with hot coffees and fudge cake. "Alan was saying we might come over for a weekend before he jets off to the States."

"Great. When's he going?

"Oh, not for weeks yet. I'm thinking of coming home for a while – it's going to be pretty boring in Dublin all on my own. Plus, I'd get the bonus of reminding Timothy that he has a sister. I don't know when I've seen him, and he's never discovered what the telephone is for."

I was hoping to end the conversation as soon as possible. So this was just an interlude, a water-testing exercise for things to come. Weeks spent indulging Sammi did not appeal to me at all. Particularly since she'd reached her teenage years, we'd found it increasingly difficult to co-exist in harmony at home. We had endless fun on shopping trips and family holidays, but it just didn't work for us at home. My coffee mornings with Alison, Lily . . .

"Hannah, Alan's really looking forward to going to the States, never stops talking about it." There was a slight pause where she was waiting for me to respond but I didn't know how to. "It makes me so mad," she moaned. "We should be his priority."

I sighed inwardly. "He has to think about his career," was my token offering.

"I know he does, but he doesn't have to keep going on about it. It's so boring to listen to it all the time."

"You're both adjusting to having a baby. They really do change your life."

"Oh, Hannah, I am probably overreacting. Dad said you would be buying some new cots for the hotel any day now. Could you hold one aside for Dan – that's if we come?"

I got a feeling that the decision was already made but I bit my lip. When I took David, I took the full package.

"Of course, love, I will."

Chapter Fifteen

Cedar Woods
Monday 13/09/04

Dear Journal ~
Me again. It's gone midnight and I can't sleep for the sound
of David and Sammi downstairs. Whenever she comes our
family seems to dissolve into two distinct parts – dad, daughter
and grandchild on one side, mother and son manning the other
fort. I'm going to buy David a bloody magnifying glass to help
in his mission to formally declare Dan as a clone of his first wife
Claire. Normally I can't handle his continuous silence about
her – then, when Sammi arrives, their séances at the kitchen
table dissecting Baby Dan's various parts make me simmer
with resentment. Watch out for your little willie, Dan, it's the
only part they haven't signed over to Claire! I know you'll think
I'm a jealous bitch but it's no fun competing with the dead for

attention. I wish David would let me into that dark corner of his life ~ I might be able to understand.

Bye for now,
Hannah

* * *

I waved Sammi and Dan off the following morning, having gone to bed early the night before. I drifted off to sleep to the drone of conversation in the sitting room below. Father and daughter stuff – it was nice, though, once it got past the Claire factor.

David came to bed around one o'clock. He patted my back casually – there was no sense of him lurking with intent. A brief memory of him arriving in Drumcondra with condoms flashed across my brain.

"'Twasn't the worst of days, after a bad start," he said smugly. "Sammi is in great form and Timothy is showing great interest in the hotel lately. Stayed there again last night to keep watch over the late-night revellers."

"We need to talk about that," I murmured sleepily beneath the duvet.

At least twice a week I went to visit my mother, and it was convenient to make this morning one of them en route to the hotel. I hated admitting it but it was always a duty visit. Seeing her depressed me. After my father's death she lost all interest in the hotel and in life. I don't know if it was his death that extinguished the light – it was more likely that Dad had slapped her hardest at the reading of his will. Imagine that, *after* he died. It later emerged that Dad had changed his will in my favour some months before he died. I shuddered as I remembered Cormac's vicious bile at the hotel bar several years after the event.

"Why the fuck do you think he changed it? You were his route to David Joyce, Hannah! Cope with it! I remember it clearly – Dad ringing his old pal George Brennan that weekend in Donegal to get him to check that you were there with David. Look at what he did to Mammy – he never saw her, or you for that matter, as anything other than an essential ornament for the hotel. The perfect hostess, the antidote to his raucous, belligerent ways."

Louise, standing quietly in the background, blinked back the tears. "Leave it, Cormac, will you just leave it!"

Louise was not the only one to cry that night. I shed bitter tears in the hotel laundry where the glistening new leisure centre now sits. Not at Cormac's barbs but at a sense that my precious memories of that night overlooking the sea at Bunbeg were being violated. My precious, love-filled, wildly orgasmic night. How could you, Dad . . . Cormac . . . surely not David . . . surely not . . .

Every conversation I had with my mother seemed to revolve around Cormac. We sat in her cosy well-ordered sitting room that she dusted every day, except on Sundays. My mother was always very disciplined, something my brother or myself didn't inherit. I envied her will power. Nothing tempted or swayed her. For example, she never ate after six o'clock. She never said: "Oh, go on then, I'll just have one fun-size Mars bar," or, "You only live once." She was more likely to say, "No, thank you, I never eat after six," and you knew by her tone and the firm line of her thin lips that she meant it.

I had suggested that she join a reading group or some retirement group but she refused, adamant that she didn't need to. Her days were long stretches of nothingness broken up by three meals. And, so, over the years I found myself inventing things to take her out of herself. I felt the strain of always having to be the one that visited her to see that she was doing okay. It was acceptable for Cormac to visit when he felt like it. Somehow his excuses were more valid than mine.

"How is Timothy getting on in the hotel?" she asked before I got a chance to take off my jacket.

"Why do you ask?"

"Why can't I ask about my grandson?"

"Oh, no reason, he's getting on fine."

"He came to see me today – he asked me for a loan."

An uneasy, queasy feeling surfaced from the pit of my stomach. "Did he say why he needed the money, Mammy?"

My mother beat an immediate retreat. "Oh, I've said too much. I think I promised him that I wouldn't say anything."

"I'll make us some tea." I felt the slow, heavy thud of a headache coming on.

We sipped it in silence. Indignation and rage rose steadily within me while unpleasant questions and fears ballooned in my mind. Why couldn't Timothy have told me he had come to see his grandmother – what was he hiding from me – was Erin in trouble? As best I could, I made light of the matter – I didn't want Mammy picking up on any tensions in our home for fear she would embark on one of her self-appointed rescue missions. My vocal chords seemed to tighten and I just couldn't speak. The antique clock above her fireplace tick-tocked steadily along . . . Soon, soon, I promised myself, my time would be up.

My mother sat regally, wearing the same pearl stud-earrings she had worn for as long as I could remember. She was old and fragile and I couldn't be upsetting her, voicing stupid old grievances that I carried around with me. Somehow, it was never the right time to speak your mind. Time for some trivia, Hannah, I decided, or you'll end up listening to Mother's "poor me" voice on the phone later on – nobody cares about old people these days and all that . . .

"Did I tell you that Vincent has left Lily?"

"No. It doesn't surprise me, though – I always thought he was a slippery-looking character. As for her, she's fooling nobody with her peroxide-blonde hair – cheap as you could get, that one. You really should choose your friends more carefully, Hannah."

"I'm sorry I brought it up now – I should have known you'd go off on one of your lectures."

Soon, I could excuse myself from the dreary monotone that was my mother's voice. I yearned to relive with her those heady excursions to Granny's home near Tarmonbarry on the banks of the Shannon when, for once, she would shed her cloak of rigid formality. She would become a "real Mammy" then, splashing in the waters, racing up to buy cones from the ice-cream vendors and reading us bedtime stories into the wee hours of the night. It took Tarmon to bring out her inner child and we loved it, cherished those moments. I massaged my forehead, longing to close my eyes and blank it all out.

"So," my mother said to break the gloomy silence, "have you any more news?"

"No, Mammy, no more news."

* * *

I entered the hotel foyer at twelve noon. A coloured girl

eyed me quizzically from reception as I went directly to the office. Let her look, she'll get used to it, I thought. That's the way the hotel trade was going. Giselle Boateng – that's what her badge said. You could no longer keep track of who was working for you, the turnover of staff was so fast.

David was sitting at the desk.

Customary rule obeyed, I noted to myself. He never wore the same suit two days in a row. Business-conscious was how he described it, and it was true. David left the matter of his casual clothes to me and The Coffee Triangle had much fun in Marks and Spencer pondering over what colours would complement my husband's best features.

"Lily was on the phone," said David, looking at me directly. "Going mental about Vincent – waste of time, he's going tomorrow anyway – Sinéad has earmarked a nice bungalow out of town. Threatened to ring the Council, Lily did. Some nonsense in her head about me giving backhanders to Vincent."

"It's good that he's going, David – at least we will be out of their lives."

"You didn't tell me about Timothy and Erin," he said, his gaze unwavering.

I felt myself flush with indignation. "When do we *ever* get to tell each other things these days? I mean, when do we get time alone to do just that?"

"Well, as a start, we're going to handle this one together." David picked up the phone to reception. "Giselle, could you get me Timothy, please?"

Timothy materialised at the door. I don't know if it was just motherly pride but I thought he certainly had turned into a handsome young man. Timothy was nearly twenty. Three months after marrying David, I was pregnant. As

Brenda would jibe at me: "Not bad for a late starter!"

Timothy stood six-one in his stocking feet but today he looked smaller under the intense stare of his father. He shifted uncomfortably and sought to hide his guilty expression by coughing and looking at his feet. He had David's dark eyes but when he laughed I always saw a glint of my brother in him.

"Yes, Dad, eh, Mum. What is it? I'm just stocking the barroom –"

"You've been using guest bedrooms to have sex with Erin, haven't you?" said David, raising his voice. An uneasy silence followed. "Are you just going to stand there now saying nothing?"

"David, please, not so loud."

He got up and advanced ominously towards Timothy, causing him to step backwards.

"Look, Dad, I can explain, if you'll let me –"

"I'm not looking for an explanation, I want an answer. Have you been sleeping in Room 50 with Erin?"

"Well, yeah."

David's breathing was laboured. His face was flushed, his trademark white shirt damp from perspiration. He paced up and down on the beige carpet.

"Good. I knew anyway. I went through some of the footage on the CCTV cameras and saw you going up the stairs and into the bedroom with her. It was you in the bedroom next to Mr Goodman – the room he had pre-booked. He couldn't sleep because of the racket you were making. Your mother didn't charge him for the room because of you. Keep this up and we'll have no bloody guests left!"

"Timothy –" He shuffled from foot to foot and wouldn't

look at me. "Timothy, how could you?"

"Oh, look, we didn't plan it like that, it just sort of happened." He hung his head in embarrassment. The air was charged with tension and stale air. He broke the silence to say, "It won't happen again."

David sat back down. He was silent for what seemed like an eternity.

"You're right about that. Consider yourself finished as of now. I'm not having you working here in the hotel and you carrying on like that."

I looked from father to son and back again, the air sticky with tension. Timothy appeared on the verge of saying something but his opportunity passed.

"You know your mother and I have been waiting patiently since last year's Leaving Cert to see you doing something with your life. We'll support you through college if that's where you want to go, but you're finished here and the money that comes with it is finished too."

"Ah, come on, Dad, that's way over the top!"

"That's what we've decided, Timothy. There's no going back. I'll be telling Erin that she won't be getting any more casual work at this hotel. It's enough to have to listen to your Uncle Cormac in the bar most nights. Do you want to go the same road as him?"

Timothy stood upright suddenly, his fists clenched. "Stuff your job, Dad, and your college support. It's okay for you to drool all over Vincent and his bit on the side but, ho, it's a crime when your son does pretty much the same with his daughter. Bollocks!"

"Vincent is a paying customer," said David in a determined, steely voice. "Our position is quite clear and I'm not going to repeat it for you. And the prohibition on your sex sessions with Erin or anybody else for that matter includes our home. Now, I have work to be getting on with."

David swung open the office door, drawing in a gush of fresh chilly air. He marched purposefully out and slammed the door after him.

So much for *we'll* tackle this together, I reflected bitterly – David doing all my talking – "we" – "our position is" – no different to my father. Different approach and tactics, the same result. Decides what your medicine will be and you take it. All of it.

My computer hummed loudly in the otherwise hushed office.

Timothy cleared his throat and moved closer to my desk. "I'm sorry, Mum."

Memories of Timothy and Erin playing at Mulligans' Montessori school surfaced. Brick-building and painting each other's faces to the point where they were almost unrecognisable. "You really shouldn't have, Timothy . . . Erin's having it hard right now with her dad moving out . . ."

"Yes, I know, we were just going to talk about it. She was crying in the kitchen and I just suggested that we go somewhere quiet to talk and then it just . . ." he shrugged awkwardly and cleared his throat again, "happened."

I touched his bristled cheek. "Oh, Timothy, what are we going to do with you? I hear you borrowed some money from your grandmother – do you want to tell me what that's about?"

Timothy shuffled awkwardly from foot to foot. "There's nothing to tell."

"Why couldn't you have come to me or your father if you wanted a loan? You really shouldn't be hassling your grandmother."

He sighed with exasperation. "Mum, it's between Gran and myself – you should learn to mind your own business."

I swallowed down the caustic remark that ballooned inside me ready to be voiced.

"Fine, then," I said, walking away from him.

"Can I take your car?" he asked.

"No, it's best that you don't right now. Walk, the fresh air will do you good."

Chapter Sixteen

Cedar Woods
Tuesday 14/09/04

Dear Brenda,

I hope you remember me, Hannah Joyce, sorry, Duignan ~ we were best friends in college. In ways it only seems like yesterday. I'm not much good at tallying the years but it's quite a while ago now.

I am sorry that I didn't go travelling with you that summer and I never did apologise properly to you. I feel I have let you down badly. You were always such a good friend to me. Well, you were right ~ you said I would regret not going off with you and right now I do. I just wanted you to know that. I could have gone off for the summer with you and still have married David, but no, I was too insecure. I didn't think he would wait for me.

Also, of course, my father had just passed away. It all

happened so suddenly ~ it was such a shock to us. We weren't expecting it, though he had a heart condition. I felt I had to go back to Castletown and help out ~ my mother just couldn't cope on her own.

So while you were packing your rucksack to go travelling, I was laying out my wedding dress.

Remember all those nights we stayed up planning our trip, wondering where we were going to get the money to fund it? You were always so positive. "Something will turn up," you used to say.

I remember you sent me a postcard from the South of France. You wrote that the air was scented with pine trees and lavender. You went to discover new things while I settled for the familiar and safe.

I'd love us to meet up again. I'd love to hear all about that trip and see your photographs. Are you a teacher now? Did you get married and have children? I do hope you get this letter. I'm just curious to find out. Perhaps you met the love of your life while travelling. I have all these romantic notions that your life turned out wonderful while mine is just very ordinary.

All the best for now,
Your old pal,
Hannah

I addressed my letter to Brenda's mother in Drumcondra. I smiled as I thought that, if I could be sure that Brenda would be the first person to open it, I would have included some more detail. Hopefully, her mother would still be living there and she would pass it on.

Chapter Seventeen

At first I thought I was dreaming and in my dream there was a phone ringing. A loud piercing sound, summoning me to answer it immediately. Then, I realised it was in the bedroom. I opened my eyes and made a stab in the darkness to pick up the receiver so I could hush it up. My first coherent thought was Timothy. Was he in trouble? I fumbled in the darkness and grabbed the receiver.

"Hello?" I said as I sat up, my heart pounding hard against my chest.

It was Jasmine, my nine-year-old niece.

"Jasmine, pet, what is it?" I whispered into the phone. She was sobbing so hard I couldn't make out what she was saying. I threw back the covers and got out of bed.

"Who is it at this hour?" David asked sleepily.

"It's Jasmine," I whispered. "She's upset."

David pulled the covers over his head. To him this was

89

like a repeat performance of a similar scene we had six months ago.

Simultaneous feelings of relief that it was not Timothy and annoyance that it was my troublesome brother ran through me. "What is it?" I asked her gently. In the background I could hear her mother shouting at Cormac.

"Please, Auntie Hannah – please come!" she said through her sobs.

"Don't worry, pet – I'm on my way over," I whispered into the phone. "You just hang on – I'll be with you in minutes."

I started to dress.

David sat up suddenly in the bed.

"You're not going to improve anything by going over there again, Hannah, you know that. Jesus, Louise was long enough with him before they eventually married. Leave them to sort it out themselves – it's their own dog-pooh."

"I don't care about them, David," I said firmly. "There's a child involved. That's enough for me. I'm going over and, depending on how I find things, I might bring Jasmine back."

I checked Timothy's bedroom, saw his long-limbed shape under his duvet. I longed to go over and kiss his forehead, run my fingers through his hair like I used to do when he was little.

It was times like this that caused me to regret not having more children. Perhaps then I wouldn't have spoiled Timothy and indulged Sammi's tantrums so much. David felt we had enough with two. Downstairs I grabbed my car keys and bag and quietly left my slumbering household.

Here I am. I heard the words quite plainly in my head. Sometimes I had to remind myself that this was it. This was my life. I stifled a yawn. It was late, almost one thirty in the morning – this was very late for me.

I sat at traffic lights waiting for them to change. I was really annoyed and my annoyance was growing, solidifying into a great lump at the pit of my stomach. I had work in the morning – I shouldn't have to do this. It was so unfair. That was the steady chatter that was going on in my head. Round and round it went. This endless circle. Why had I always to come to the rescue? Why couldn't my brother just grow up like everyone else?

Eventually, the light turned green and I pulled off. I hoped that Jasmine was okay and not too frightened. It must have been six months ago since their last big row. On that night the Gardai had to be called. Jasmine didn't deserve them as parents. What was I to do? I couldn't play God, or Judge Judy for that matter, but I'd have liked to. The next set of lights turned green as I approached and a little smile settled momentarily on my face. "Nearly there," I muttered to shake the sleepy feeling away. My eyelids felt droopy. I longed to park my car and just continue where I left off in my sleeping.

My body tensed as I took a left into the leafy enclave where Cormac and Louise lived with their only child. Cormac had sold the Bed and Breakfast almost immediately, not pausing to consider Mary Drake who had worked for my parents since the day they bought the Castletown Arms. The fact that she was his godmother meant nothing to him. Wordlessly, David had given Mary a rent-free suite at the hotel and she still pottered around the kitchen there despite her advanced age.

The site was the second bequest to Cormac in Dad's will and he boasted of his cleverness in getting David to build this magnificent house in lieu of taking his ten per cent share of the hotel profits for five years. If he sobered up long enough to count up the figures, he'd surely find that David gave presents for nothing to nobody. God, how hard David tried to buy him out altogether when the five years ran out! But Cormac was unyielding. It seemed he took great fun out of being a nuisance to David and it blinded him to the generous offers that he made.

"Christ," David would say, frustrated at his and his solicitor's inability to crack Cormac on this one, "there he goes, swanking round the bar, getting ten per cent of the profits of a much different and bigger hotel than we inherited and there's nothing we can do because of a technicality in your father's will!"

As I got out of my car I looked up at Jasmine's bedroom window and saw her peering between the curtains. She had been waiting for me.

Cormac answered when I rang the doorbell. He opened the door wide. "Ah, sis," he said and waved his arm with a flourish as he allowed me to enter.

I walked in, ignoring his clownish gesture.

My brother and I had a very polarised relationship. In every way we were opposites. He was the troublemaker. I was the peace broker. It had always been the same.

"I came to see Jasmine, she called me," I said firmly. "You really should arrange a baby-sitter for nights like these – you're destroying your own child."

"Bravo!" said Cormac, glassy-eyed.

"Cormac, I'm tired, you're trying my patience. Last time, after the Gardaí had to be called, the social workers visited me. I didn't make a statement. You won't be so lucky next time. Now, where's Jasmine? I'm taking her out of here for tonight."

"Auntie Hannah!" Jasmine cried, running downstairs, her light brown hair loose around her face. She wasn't wearing her glasses and she looked cross-eyed at me. I hugged her and kissed the top of her head while she wrapped her arms around my waist. "Mummy and Daddy were fighting," she said, her face pressed into my breasts.

I bent down and looked into her anxious blue eyes. Her hair was silky to touch and, gently, I pushed strands of it from her face. "You look tired."

She yawned. "I'm not really," she said defensively.

"It's very late for a pretty little girl to be up."

She smiled at me and hugged me tighter.

"Would you like to come back to our house, Jasmine? Or we could go to the hotel if you'd prefer that?"

"That won't be necessary," Louise's voice came from behind. Her mascara was smeared, a sure sign that she had been crying.

Louise Moran, the blonde hussy from the housing estate, as my father used to say. It wasn't true. Louise was a year older than me and had started dating Cormac around the same time I left to do my teacher training. The courting period was to last almost fifteen years, although my brother dumped her several times over those years. He always came back and she always accepted him back willingly.

"Have you no pride?" I used to ask her. "Can't you see that he's using you? Maybe if you said no for once he might treat you better?"

"Pride is one of the Seven Deadly Sins, Hannah, and, anyway, I love him. It's as simple as that."

Some years back, before they married, Louise confided in me that she was having trouble conceiving a child. She had stopped using contraception and, as her periods continued to arrive like clockwork, initial feelings of puzzlement gave way to concern.

"I went to a specialist in Dublin. He's put me on a waiting list for fertility treatment. I can't wait to start. I so much want a baby of my own."

"Does Cormac know anything about this, Louise? I mean, he won't marry you just because you're pregnant. He needs to get his head sorted before he even thinks of becoming a father."

"I don't think you're listening, Hannah. I've been with your brother years now and have never put any demands on him. I've got lots of love to give and I want to be a mother. If Cormac doesn't want to marry me, that's fine. He can opt out of being a father if he can't get his poor head sorted. But what about me?"

So Cormac and Louise eventually married. They had a lavish reception at the Castletown Arms, attended by nigh on three hundred guests. Not a penny changed hands, Cormac having negotiated a deal with David using his ten per cent share of the business. Two years later, Jasmine was born.

"Jasmine phoned me – I came over because she was crying," I started to explain.

"I'm sorry about this," Louise said, without making eye contact with me. "It seems me and Cormac can't have a conversation any more without it turning into an argument."

"It's no bother for me to take Jasmine for the night, Louise – give you time to sort out whatever is going on between the two of you."

"Thanks but no. This is her home."

"You can come also, if you wish."

Louise took Jasmine's hand and led her away. "Tell you

what, let's sleep together in my bed," I heard her say, as they made their way upstairs. "And if you're really tired tomorrow morning, you can stay home from school. Just this once."

Louise had expertly deflated the situation and I immediately felt that I should have remained in my warm bed with David.

I returned to the living room where Cormac was sitting, looking dopily contemplative. He held a large glass of whiskey in one hand and stroked the glass silently with his free fingers. A half-full bottle of Jim Beam whiskey stood on the coffee table.

I was angry that my rescue mission was petering out. Helpless in the face of an addictive brother and a woman who lacked the courage to get up and leave or make him leave.

"Pondering life again, Cormac?" I said with an edge to my voice. "You should be living it or at least have the good grace to let others live theirs."

Silence for a moment.

"Hmm . . . let me see now . . . are you living your life? Teaching certificate, never used . . . Weren't you to go on a world trip with that Brenda?"

"You'll get a long way by switching the spotlight onto me, brother," I said, anger rising at the truth of his words. "Take a long hard look at yourself or is that too difficult for you?"

"Ah, poor sis . . . running around dutifully after David Joyce during the day and stuck in *my* house in the wee hours of the night offering her pearls of wisdom. Can't stop yourself interfering. Why can't *you* get a life?"

"Look, my only concern in all of this is my niece. You and Louise are adults with choices. Jasmine phoned me – she told me you two were fighting. What was I supposed to do, hang up and go back to sleep?"

"It's what I would have done."

"Of course you would, you selfish bastard!" I shouted back.

"Now, now," he said and grinned, pleased he had got a reaction.

"I think it's best I go now – there's nothing further I can do here – it's such a pity – for Jasmine, that is," I said levelly.

"Have a drink with me before you go, Hannah . . . I think I've some gin in the drinks cabinet." His voice had become needy, pleading almost. He was on his feet now, a little unsteadily.

In that moment, I thought I could see the fight draining from him.

"I'll make myself a coffee and sit with you a while," I said, "but not for long. I'm working in the morning."

"Yeah, work . . . the Castletown Arms Hotel . . . wonderful, isn't it?"

"You never wanted the hotel, Cormac. You'd have sold it in a jiffy. Look at all the opportunities Dad gave you. Stop feeling sorry for yourself."

"Opportunities – yeah – all I wanted was the chance to breathe, be listened to – know I was being heard. You're right about the hotel, though. I would have sold up – it has suffocated us all far too long."

"That's a little bit rich for someone who has clung on with determination to his share over the years. Always hovering around the place, the bar mainly, that is . . ."

"It was my inheritance. It should have been split evenly or left to Mammy to decide what's best after her day."

"You've been carrying this for over twenty years – let go

of it! It's done."

"It's more than twenty years, sis. I walked in Frank Duignan's shadow as a boy and I continued to walk in his shadow after he died, especially once news of his will spread."

Cormac was looking vacantly at the floor.

I waited for him to continue.

"It wasn't about the hotel . . . but the humiliation . . . the locals . . . 'He'd never have been up to it, hasn't got it' . . . bastards . . ."

"You're still young, Cormac," I said softly. "You can continue to walk in Dad's shadow or you can move on. It's time to move on . . . Are you listening, Cormac? Don't go to sleep on me now . . ."

But he had drifted off.

I closed the door softly as I didn't want to disturb Jasmine, safely tucked up with her mother sleeping. Children are so much wiser than adults, they really are, I thought. I felt tears streaming down my face and realised that I was crying.

"Nobody's perfect," I said softly to myself as I walked towards my car.

The night air was velvety black and so calming after the charged atmosphere of the house. My favourite time was evenings. Then, the day was done – over with. It couldn't be changed but tomorrow was all brand new. Ready for me to start again. The only problem was I kept dragging all my yesterdays with me, bringing them into my tomorrows. I wished I could just forget them.

Oh, the hours we worked, building up the business! I felt all those years were wasted. Sure, we had a thriving hotel but at what cost?

I looked up at the night sky and marvelled at the wonder of the stars. Wasn't the sky a mysterious and wonderful place? And it seemed so peaceful up there. A part of me wished someone would lower down a ladder and let me climb up . . . let me, Hannah Joyce, discover something about the Universe.

"Where do I start?" I whispered, careful not to disturb the hush of the night.

This endless pull of my family and their domestics was weighing me down so much. I closed my eyes and for a moment imagined myself climbing up on that ladder and disappearing into the velvety darkness. Oh, the peace of it all! I longed for some real freedom. Just to walk away from everything.

Three thirty in the morning. There was not much point going home. The car hummed effortlessly along the road to the Castletown Arms.

* * *

"Mrs Joyce . . . what are you doing here at this hour?"

Desmond Feeney had answered the hotel door. We had taken him on two years back when David conceded that we needed managerial support to oversee our vastly extended business. Desmond came directly in the aftermath of his graduation in Hotel Management, on yearly renewable contracts.

"This is strictly a temporary position," David had told him. "Our intention is that our son will eventually take on the role of duty manager in the hotel."

"That suits me, Mr Joyce – it's a great opportunity for me to learn."

Tonight, Desmond looked fraught and anxious. He'd interrupted dealings with two well-groomed middle-aged men and a tall blonde-haired girl at reception to answer the door. They seemed to be arguing over something – the girl kept prodding one of the men in the chest aggressively.

"Is everything okay, Desmond? I hadn't expected to see you around at this late hour. Who are these people – is there some trouble afoot?"

"Eh, they're overnight guests – there's another one in the toilet. Just settling their bill."

"At four o'clock in the morning? I don't understand . . . who are they?"

"Actually, I don't think we have their names. You know that Belmullen Electronics have block-booked Rooms 61 to 63 for the next twelve months? They're constantly flying their executives back and forth to oversee the opening of the new extension to their plant. These people have to catch an early morning flight from Dublin."

"Okay, but we really should be getting their names and some personal details – it's too loose. Why would they be paying – would we not be billing Belmullen?"

"We are, but they have to sign for it . . . accounting procedure for the company."

"Okay, I'll have to talk to David about this. You shouldn't need to be out of your bed at this unearthly hour just to capture a few signatures. Aren't you back on at eight o'clock? Make sure you get a few hours' sleep after you've finished with them."

Chapter Eighteen

The shrill ringing of a phone jerked me from a restless slumber.

"Mrs Joyce, you asked me to give you a call at seven thirty when you came in last night. I'm going home now." It was Dennis, the night porter.

"I did too. Wish I hadn't. Listen, Dennis, before you go, there's a work uniform of mine and black shoes in the office downstairs. Could you bring them up to me?"

"With you in a minute, Mrs Joyce."

Minutes later, I was in the kitchen asking the breakfast cook to prepare fresh orange juice, poached eggs, toast and coffee for me.

"I'll have it ready in ten minutes for you, Mrs Joyce – are you having it in the staff dining room or the main dining room?"

"The main dining room for Mrs Joyce," came a voice

from behind.

Mary Drake. Eighty-five. Same age as Dad would be now. Still pottering around our kitchens. Anybody needing to write a history of the Duignans and this hotel would just need to sit down with Mary.

"I've been hearing bad things about you, Hannah Duignan," said Mary, scoldingly. So much for my married state but when someone rears you from the cradle . . .

"And what are these bad things, Mary?"

"Dennis tells me you came into the hotel at a quarter to four this morning and here you are on the go again. Are you trying to kill yourself?"

"Not at all. It was just one of those nights. Things came up. Had to be dealt with."

I was not going to tell Mary about Cormac. Selling the B&B from under her feet had hurt her badly. I made my excuses with Mary and brought my breakfast to the dining room. It was almost empty.

"Hello, Hannah."

"Vincent . . . you're up early . . ."

I felt lost for words momentarily. Vincent was always a background person in my life. When I went to visit Lily, he might be there, but you'd scarcely know it.

"Would you like to join me?"

"Well . . . it would be rude not to," I said, looking around the deserted dining room.

An awkward silence followed as we ate.

"I believe you're leaving today," I said stiffly.

"That's right. We've rented a house on the edge of town."

"That's nice. At least your wife and daughter will get to see you walking around together, know you're alright," I said with venom. My feelings for Vincent were see-sawing between intense loathing and a mild curiosity as to why he had left.

"Maybe it's not such a good idea for us to be talking."

"Oh, don't mind me, Vincent. It's just that I get to see the hurt on the other side. Lily is my friend and your staying here puts that friendship at risk. Why couldn't you have taken a bed in one of the local guesthouses?"

"Aah, I thought here would be more anonymous . . ."

"Walking around town with a girl young enough to be your daughter doesn't look like someone seeking anonymity to me."

"Her name is Sinéad and we are in love."

I struggled between an impulse to add further to the rumours about Sinéad and a natural reluctance to spread gossip. But my loyalty was to Lily. I didn't even know Sinéad. Eventually I blurted it out.

"Look, Vincent. All I can say is that I don't like what you're doing. This girl comes with a reputation and a history of sleeping with married men. You're a fool. It wasn't a good idea to join you – I'd better get on with my day's work."

* * *

The dining room was filling up nicely as I left. David had asked me to check in with the painters this morning. The reception area looked totally uninviting. We had planned to get the painters in to do it at night but we were conscious of the extra cost involved so decided to put up with the inconvenience caused by them during the day.

"The numbers coming in for lunch are down since they came in, Hannah. They're getting in the way of people. You know John Devery better than I do. Work on him, get them to wrap it up."

I smiled to myself. That's exactly what John Devery would have wanted me to do, back in our teenage years. Work on him. We went to school together and he was my first boyfriend.

"Well, hello there, Mrs Joyce. To what do I owe this pleasure and so early in the morning?" said John, his eyes twinkling mischievously.

I felt that he was mentally undressing me as we stood together all these years later. Oh, he had caressed my developing breasts when I was fifteen but he got a reddened face for trying to push his hand down my school skirt. Today I noticed the fine lines at the corners of his eyes and the silver emerging in his blond head. I knew if my hairdresser didn't pay some attention to mine, we'd be in the same grey boat. John was a well-built muscular man and I had always found him very pleasing to my eye.

I strode towards him across the carpeted floor. He was wearing white overalls but still looked attractive. "Hi, Littlejohn, I've been hearing rumours about you."

John grinned – he wouldn't succumb too easily to my teasing about his schoolyard nickname. Invariably, there was a sexual innuendo to our conversations, driven by him, mostly. It was his way of telling me that he could still mark me down as one of his conquests all these years later. It was harmless fun, wasn't it, kind of flattering and nostalgic? He continued to spread a dustsheet and I had to move out of his way.

"I hope they're really bad."

"Marian said you're very good in the kitchen."

Marian was also in our class. John sat beside her in sixth

class and was constantly playing practical jokes on her. One time after the weekly school swimming session Marian could not find her knickers and had to return to class red-faced. Nobody knew why she wouldn't join in at playtime that day until John suddenly produced her underwear from his pocket in front of the whole schoolyard. He got a week's suspension for his prank but it was nothing to the ribbing Marian endured for years afterwards. "Wearing any today?" the boys would shout.

He was standing beside me now, a little too close for comfort.

"I've got what it takes," he said.

I inched slightly away. He grinned at me like he'd received the message loud and clear. John was one of those people you could call young at heart. He flirted outrageously with every woman.

"You'd want to be careful. She's married."

John snorted. "Was she really praising me? You can be honest with me. She nearly wet herself when I landed on her doorstep. Never thought when she rang Brush Strokes for a quotation that John Devery would land on her doorstep after all these years!"

"Yes, she said you're the best." He snorted again and I had to ask. "What's so funny?" I knew by the devilish glint in his eye that he was up to something. He didn't reply so I persevered. "You didn't do anything you shouldn't have?"

John closed the slight distance that had grown between us.

"Depends what you mean by that," he said, pleased with the fact that I was interested. "She went to Spain for a week's holidays and when she came home she was furious that the kitchen wasn't the exact shade of green that she wanted."

"Oh dear," I said sympathetically.

John's eyes twinkled at me and I knew he was squaring himself up to tell a good story.

"Marian gave me a piece of wood and she told me she wanted the kitchen painted in the same shade. When she got back from Spain she kept holding up this damn bit of wood and saying to me: 'Take a good look at that, John – can't you see they're not the same colour?' I have to tell you it was the ugliest green colour I had ever seen. She has no taste, no taste whatsoever."

His breath was a pleasant mixture of toothpaste and coffee.

"So what happened?" I asked.

"That's what money does. It turns some women into awkward bitches. Now, you're not like that."

"You're not answering me, John Devery," I said, aware of his lecherous gaze. Those dancing eyes . . . This fellow is almost back in that schoolyard, merging too close during our kisses . . .

John looked around him. Two of his employees were bringing in ladders, paintbrushes and buckets of paint. Another was starting to sand the wall. He shook his head and turned his attention back to me. "Where was I?" he asked and then he smiled. "Ah, yes, Marian."

"What did you do?" I asked, eager for him to finish his story.

"I painted the piece of wood the same colour as the kitchen. Sure, the woman is colour blind, couldn't tell the difference."

"Crook," I said in admiration. "Now, let me assure you that you won't be pulling any stunts like that here. You'll have me *and* David to deal with. When will you be finished?"

"End of the week, Hannah. Say Friday. Will you come round to pay me in person? I might even buy you a drink."

"Just you make sure it's Friday – forget about drinks and drinking until then."

John Devery. All suggestion and titillation, not much else. Provocative bastard, I thought to myself. Yet I had participated.

Why?

The settled Hannah Joyce . . . married to the sexy, successful love of her life.

Chapter Nineteen

Castletown Arms
Thursday 16/09/04

Dear Journal ~
It's me again. Outside my window I can see the garden, swathed in fog, giving the place a mysterious air. The day will probably brighten up to be glorious. September always heralds change. Another day is beginning. David is probably awake now. He will see that I am not sleeping beside him.

Anything is possible. I do believe that any ordinary day can bring a new beginning. Perhaps Vincent is calling Lily now or else taking a trip out to their house. Perhaps he's phoning Sinéad. Perhaps he's just going to get on with his day ~ ignore the chaos that's happening all around him. I wonder is he tempted to leave ~ pack a bag and leave it all behind him?

My world is so out of sync. What I plan and what actually

happens are never the same. Last night I was so tempted to leave. I really wanted to, only I had no petrol. This morning I am full of regrets. I could have pushed myself. I could have looked for a petrol station. I mean, lots of stations are open all night. I had my wallet. I could have done it, but I'm such a coward.

I just don't have that reckless streak. My mother is old and fragile – she isn't up to this. I mean, Cormac seldom goes to see her and I suspect when he does it's because he's looking for something. Then there's Timothy. I just wish he'd talk to me. I worry about him. He seems to have no ambition ~ he's so laidback and carefree. Oh, Lord, I almost forgot, isn't Sammi coming home with the baby? Alan is off to the States. I couldn't possibly go, not now, she needs me. I could take the baby for a few nights and let her get some sleep.

And then there is David ~ we badly need to talk. So engrossed in the hotel, he cannot see that I am hurting and need more from him. What is it about us that we take the precious things in life ~ love, warmth, communication ~ for granted?

I have argued my case on why I can't leave home. This is my home, these people are my family and I simply cannot walk away from them.

Bye for now,

Hannah

I closed my journal tightly and returned it to my bag. I sat quietly in the house at the rear of the hotel. It was empty these days. These were David's living quarters when he came to Castletown all those years ago. It was now my private retreat, a place where I could escape the bustle of the hotel for a short while and scribble a few notes at my leisure. Where would you be now, David, if I hadn't become part of your life when you came here? You and Sammi.

Hardly here . . . the Berkeley Court, Jury's, who knows?

My mobile rang. It was my mother.

"Hannah, where are you?" she asked irritably. She hated calling mobiles because of the cost – secondly, she liked to think that I spent all my time in the hotel.

"Eh, having coffee with Alison." A lie, but I was hoping she would excuse herself and postpone whatever it was she had to say to me.

She tutted. "It's well for some."

I knew by her tone that she was cross over something.

"Why did you go around to Cormac's last night?" she challenged me.

"Well –"

"You should mind your own business and stop interfering!"

I heard her voice quiver. I really didn't want to upset her. "Mammy, will you just let me explain?"

"You know what he's like when he's had a few drinks."

"You're upset, I'll –"

"Upset? Of course I'm upset. Wouldn't you be if you were woken at four o'clock in the morning?"

My mother always kept a box of tissues beside her, and I heard her sniffing into one now. I loved my mother, she was great, but she'd got this thing about Cormac. She thought he could do no wrong.

"You mean Cormac phoned you at four this morning?" I heard myself repeating her words. If Cormac had waited until morning to phone her, those memory cells would have been eroded and he'd have forgotten. That's why he had to call her while it was still fresh in his head. Old resentments started to bubble up inside me.

"Yes, Hannah, that's what I said. Have you been listening to a thing I've said? I was sound asleep and the next thing the phone rings and I think to myself who could that be at this hour . . ." She was crying now and I had to feel sorry for her.

"Jasmine phoned me – she was upset –" I started to explain.

"Hannah, you just can't do that," she butted in.

This always happened: Cormac did something bad or stupid and I ended up taking the blame. She was having the conversation with the wrong person. I wasn't to blame. I didn't wake her from her slumber. She continued to sniffle and I waited for her to finish. My mother didn't need me upsetting her – Cormac did enough of that.

"We'll talk later," I said in a conciliatory tone and then switched subjects rapidly. "I'm just on my way in to the hotel – jobs to do," I said as I opened my car door.

"That's good – I always say if you want something done you're better off doing it yourself," she said, then added nostalgically, "I remember when your father and I were running the place, we never left it . . . never could."

"That's the way it was alright, Mammy." I had to keep the status quo – there was no point in upsetting her more.

"You go along, dear, we'll talk later."

*　　*　　*

"David, got a minute?"

"Hannah, you didn't make it home last night. How did it go?"

"Oh, I should have listened to you. I don't know why I bother. It was so late when I left, I came directly here. The painters say they will be out by Friday week."

"Good." David returned to examining some paperwork at

the desk.

"David, you know this contract we have with Belmullen Electronics . . . what arrangement did you reach with them?"

"I thought you knew all about that. It's been in place for nearly two years. Belmullen pay twelve hundred euros weekly to block-book the three rooms for their executives. They also fly in some of their more experienced foreign workers to help with the training and set-up of the new assembly lines. The money is paid into the hotel bank account monthly in advance – any extras are invoiced to the company. Actually, Cormac's Louise handles the account from the Belmullen end."

"We don't seem to maintain a record of the *names* of the people who stay here."

"No, it's a room-only basis, somewhat like renting out an apartment, I suppose. Saves a lot of checking in and out. Is there something wrong?"

"No, I just needed to get an understanding of the thing – I met some of their men and a lady leaving here at four o'clock this morning. I thought it strange at the time, but now you've filled me in, it makes a bit more sense . . . David, I was just looking at your wardrobe the other day – you seem to be running low on white shirts, and a few new ties might freshen up your suits. I'd better go on a shopping trip."

"I don't suppose *your* wardrobe will be extended as a result of this trip?"

"You never know. I might see something – you won't need to remortgage the hotel, though."

"Coffee Triangle day out?"

"That's about it."

"When?"

"Tomorrow."

111

* * *

Driving through the town on my way home, I noticed Jasmine waiting outside the school gate alone. She waved smilingly at me and I continued on until my dashboard clock caught my attention. Half three – school finished at three o'clock. Soon, I was back at the school and Jasmine was getting into the front passenger seat.

"I thought your mammy was letting you stay home from school today, pet? What happened? You were up until all hours last night."

"Mammy was working and Daddy had to go to Dublin again. There was nobody to mind me so I came down to the school. I didn't care – I don't like staying at home, I don't like the fights."

Jasmine looked pale and bleary-eyed despite her brave front. She seemed to carry an air of resignation, as if the way her parents behaved towards her was the way things went for children so she might as well get on with it. Deep down, surely though, she knew this was not normal. A surge of anger towards Cormac and Louise rose within me. I'm really going to have to take a firm lead in this, I thought. It just cannot go on any longer.

"Did you have your dinner, Jasmine?"

"No, Mammy packed some Billy Roll sandwiches for me this morning. I ate some at big break and gave the rest to my best friend Sheila. Her mammy never packs any food for her, she just brings Tayto."

Like attracting like, I mused resentfully.

I would have loved another child, a daughter, but it just didn't happen for me. It was baffling that I conceived so quickly with Timothy, sooner than I wanted to, and nothing happened afterwards. We didn't want another child immediately but I came off the pill when he was four.

But I dismissed David's suggestions that I was being over-protective towards Jasmine – that I was compensating for my own loss.

"Let it go, Hannah," he would say. "It's not ideal, but there's a lot worse than Cormac and Louise out there, isn't that what the social workers told you? She's got a fine home, the best of clothes and toys – goes off to Spain at least twice a year on holidays. The picture is not as bad as you paint it."

I was not going to let it go. Men just didn't understand. No mention of Jasmine's friends there, David – you don't see them coming round in droves towards her "mod cons" house, do you? Yes, Jasmine has all the latest toys and gadgets to play with – alone.

"Auntie Hannah, could you bring me to swimming training in Athlone this evening if Mammy and Daddy can't? I need to go – I won't get moved up to the Seals if I keep missing training and I want to stay in the same group as my friends."

I rang Cormac on his mobile.

"God, I'm sorry, sis, you're right . . . I was due to pick her up today, shit, I got it mixed up . . . You'll take her to swimming . . . Yeah, that's great . . . I could be there in an hour but if you're volunteering . . . Yeah, I'll ring Louise and I'll pick her up at your house later. Nine o'clock, that's fine."

That's settled then, I thought triumphantly. I'd known that Cormac would roll over easily – if I rang Louise, she would switch into Earth Mother mode immediately and I would not get a chance to spend the evening with my niece. Louise was no better suited than me to be the goddess of fertility and life. You might have a point, David, but if you weren't joined at the hip with our, no, *your* hotel, you might be able to see that I have needs too.

Jasmine's eyes lit up with joy when I returned with the news. "Great," she exclaimed, planting a big kiss on my cheek. "Swimming is at seven so, yeah, we have time for bowling – and, yes, I'd love a Chinese. I packed my swimming stuff this morning, so we don't need to go by the house. You're the bestest auntie in all the world!"

* * *

"Okay, that's half an hour bowling and half an hour in the children's adventure area. That's fifteen euros in all. Size five shoes for you and small size thirteen for your daughter."

Jasmine giggled when I didn't correct him – no harm in playing out the mother role for the evening.

"And you want the barriers up on the bowling alley." The attendant twitched his nostrils. "I see you've got some Chinese food with you there – I'm afraid that cannot be eaten here – rules. We have our own fast-food service over there."

Minutes later we're tucking into our Chinese food. A five-euro bribe had yielded a sudden change of heart and two pristine-clean plates. Chicken Szechuan for Jasmine, Beef in Black Bean Sauce for me.

Then we played bowling.

"I think we should take down the barriers for your shots, Jasmine. One hundred and two against seventy. You don't need any extra help. Next time you'll have to give me a head start."

Later, I sat watching her head disappear among the coloured balls and resurface like a mermaid from the sea. She

114

had quickly joined up with a little coloured girl, probably the same age, and soon they were trying to outdo each other with gymnastic poses on the climbing frames and slides.

"We are celebrating today," her mother told me. "We've just got news from Justice that we can remain in Ireland. We came here four years ago from Nigeria and were staying in a caravan all that time in a specially built site. Now we can rent our own home and I can look for work. I took out my medication this morning and flushed it down the toilet. My depression lifted the moment I opened the letter."

"That's wonderful news for you. Would you like a coffee while we watch?"

"That would be nice. My name is Funke by the way. I overheard your little girl call you Hannah."

Eventually, the two little girls emerged from the sea of balls. My earlier tip to the attendant seemed to have gained them extra time.

"Bye, Jasmine!" the little girl shouted on the way out.

* * *

Jasmine's alter ego emerged once we entered Athlone Swimming Pool. She did not accept my outstretched hand as we walked together across the car park, a fixed look of determination imbedded in the contours of her little face. It was time for discipline and focus and it was as if I was being afforded a glimpse, a preview maybe, of Jasmine as a young woman in the future. She moved gracefully and powerfully through the seemingly endless laps, only pausing to hear the instructions of the poolside coach.

"She's one for the future, this girl," the coach remarked on noticing my interest. "It's a pity she misses so many sessions, she has real potential . . . a certainty for the National Community Games if she practised that little bit more."

One of the children shouted from the pool. "Liam, are we practising our dives and turns this evening?"

In the car on the way home, Jasmine yawned repeatedly and gave little sighs of contentment. "Liam's picked me for the Gala in Limerick next Sunday. I hope Mammy or Daddy can bring me."

"You ring me if they can't, pet," I replied. "We'll work something out, make sure you get there."

Soon she was asleep, occasionally twisting and scratching her nose as the Clio hit bumps on the road. I could've been teaching you today, girl, marking your copybook, I thought as I surveyed her school pinafore and small navy cardigan. "You've got my nose and all, girl," I whispered as I gave way to a self-serving interpretation of her little features. I felt more comfortable adopting the maternal mode with Jasmine – the age difference and her neediness meant we slotted more easily into the mother/daughter routine than I had ever managed with Sammi.

Cormac collected her spot on at nine with a predictable "Thanks, sis, I owe you one!" and a wave in the driveway.

I took out my journal before retiring for the night.

Cedar Woods
Thursday 16/09/04

Dear God ~
Thanks for sending Jasmine my way today.
Bye for now,
Hannah

Chapter Twenty

Next morning we set out for the Big Smoke, as my father used to call it. We usually took it in turns driving on these shopping expeditions to Dublin. Lily was the fearless one among us – she liked to drive. Today Alison and myself gladly let her at it. I sat in the back seat, looking out at the passing mosaic of fields. For years the landscape had remained almost the same and now everywhere you looked the earth was being dug up and concrete was being poured in. Soon, the distance between Castletown and Dublin would be one urban sprawl.

I had really needed this trip. We were long overdue a day away from the unrelenting suffocation of Castletown. Alison had needed little persuasion. Getting Lily to complete our triangle had been more difficult . . .

* * *

"Come on, Lily, it will do you good," I had coaxed.

"What would I do in Dublin?" she'd asked.

"Take a day to yourself – you don't have to do anything," said Alison.

"I don't know . . . I'm not sleeping well. I don't know if I have the energy for a day in Dublin."

We were sitting in Lily's kitchen having coffee. She was hibernating from the world. Alison was even doing her shopping for her.

"Let's go out to the garden," Alison suggested.

Lily brightened as she started to explain what was happening in her garden. Underground there was another world living: spiders, centipedes, beetles, earthworms. I wasn't aware of them until Lily told me about them.

"Gardening has always been my salvation but not this time." A watery smile flitted across her face.

"Your garden looks great," I said.

She nodded in agreement.

Alison tilted her auburn head. She was wearing sunglasses and they added a touch of glamour to her. "A day away from here will do you good."

Lily had smiled wearily at us, knowing that we weren't going to give up on her. "Okay, so."

* * *

Now, here we were on the Quays – as usual there was a tailback.

"Let's get coffee first, then we'll decide on a plan of action," I said from the back seat.

"Hannah, remember the time you parked in one of the

car parks beside Debenhams and we went back to the wrong one?" said Lily.

"That's right, oh, will I ever forget it?" I said, remembering the panic I'd felt as we fruitlessly walked up and down and around each level looking for David's car.

"We're much smarter now," Alison laughed. "Now we actually take note of which car park we drive into."

Once we stowed the car away we set out for Henry Street.

"Damn!" said Alison. "I shouldn't have worn these shoes!"

"But they look good," I remarked, taking in the uncomfortable-looking but stylish shoes.

Lily just frowned. She was dressed sensibly in runners and tracksuit bottoms, which of late had become her usual attire.

"Now, where can we get a decent cup of coffee?" she pondered once we'd reached Henry Street.

We liked the look of the first café we came upon, so we went inside and soon were fortifying ourselves with coffee and scones.

"I'd hate to live in Dublin," Lily remarked.

"You liked Dublin, Hannah, didn't you?" Alison asked.

"Oh, I did, but I didn't really appreciate it at the time. I should have gone to more art exhibitions and plays and stuff like that."

Lily pulled a face. "Hindsight is a wonderful thing. If I could have seen into my future I definitely would have done a lot of things differently."

There was a small pause while we digested that thought.

"So what's the plan?" Lily asked abruptly.

"I have to buy a few bits in Marks & Spencer for David,"

I said, "and I just might get myself something new. And I'd like to get my little niece Jasmine something."

Lily poked me in the side. "You'd better not forget your grandson!"

Alison laughed. "Yes, imagine you're a granny!"

"Ha, ha. I wasn't forgetting that fact but I don't need reminding today – I'm not leaving town without some sexy underwear."

"What for?" Lily asked.

"Oh, you just wait and see." I tipped my nose.

"Hmm – it's like that, is it?" said Alison.

"Right, underwear it is," Lily said briskly, then checked her watch. "Where to first?"

"The ladies'!" we two chorused and started to laugh.

"I could do with a new pair of shoes," Alison said as we took the elevator to the third floor.

"Another pair!" Lily exclaimed, turning to look at me, eyes wide. "Hannah, did you see her wardrobe lately? It's full of shoes!"

"I know, I know," said Alison. "I just like to buy shoes."

We stopped outside Monsoon.

"I'm going in here to buy a dress," Lily said.

Alison's face brightened with curiosity. "Going somewhere special?"

"I just might be, Alison! You're not the only one that can have some fun!"

Alison and I exchanged looks. Excellent – Lily seemed to be coming out of her shell. In the shop Alison took on an efficient air and started to flick through clothes rails like some fashion guru. "Casual or formal? Day or evening?" she asked Lily.

"Formal – but daywear."

Alison rummaged further. "What do you think?" she asked, as she pulled out a pink linen dress and held it out to Lily.

Lily made a face. "I'm not sure."

"Try it on," I suggested.

"What's the occasion?" Alison ventured to ask as she led the way towards the fitting rooms.

"I've been invited to my brother-in-law's wedding and I need a new outfit for it. I wasn't going to go but . . ."

"So when did you decide you were going?" I asked.

"Just now."

After several fittings Lily finally decided on the pink dress that Alison had chosen at the beginning. She eyed her lissom figure in the mirror again. I could tell she was putting on a brave face.

"Lily, you look fantastic, doesn't she, Alison?"

"Yes, you do. But, Lily, are you sure about going to this wedding? Vincent will be there with *her*."

Lily marched back into the cubicle. "I know he'll be there but life goes on. I'm not going to stay at home just because we're not . . . together . . ." Her voice trailed off.

"Damn right. I'll come along if you like?" I offered.

"Thanks," came Lily's voice from behind the curtain. "I haven't decided – perhaps myself and Erin will just go together."

Back on the street again, Lily asked, "Where to now?"

Alison linked her arm. "You're on a roll today."

"I sure am and we have no time to waste. So, where to next?"

"You'll have to get some shoes to go with the dress, won't she, Hannah?"

I smiled knowingly at Alison – any excuse for her to get

into a shoe shop. "Of course."

After trailing through several shoe shops and numerous pairs of shoes, Lily announced that she had seen a nice pair in Smith's window back home in Castletown.

"Now you tell us!" I said wearily.

"A hat," Alison announced. "For a wedding you need a hat, Lily."

"Later!" said Lily. "How about a coffee break?"

We trudged into the first café we came across, laden with shopping bags, and found ourselves queuing even though the lunchtime rush should have been over.

Finally seated with coffee and sandwiches, we felt ourselves unwind again.

Alison sighed and leaned back in her chair. "Shopping can be hard work."

"I've been thinking about leaving Castletown," Lily said abruptly.

"Oh, Lily, don't say that!" said Alison.

Lily shook her head. "Oh, don't mind me! I'm just confused and angry."

"It's early days," I cautioned. "You don't want to do something that you'll regret."

Alison nodded in agreement. "Come on, Lily, have a sandwich, it will keep your strength up. Hannah still has to get to Marks & Spencer's and buy that sexy underwear for whatever she's planning."

"Oh, come on, Hannah, you can tell us," said Lily. "Alison and myself are good at keeping secrets."

I laughed and felt tempted to tell but then cautioned myself. No, it was early days.

Ten minutes later we were zigzagging our way across Henry Street. We made our way into Marks & Spencer's and

I headed towards the men's department. I picked up two shirts, a polo shirt, some ties and a pair of chinos for David. Then I met up with Lily and Alison in the women's department. Apart from the sexy underwear, an equally sexy nightdress wouldn't go astray.

More concentrated shopping followed. We didn't rush around from shop to shop like years ago when we had to be home for the children. Now, we had the whole day to squander. We planned to eat in Furey's on the way home. There we could chat and analyse our day's purchases.

Something about that day in Dublin reminded me of my college days. I recalled a day that Brenda and myself took the bus into town to get our passport photos taken in Woolworth's. We'd been at a party the night before and we couldn't stop giggling from lack of sleep – we were so young and innocent. I felt a guilty pang, remembering Brenda's hurt expression when I told her that I wouldn't be going travelling with her.

I picked up two lipsticks from the Lancôme counter in Arnotts. "I'll have these," I said to the sales assistant.

"Hannah, you should have tried out the sample colours," Lily reprimanded me. "Seen if you liked them first."

"Yes, I suppose I should have," I said. "Where to now?"

"Home," Alison suggested. "Or, Furey's rather."

"Good idea," Lily said. "Let's get going before the traffic gets really chock-a-block."

* * *

At Furey's we stopped to have dinner. The food was delicious there but you did have to wait so we decided to order a bottle of wine first thing.

Lily and Alison always looked to me for a good wine recommendation and, as always, I protested. "I haven't a clue about wine – usually I let David choose!"

But they insisted I do the honours and I ended up choosing a mid-price Australian Shiraz almost at random.

"That's what we should do," Lily said, sipping appreciatively at the one small glass she allowed herself since she was driving. "We should go on one of those wine-tasting trips, somewhere nice like Italy. What do you think, girls?"

"Hey, Alison," I said, "didn't your neighbour Susan go on one and come back with a lover and ditch the husband?"

"Yes, she did." She grinned mischievously. "It could be a bit of fun. Great idea, Lily – why didn't you think of it before?"

"I might be able to get us a good deal," I said. "We know some hoteliers in Italy. So if you're on for it, then so am I."

We chatted happily about this scheme until our food arrived.

"I'm exhausted," I said as we started to eat. "But it's a pleasant exhaustion."

"Me too," Alison replied.

"I must say I enjoyed my day," Lily said.

The drone of the *Six-One News* hummed in the background. I paused suddenly with a piece of steak hovering on its fork near my mouth . . . Had the reporter just said something about the Castletown Arms?

Lily and Alison were suddenly alert, listening.

". . . *a sensational report in today's* Evening Herald. *Gardai are investigating reports of a lucrative prostitution racket that is alleged to be in operation there for the past two years. The Castletown Arms, which is one of the midland's*

leading hotels, is owned by David and Hannah Joyce. Cormac
Duignan, brother to Mrs Joyce, is a minority shareholder in the
business. Nadia Constantine, a Russian native, is the main
subject of the Herald's exclusive article, which explores the
seedy world of people trafficking and prostitution. The Vice
Squad have set up a special unit in Athlone to handle the
investigation. Superintendent Matthew Kennedy has been
appointed . . ."

Chapter Twenty-One

I sat in shock as I read the *Evening Herald* exclusive. The headline echoed violently in my brain. *Lucrative Prostitution Ring Smashed – Vice Girl Nadia Exposes Corruption and Racketeering in Midlands Hotel – See Our Exclusive on Pages 4,5, 6 and 7.*

The front page showed photographs of the Castletown Arms and "Nadia". I gasped as I recognised her as the girl from the hotel foyer the other night. On the inner pages were photographs of David and Desmond Feeney. There was also a blurred picture of a man going through the back entrance to the hotel underscored with the text: *"Punter enters vice lair."* I looked frantically over the various headline articles spread across four pages, not knowing where to begin. *Nadia – My Horror Story, Respected Local Businessman also Subject of Investigation into Planning Irregularities, Estimated Turnover of EUR 2 Million Annually,*

Two Men and a Woman Helping Garda Enquiries . . .

Where should I start?

"Lily, could I borrow your mobile? I left mine at home this morning."

"Yeah, of course . . . it's out in the car, I'll get it for you."

I overheard a whisper in the background: "That's his wife over there . . . Hannah Joyce . . ." What did I expect? Furey's was a renowned stop-off point for midlanders going to Dublin.

"No, Lily, I'll go out and get it. It'll be more private. Do you mind if we go then?"

Outside, in the car, I rang David.

"Hannah, where in God's name are you? Have you heard –"

"Yes, I –"

"I've been trying to reach you since morning – I got only three hours' notice of intention to publish – couldn't block it – Declan Burke sought a temporary injunction to delay it –"

"What's it all about, David, I –?"

"You mean you haven't twigged already? It's about Cormac, Louise and Desmond Feeney. Bastards! The Belmullen Electronics thing was a front, a scam. The three of them are down at the Garda Station. Get home quick, Hannah – I've got to go."

* * *

I sat silently in the rear of the car as we made our way back to Castletown, the peace of our leisurely day out violently shattered. Told from her angle, Nadia was one of six East European women who had came to Ireland on a promise of employment in the catering sector. They soon found themselves in the grip of unscrupulous people who threatened them with imprisonment, deportation and all sorts of unpleasant things if they did not co-operate. Anything to dump your shit on somebody else, I thought grimly, remembering the elegant, aggressive blonde in the hotel foyer. This is a revenge mission, no doubt. The women were paid thirty euros an hour, the balance of the punters' investment of two hundred euros per hour going to a Mr Big, presumably Cormac, via a link person at the hotel. Desmond Feeney.

I got out at the hotel. "Thanks, Lily, Alison," I mumbled and made my way inside.

David was in his office, his jacket and tie removed.

"Come in, I've just finished up with Special Branch and the Criminal Assets Bureau – they've been here for nearly five hours – I'm spent. This has been going on for near on two years right under my nose. A credit of five thousand two hundred euros monthly has been going into our account for the past twenty-one months – in payment for the rooms. The original standing order was set up by a person with a bogus name and address. The money was paid into the bank monthly in cash. The Gardaí are convinced that Cormac set the scam up but can produce no evidence . . . Jesus, we've been had, Hannah."

I started to recycle the *Evening Herald* reports into my own words. "But how, David? Six women, entertaining a stream of clients right here at the hotel – how could we have missed it?"

"Guile and sheer good luck on your brother's part. The women came into the gym in threes at the start of their shifts. Did their workout and then made their way up the corridor leading to the bedrooms. The customers could have come in any way they liked – the gym, the side entrance, even in front of our noses – they'd blend in quite easily with people attending functions and meetings in the conference room upstairs."

"And where does Louise fit in?"

"Fucking nowhere as far as evidence is concerned. Our file on Belmullen has gone missing and there isn't an iota of evidence at the factory. Alfred Bantam, the managing director, knew nothing about the whole thing."

"But how could that be, David? Didn't you wine and dine him regularly as a thank-you for his patronage?"

"But of course. Belmullen also had an ad-hoc arrangement where they could book other rooms at short notice. That was a separate account and Louise handled it at their end. Alfred assumed I was thanking him for the legit account."

"Poor Louise, maybe she didn't know what Cormac –"

"Aw, give it a rest, Hannah! The Criminal Assets Bureau conservatively estimate that your brother might well walk with a two-million-euro profit on this. But all of the evidence is circumstantial. Their only hope is that Nadia will testify against Cormac. The other five have disappeared without trace. Fuck Louise, fuck the pair of them!"

"Look, David, you go home, you look all in. I'll stay here. But what's the bit about the planning permission?"

"Oh, that's a whole different ballgame. Some crank wrote anonymously to the Council. Said I was backhanding Vincent and others. Coincidence – bloody inconvenient timing at that coming together with this scandal." David walked wearily through his office door.

* * *

"Thank you, Matthew . . . Yes, I understand it's all off the record . . . I really appreciate it . . . No, not a word to anyone. I really needed to know."

I replaced the receiver in its cradle.

A hugely professional operation, Superintendent Matthew Kennedy had called it. Incredibly simple, yet ingenious. No state records, no passports or driving licences to match the details supplied to the leisure centre – these women simply didn't exist. No apparent Social Welfare claims – why bother when you could pocket two thousand euro per week? Matthew confirmed the Criminal Assets Bureau's estimate of Cormac's gains, saying that two million was a conservative estimate of his profits. These women were highly professional – they operated to a strict procedure: cash only, no local customers, no personal property left on the premises, no criminal records, no matching fingerprints found on the state's records . . . nothing.

Except Nadia – what caused her to break cover?

"The three of them – your brother, his wife and Feeney – are playing a blinder. They have their solicitors present. Threatening to sue for false arrest, they are," were Matthew Kennedy's final words.

Timothy's number came flashing up on my mobile.

"You heard, Mum?"

"Yes, Timothy – did you know anything at all about it?"

"Not a notion, Mum – but hell, what a sting, you'd have to admire them!"

I frowned worriedly at his attitude. "There's nothing admirable about it – they could regret it in the long run. Who's looking after Jasmine?"

"She's with Gran. I'll tell you, she's amazing, Gran is. Must be some mistake, she said, and carried on as if nothing had happened."

Typical Mammy, I thought. In total denial that her Cormac could even contemplate wrongdoing, let alone do it. Secretly, I preferred to remain in denial on this one myself – the consequences were too awful to imagine.

Lily too . . . instinctively I felt she had some thing to do with the planning permission accusation, an idea I found hugely disturbing. Could she possibly have written to the Council and then brazened it out with Alison and me in Dublin? Was she capable of that?

* * *

I returned home to an eerily empty house. No sign of David and Timothy. I felt a strange sense of unease and started making some telephone calls. Surely this was a night for the family to close ranks, stick together.

Mammy's cutting voice came across the phone: "If it isn't Hannah, off shopping in Dublin while the family business collapses! You were with that Lily one too – I bet it was her that tipped off the Council. Sad old cow! Just because she cannot keep her husband in check."

I bit my tongue against a hostile reply – Mammy had this knack of forgiving errant husbands their sins without giving a thought for her own gender. She never forgave Mary Robinson for depriving Brian Lenihan of presidential office.

"Is David or Timothy over there?" I asked.

"No, just me and Jasmine – we're off to bed."

"You're taking this very calmly, Mum – aren't you worried about it all?"

"I don't believe a word of it, Hannah. Declan Burke rang me – he's looking after Cormac and Louise. He says there's not a shred of evidence to link them to any of the *Herald*'s allegations."

"I hope you're right, Mammy, I really do. Give my love to Jasmine. Call me if you get any news – I'll do the same."

Chapter Twenty-Two

David returned about four in the morning with Timothy.

I stirred sleepily, peering at his silhouette in the dark. "Where were you? I was worried sick about you."

"I went back to the hotel with Timothy to search for that file. Nothing doing, though. Look, let's sleep on it. I'm going in to see Declan Burke in the morning. He feels that I need to prepare a damage limitation statement, as he calls it."

"Okay, I'm going to call by Lily to ask her about the anonymous letter to the County Council. I'll never speak to her again if I find she did that to me, to us . . ."

David's shallow breathing told me that he was already asleep.

* * *

I awakened to the sound of the shower running in the en-suite. Eight thirty. David had picked out his best outfit, an expensive Hugo Boss number with same-brand shirt, tie and shoes. He emerged from the shower, towelling his greying locks vigorously. "I'll show them all who's *Boss* today." He laughed manically at his feeble little joke. "Are you coming in today?"

"After I deal with Lily first. What's with your best outfit?"

"The media, Hannah. They were all over the place yesterday. I want them to see that it's business as usual – let them know that the Joyce family won't be bowled over by the begrudgers. See you later."

David turned out of the driveway in his Mercedes 520. Within minutes I was pointing my way towards Lily's house.

She was flying round her garden on her sit-on mower. I shouted as loudly as possible to be heard.

"Can you turn that off? I need to speak with you!"

She shut it down and came towards me.

"I get the feeling this is not purely social, Hannah. It's about the article in the paper, isn't it?"

"Did you do it, Lily? Write to the Council about the planning permission?"

"I did. Not sorry about it either."

"Look at the harm you've caused. David will sue you if, no, *when* he gets to hear what you've done."

Lily laughs disinterestedly. "Don't think so, Hannah – there were no backhanders but that was only because Vincent refused them. So don't you go preaching to me about harm. The only real victims in this are Erin and me. A little embarrassing for your David, maybe even you, but that never killed anybody."

There was nothing more to be said. Lily had gone and

revved up her lawnmower once more and I was left with my tears in her driveway.

* * *

"Mammy, are you driving? Switch on the news headlines. They're coming up at ten, before the *Pat Kenny Show*." Timothy rang off abruptly.

I pulled up on the hard shoulder. A bit about Iraq . . . oil prices . . . I stiffened as I listened.

"*Garda sources in Athlone have confirmed that Nadia Constantine, the Russian woman at the centre of yesterday's sensational* Evening Herald *story, has disappeared and is presumed to have left the country. A spokesperson told RTÉ News that an anonymous phone caller, using a special reference number known only to Nadia and Vice Squad detectives, has advised that she will not be making any statement on the matter to the police. Ms Constantine's story regarding the operation of a brothel at the Castletown Arms Hotel was the lead story in yesterday's sensational* Evening Herald. *Two men and a woman, who had been helping Gardaí with their enquiries, were released without charge at nine thirty this morning. Mr Declan Burke, solicitor for David Joyce, owner of the Castletown Arms Hotel has advised our reporter at the scene that his client has no comment to make at present but will be making a statement over the coming days . . .*"

Timothy rang back. "What do you think, Mum? It looks like it could have been one big hoax. Dad is threatening to sue the *Evening Herald*. The Vice Squad reckon they will never trace these women, if they ever existed, that is."

"It could be that alright, Timothy, see you later."

My thoughts drifted to the blonde woman in the foyer.

You were real, Nadia, weren't you, but where are you now? I suddenly felt cold despite the unseasonably warm weather.

* * *

The weekend came and went quite quickly. Sammi, Alan and Baby Dan came on their promised visit. Sammi waxed lyrical about David's expertise in defusing the "vice den" situation.

"Did you hear his interview on the local radio, Hannah? I hope he sues the *Evening Herald*. They could have ruined him."

Us, Sammi, I think silently. They could have ruined *us*. I listened in to David's interview and reflected on the grim ironies of life. David read directly from a statement drafted by Declan Burke. The whole thing was an elaborate hoax, most likely inspired by a rival consortium that were seeking to build a hotel on land overlooking the golf course. The *Evening Herald* had back-pedalled furiously as the week wore on and their exclusive story disintegrated before their eyes. A muted apology was published in their Saturday edition with a grudging oblique reference to the mystery of the rented rooms. Belmullen Electronics refused to comment. Cormac held court in the hotel bar over the weekend as backslappers gathered round him like bees around a honey pot to commiserate with him on his ordeal. David paid up the last three months of Desmond Feeney's contract as he decided it was best to "move him on". It seemed that the only casualty of the saga was my friendship with Lily.

"Hiya, Hannah."

I turned to face Superintendent Matthew Kennedy in the hotel self-service.

"Join me for a coffee?" he asked.

"Sorry, Matthew, I'm up the walls just at the moment."

"I can imagine. And no doubt recovering from last week."

"It was a hectic week for us all, Matthew. Any news of Nadia Constantine?"

"No, vanished without trace. She'll probably reinvent herself somewhere else with a new identity . . . that's if she's lucky – say, was David at home with you on the night the story broke?"

"Yeah, we stayed in for the night. It was a hell of a day."

"'Twas that alright. Well, I'd better be off then."

Chapter Twenty-Three

"Helen."

"Mrs Joyce. What can I do for you?"

"I was hoping to drop in on you for some therapy tomorrow, a massage, maybe. I'm putting myself in your expert hands to eliminate all my pains and aches."

"Glad to hear it. I'll do it myself. What time suits?"

"Eight in the morning – I hope that's not too early."

"Not at all. We have another appointment at that time already but Boris can take that one. Eight o'clock then. See you tomorrow."

Helen is the manageress of our sparkling new leisure centre, which was added to the hotel three years back. I was glad she'd suggested herself instead of the muscular Boris. I hadn't fancied at all the idea of him with his paws or for that matter his eyes going over my sagging bits. But the events of the past week convinced me that there was no time better than the immediate to put my plan into action and the massage was the first step in that direction.

* * *

"Good morning, David."

"Eh . . . yeah, same to you," said David, squinting sleepily at the kitchen clock. Six thirty. "Have you got your days confused? Isn't it me that's on early today?"

"It is surely, Mr Joyce, but there's no rule against a lady pampering her nearest and dearest before he ventures out to the mean streets of Castletown. Now sit yourself down – I've cooked you a nice breakfast."

David eyed me suspiciously. "Is this your way of telling me that you spent a small fortune in Dublin last week? I noticed you scooping up the credit-card bill into your bag last night."

"No, nothing like that at all. You've just reminded me, though, that I never unpacked your stuff. I'll get the bags from the wardrobe."

Minutes later I was laying the kitchen table as David had quickly taken over the breakfast counter to examine my purchases from Marks & Spencer. He picked out a white shirt and a striped grey tie.

"I think I'll put these on today," he said. "By God, you've got me a Lacoste polo shirt too. You'll have me competing with the posers at the Golf Club."

"Think of yourself as worth it," I said, kissing his head.

We ate quietly for a while.

"David, you know Timothy is going to the International at Lansdowne Road tonight?"

138

"Yeah, I'd forgotten about that. He's still got the hump with me over Erin. You're not suggesting I give him the car, are you? Is that where this is leading?"

"No, not at all. I wouldn't give it to him myself. Show me a fellow his age who won't have a few pints in Dublin 4 tonight and you've got a rare species. No, he's staying overnight. Four of them have taken a room in Jurys on the Quays for the night."

"No problem with that. The ground rules are for home and business. He's only nineteen, after all. I'm not trying to control what he does outside the house."

"That puts you and me together tonight, David . . . just the two of us . . . alone."

Our eyes met across the kitchen table. I held his gaze with burning intensity as he cleared his throat to speak.

"And what time would you want a fellow home at?"

"Not later than six o'clock."

"I'll have to be there then, won't I?"

* * *

Giddily I reflected on how easily David had succumbed. No objections at all.

A wave of smugness came over me as a memory of Brenda shot to the forefront: "You may be part chastity, Hannah Duignan, but you're all temptress, no doubt." Embarrassing at the time but wonderfully reassuring right now. I gave David enough time to get a head start and made my way towards town in my Renault Clio.

Once Sammi and Timothy's schooling was past, David suggested we downsize our second car. I had reservations at first, but I needn't have worried. The inventiveness of car-makers these days! It was certainly a case of "love at first drive". Timothy got into the spirit of things and bought me a stick-on magnet of some Arsenal footballer for the dashboard. "It's Thierry Henry, Mum – have you not seen him cruise round the Paris streets in the Renault advertisement? Women . . . ye take so much for granted!"

I parked the Clio a little bit away from the hotel and sneaked in the back gate to the leisure centre.

The reception desk was vacant and I paused to look at the members going through their programmes. The gym opened at six in the morning when the truly body-conscious went to work. I noticed a young girl in a leotard that almost seemed part of her body as she ran at high speed on a treadmill. Instinctively, I felt around my waist, suppressing a vision of Hannah Joyce in the same costume. Not exactly French and Saunders, but most forty-something mothers will know what I mean. You can control your thoughts, Hannah, the therapists say – she'll probably have a lettuce leaf and some cucumber for lunch – yeah, that's better now, Hannah.

"Okay there, Mrs Joyce?"

I turned to see Helen behind me. She sensed what I was thinking.

"Don't compare yourself to her, she's the exception. Latest medical research says we should be aiming for the 'body normal'. You won't see too many like her around."

"I'm glad. Thanks for taking me at such short notice – I was dreading you'd leave with me Bulging Boris."

Helen laughed while looking towards the brooding muscle-bound monster in the background. "You needn't worry – he's taking the other appointment. He's not too bad

– actually he's very good, particularly where sports injuries are involved. The girl in the leotard on the treadmill is his girlfriend – they're both from Poland. This brothel affair spilled over into their lives last week – the Immigration Squad had them in, but luckily their work permits were in order. Got a search warrant for Boris's flat, they did – thought they might pick up some clues on our East European women. Now, a full body massage was what you wanted?"

"That's right."

"Okay, come this way. I've made some preparations."

I followed Helen to a semi-darkened room lit up only by candles scented in rosemary and lavender. Behind a curtain I took off my clothes and Helen handed me in some hot towels as wraparounds.

"Now I want you to lie out here face down and relax to some music. This is my treatment table. I will be leaving you alone for ten minutes so you can unwind totally, wash away the tensions."

Once inside the room, Helen's voice had dropped several decibels and the tone was soft and soothing. I lay there prone while she went away and soon the music of Enya wafted softly across the room. The towels were exhilaratingly hot and my nostrils twitched agreeably to the intense aromas . . . was there a hint of eucalyptus in the air? I found myself nearly drifting off to the sound of "The Celts". Suddenly, my escape from reality came to a halt as I became aware of a presence in the room, a hoarse breathing that sent impulses of fear coursing through my body like electric shocks. I turned round to see a giant shadow and instinctively jumped from the table, my towels falling away. A male voice emerged from the shadow as I adjusted my eyes to the poor light.

"Excuse me, am I in the right place? Is that you, Miss –"

"Aaagh! Aaagh! Helen, Helen, get him out, get him out!"

Helen came rushing in and – unfortunately – switched on the light.

I stood there naked, transfixed.

Murdoch Goodman . . . in his shorts.

* * *

"You can come out from behind that curtain now, Mrs Joyce. He's gone."

I stepped outside gingerly in the dressing-gown that Helen had passed in.

"Sit down there, drink this," she said, offering me a cup of Ballygowan.

I had heard muffled talking from behind the curtain, an East European voice asking Murdoch to leave.

"It was a genuine misunderstanding, Mrs Joyce," said Helen. "Mr Goodman was booked in with me initially but I switched him over to Boris after you called. He just walked into the wrong room, that's all. Poor man is terribly embarrassed, can't stop saying sorry even though it's not his fault." She paused for breath. "I'm really sorry about this, I feel awful, I don't know what to say . . ."

I sipped my Ballygowan quietly. Eventually words tumbled out. "At least *he* was wearing *something* . . . How will I ever be able to face him again?"

"You probably won't have to – he looks like someone just passing through – I've never seen him before."

"I wish, I wish, Helen. He's a regular." I filled her in on

how Murdoch came to be here in the first instance. "Curse Timothy and Erin for taking the man's orthopaedic bed – none of this would've happened!"

Helen held her head silently in her hands. "Look we can cancel this, if you wish, do it another time."

"Is Mr Goodman going ahead with his?"

"No, he made his excuses and left. I think he's in shock himself."

"I'll go ahead with it then, Helen. I think this is the best place for me to be right now."

* * *

I emerged from my treatment an hour and a half later feeling supple and relaxed. Helen was a consummate professional and I complimented her on her articles on diet and nutrition in the local newspaper.

"Thanks, Mrs Joyce. I never got the chance to write it this week. The phone hasn't stopped ringing since . . ."

"Since Nadia and her friends. No need to be embarrassed about saying it. It's a real puzzle, isn't it?"

"It sure is. Six of them coming in here – regular as clockwork. You could set your watch by them. Very disciplined, they all were – went through their paces and never mixed with anybody. Then, whoosh, they're all gone . . . vanished into thin air like ghosts in the night. Strange, though, none of them spoke a word of English while here. Yet Superintendent Kennedy says that Nadia was a fluent speaker."

Now, as I made my way towards the office, I shook my head, banishing the thought of Nadia, only to have her replaced by the image of Murdoch in his shorts. Recalling the look of confusion on the poor man's face, I began to giggle. See the funny side, Hannah – it'll make a great story for the Coffee Triangle some day. "Oh God!" I groaned aloud, recalling that the Triangle was missing one of its sides . . .

"Come in, honey," David said. "I'm just fixing up Mr Goodman's bill – Laura on reception has gone walkabout."

I could see that. I could also see Murdoch Goodman. Again. Sitting there. I wanted to run but my legs wouldn't move. Our eyes met and he looked quickly away.

"Now, let me see," David was rambling on to nobody in particular. "Overnight stay charge including breakfast – total value ninety euros, charge waived in view of special circumstances, telephone calls nine-seventy, massage seventy euro, charge waived . . ."

Murdoch sat silently, looking at the floor.

I should have told David that Murdoch hadn't actually had the massage but I couldn't bring myself to speak.

Obviously, neither could Murdoch.

"That's nine-seventy you owe me, Murdoch, and you've hit me for one hundred and sixty euros. That's your golfing loss recovered through the back door. Wonderfully generous woman, my wife, wonderful."

*   *   *

I watched while David drove away to his meeting with the Golf Club Committee.

David's latest project was about enticing the Irish Amateur Championship to Castletown for 2006. "It'll be a huge boost for the town if we get it," he enthused.

I admonished him before he left. "Don't forget this evening – our evening. Six o'clock – the lady is not for waiting."

I phoned Giles in the kitchen. "The coast is clear!"

"Madame? I do not understand."

"David has left. Can you come with the food?" Giles is our head chef and came to our hotel four years ago. He is from Bordeaux in France. The hotel was upgraded to four stars soon afterwards and David attributed this to the leisure centre and to Giles's cooking.

"Got us into the *Bridgestone Guide – Ireland's Top Hundred Restaurants*," David would say proudly. "Best we've had since I came here – think of the others who came with bigger reputations . . . wasters looking for an easy ride."

David shared the same vision as Dad but like Martin Luther King, he also had a dream. A Michelin Star for the restaurant and a fifth star for the hotel. A tall order, indeed, I shuddered. Persuading him to abandon his dreams would be a taller one.

"Okay, Giles, what have we here?"

"I write it all down, Madame."

"Okay. Let me see: tiger prawns with chilli sauce, followed by Beef Wellington and finished with latticed apple-pie."

"*Oui*, yes, Madame. All is prepared but not cooked. You eat at six o'clock, yes?"

"That's right."

"The instructions and times for, eh, putting them in the oven are in the envelope. I have organic vegetables in the kitchen."

"And the wines you recommended?"

"In the kitchen, also. I put all in your car, Madame?"

"Our secret, Giles," I said, passing him an envelope of my own. "You're a star."

"But not a Michelin, Madame," said Giles, laughing to himself at his own little joke.

I made my way home to prepare for the evening ahead. Beef Wellington in the oven, I laid my black dress out neatly on the bed. Black Dolce and Gabbana underwear retrieved from last week's shopping trip, I stepped into a luxurious hot bath.

Later, I sat on my couch downstairs sipping a gin and tonic. I had programmed our new-fangled jukebox to play our favourite music over the evening. No further intervention needed. The wonders of modern technology. The clock seemed to be moving all too slowly . . .

David arrived at a quarter to six, looking a little frazzled.

"There are some outrageous jokers on that committee," he vented, pausing suddenly to gaze approvingly at me. "God, you're making me feel bad – I should have bought flowers. I've no excuses – just didn't think."

"Flowers aren't necessary. You go and have a shower. Food will be ready in fifteen minutes."

David returned in his new Lacoste polo shirt and jeans. "Not bad, eh, honey? Still size thirty-four waist with a small bit of room." He seemed to be getting in the mood.

At the table, against a background of our favourite tracks, we enjoyed our food while going back over old ground, shared experiences over the years. David seemed to pick up quite quickly that this was an "us" evening and any talk of Timothy and Sammi was confined to the positive. He watched admiringly as I removed the apple-pie from the oven.

"Have you been taking cookery classes, Hannah?" he

asked as he refilled our glasses with red wine. "This food is fabulous. You're talking yourself into a job."

"Don't you dare, Mr Joyce," I warned playfully.

"Joking . . . ahh, this is good, 'tis almost like rolling back the years . . . to Mauritius, maybe Bunbeg?" David looked at me enquiringly.

"Maybe . . . who knows?"

"Only there is a difference here . . ."

"And what's that, David?"

"You had an alcohol curfew that night, but not tonight."

"There's another difference here, though, for me at least."

"And what's that?"

"We were in lust that night . . . we're in love now, aren't we, David?"

"Yes," whispered David, gulping on his wine. "Yes . . . absolutely."

* * *

The lights of Castletown flickered in the distance through our bedroom window. I lay there, head on his chest, stroking him gently as he sighed happily, spent from his efforts in our marital bed. I loved David and I knew he liked me taking charge from time to time. Tonight was for sharing, though, and we lay there, kindred spirits, listening to the sounds of each other's breathing in the still of the room. The music had now stopped and we liked it that way.

Eventually, David spoke. "Isn't it funny, we didn't get a single phone call the whole evening?"

"That's because they were either plugged out or switched off."

We laughed together. Nothing left to chance this evening.

"David," I said tentatively. "When I was over with Cormac last week, he said some very nasty things . . ."

"Nothing new there . . . I'm having to pretend to like him these days until this controversy dies down. I wonder where he's spirited the money away to – anyway, don't let him upset you."

"Usually I wouldn't but it had something to do with our weekend in Bunbeg, and you know how important that night is to me – to us, I hope?"

"You can count me in on that one. What did he say, Hannah?"

"Dad was having us monitored that weekend. George Brennan was keeping tabs on you, us. Seems Dad sent you there deliberately as he knew our relationship was progressing. A kind of matchmaking exercise . . . push us closer together. Maintain the family interest in the hotel . . . he knew he wouldn't get that with Cormac."

"I wouldn't put it past him. Your dad was devious and cunning . . . Well, they're both scheming together now – George died earlier this year."

"Did you know what he was up to at the time, David? I'm sorry but I need to ask."

David sat up indignantly. "Hannah, I knew nothing about it. I wanted you from the minute I saw you . . . all the visits to Dublin . . . the waiting . . ."

"I know, David, and I'm sorry . . . All I wanted to know was that it was still *our* night despite Dad's scheming. Ssh now," I whispered as I pressed a finger to his lips, my free hand moving downwards, stroking, caressing until I felt the stiffness again. Kissing his forehead, I guided him inwards, making love slowly and tenderly until we got that magic fusion of body and soul that only the most intense love can bring.

Lying together afterwards, I murmured, "Are you happy, David?"

"Yeah, course I am. Why do you ask?"

"No, I mean happy, truly happy, and not just today but over the past twenty-one years. I mean – did you ever have times you were in doubt?"

"About us, you mean? No. I've never looked at another woman since . . . no, of course I've looked, every man *looks* – some stray but I haven't. No."

"Yeah, David, but there's more to my question than that. That's about the sex thing. I'm talking about being there for each other, soul mates, kindred spirits and all that."

"We work well together, Hannah, don't we, always being a team? You're not saying we don't, are you?"

"No, I'm not, but you mentioned the word 'work' there. I mean, we're getting on now. Our children are adults. Our profits for last year alone were huge. I mean, if you look at Cormac, he lives in style off his ten per cent and doesn't have to do a tap. Are we just going to keep accumulating money that we'll never spend, then keel over and die?"

"And what do you see as the alternative to that?"

"Maybe we need a change."

"Change," he said and turned to look at me in the muted light of the bedroom.

I couldn't be sure but I was hoping he wasn't giving me of those *looks* he was famous for. He had this way of looking at you when he thought you said something ridiculous.

I pressed on bravely. "I mean, we could sell the hotel. Timothy has no interest in it and Sammi is busy with her own life."

David sat upright in the bed suddenly. "You sound serious about this," he said, his face showing concern. "The hotel has been in your family for years – it was your father's life's work – it has supported you all your life –"

"But that's my point, David. Sometimes things go on too long . . ."

"I'm not sure where all of this is coming from – have you thought about this? I mean, you've just mentioned our age – we're still young, you certainly are, and I feel as good as I did when I was twenty. What else would we do with ourselves?"

"Oh, David, we could do nothing, or we could do other things."

"We can't afford to do nothing."

"Even if we retired right here and now, we wouldn't manage to spend all the money we have. I mean, we have the hotel, properties in Dublin and abroad, all mortgages paid. We've reaped the full rewards of the boom. We've done enough. Let it go."

David was on his feet now. "Look, Hannah, if you want to take more time off from work, then that's fine with me. We can hire some extra help."

"I want to take time off to be with *you*, David – listen to me!"

"I'm certainly not retiring. I love the job, it's my life."

There it was, like a bolt from the blue. The certainty of his voice . . . the slow nausea creeping up through the soles of my feet as the truth began to dawn . . . my truth, my reality. Desperately, I looked for a chink.

"David . . . what about me . . . us . . . I thought this *Evening Herald* thing would show you we don't need the hassle any more . . ."

"If we put the place up for sale now, people would surely conclude that there was substance to the story. No, I see that as more of an opportunity for us to buy out Cormac at last."

"How . . . why would he want to sell up now?"

"He might *need* to sell right now – he knows he's had a lucky escape. The Criminal Assets Bureau are breathing down his neck and he'll know well he cannot touch his ill-gotten gains . . . that is, unless he comes up with a plausible explanation for being in the money . . . it's perfect."

"Jesus, David, will you get off your mission – I want us to get out of the business – you're not listening to a word I'm saying!"

"I've been in the trade for thirty-five years, Hannah . . . You're asking too much. I can't do it . . . I'm sorry." He walked slowly from the room, putting on his dressing-gown as he left.

It was a warm September night, but I lay there cold, unmoving. I stood naked earlier that day before the eyes of a stranger and the insignificance of that whole episode rose cruelly to the surface. Tonight, I had exposed both body and soul to the love of my life and I had lost. I felt traces of David's seminal fluids trickling slowly down my inner legs and looked to the floor at my black dress and then up to my black panties that David had playfully hung on the bedpost only a short time earlier. I had prostituted myself to discover a devastating truth.

Chapter Twenty-Four

I squinted at the shaft of light that slid through a gap in the curtains as morning descended on Castletown. Sometime during the night I had hauled my naked body under our duvet. David had not come back to our bed that night. He did not need to make any further statement. I had recognised the finality of his voice the previous night. His *decision-making* voice, the one he adopted when he nervelessly underwrote multi-million loans for the restoration of the castle and the development of the golf course. The voice that emerged as he coldly advised a worker that his or her services were no longer required.

Nine thirty. I reflected grimly that at least I had slept. The sleep of the exhausted. I could smell the residual odours of our lovemaking all around me – the sweat, his semen and my vaginal fluids. My body, the sheets. Getting up, I took the sheets and my panties, dropping them from the landing onto the ground-floor below, hearing a near-silent rustle as they landed in the hall. In the shower, I scrubbed furiously for ages and eventually just stood in the flow with my back pressed to the wall, hoping that the hot water would steam the hurt from my head and heart. Rape victims are known to do this and some have unwittingly washed away the forensic evidence that would convict their assailant. Cleansing the heart would be a little more difficult, I reflected, as the electric shower powered relentlessly on. Wouldn't it be great if some whiz-kid inventor could eliminate all noise but the fall of the water?

I dressed and went downstairs, pausing to pick up the sheets and underwear. Robotically, I deposited them in the refuse bin – I could not harbour the thought that these items would ever envelop my body again.

Once in the sitting room, I hugged my knees up towards my chest and I cried. Great, big, convulsing, crushing sobs that shook my body violently as I rocked in the chair. The humiliation, the pain, the brutality of truth. A woman approaching her menopausal years seeking to recreate the magic of a distant night when youth and wild abandon had its day. Sad, shameful and sordid. I needed to shower and brush my teeth once more.

Afterwards I sat silently in my kitchen, waiting as the tears subsided slowly, and felt a strange calm shroud my body and soul. Acceptance, I think that's what they call it. This morning I had done my grieving – a grieving that acknowledged a fading of the light that was our love.

I felt compelled to go into the hotel. Goodness knows why but I was going along aimlessly.

I tasted the stagnant air of the building as soon as I entered it.

As I said, not many tourists visit Castletown for the scenery, golf and fishing being the main attractions. But we also had vibrant historical and conservation societies and David ensured that all our receptionists were trained in matters genealogical. This was a big interest for our American tourists and Giselle was putting her training to good use right now.

"I'm Barbara Joyner, this is my husband Fred. He's a Native American. My grandmother came over from Ireland in eighteen ninety-six. She was just seventeen then," she said proudly. "Never came back . . . O'Reillys, Prucklish, Castletown – yes, that's where she came from – she left her parents and a bachelor brother behind. Have you heard of any O'Reillys out that way?"

I stifled an impulse to laugh despite my mood. Giselle was Afro-Caribbean and her chances of knowing any local O'Reillys was slim, to say the least. Yet, she soldiered on.

"No, Mrs Joyner, but I have the addresses of all the specialist agencies right here. I'll just photocopy them for you and then you'll have them. I'll give you a phone number for Jarlath – he's a local historian – he'll be able to help you with your search."

The middle-aged American woman eyed Giselle suspiciously, less than convinced. "My great-great-grandfather was Connor O'Reilly and he lived . . ." She fumbled with some papers. "Let me show you on my map."

Giselle immediately produced a "map" of her own from beneath the reception counter. "Here, Mrs Joyner, take a look at this instead. This is a genealogical history of an American family that Jarlath completed last year. He managed to trace them back to 1603. They let him keep a copy so he could advertise his services."

The American lady was really hooked now. She gestured to her husband to come over. He approached reluctantly, his wiry, stooped frame in stark contrast to his wife's short, rotund figure. "Wow, take a look at this! An entire family life story going back over four centuries and on one big page! Let's go for it, Fred, darling – we could get it framed, hang it up in the drawing room . . . It'd be wonderful!"

"I don't know, Barbara, honey – it just looks like a diagram to me. How much is this going to cost? I thought we were going to the golf course today."

"Golf, what a jester! He's surrounded by hundreds of courses in Miami and they'll all be there when he gets back."

Giselle intervened. "Jarlath is a retired man – he does it mainly as a hobby. He'll take you on the train to Dublin to the National Archives Office, the Census – charges eighty euros a day plus expenses. This example cost less than three hundred, all in."

"What do you think, Fred? This is a real bit of good luck!"

"Does it really matter what I think, Barbara? Go right ahead if you want to do it. I think I'll take a raincheck on this one . . ."

"Fred Joyner, this is our thirtieth wedding anniversary and you're coming to Dublin with me. I'll pack your camera in case you get bored. This is important to me, sweetheart," she said admonishingly. "Now, one last thing, eh, Giselle, can you direct me to where I can get records of the local cemetery?"

"I think I'll phone Jarlath for you. He has those also. And if you wish, I can put you in touch with Mr and Mrs Lewis. They're from Manhattan and are here in the hotel – they're doing the same thing."

Eventually, they departed with Barbara chattering away.

"Say, Fred, do you think that Giselle has Irish ancestry – she was really clued in, wasn't she?"

I jumped at the feeling of someone standing behind me. John Devery, paintbrush in his hand, with a lustful smile on his face. "That genealogy stuff, it's really interesting. I've done some of it myself – brought up some really interesting things."

"John, you startled me . . . You'll give someone a heart attack if you keep on like that. Did you track down any rich relatives or what?"

"No, I can't seem to get past 1978 . . . 'Living Next Door to Alice' was at Number One. Do you remember that, Hannah?"

"Was it Friday you said you were leaving, John?"

* * *

A sign on the office door said: *Do Not Disturb – Interviews in Progress*.

Life goes on for David after Desmond Feeney, I thought bitterly. I scanned the list of candidates – six in total – who made the short-list. I had left all the hiring and firing to David once it came home to me that I was merely there as an observer, to rubber-stamp his decisions. At least two women made the short-list this time, I mused.

My mobile rang.

"Hi, Hannah, it's Alison. Did you know that David and my Eddie are off to Lahinch for the weekend to some golf tournament – the amateur championships, I think?"

"No, didn't know a thing about it but that's no surprise at my end – your Eddie, though, that's a turn-up for the books. What brings him down there?"

"Well, you already know that your husband is busy lobbying for the championships to be held in Castletown in 2006. Eddie is promised the contract for the building of the new bar and clubhouse if things go to plan. Vincent is going too."

An old familiar rage started to kindle inside me. I wanted to suppress it, dampen it down, but couldn't. The husbands of your two best friends – one of them staying at the hotel for days before I knew it – and now the three of them waltzing off to Lahinch for the weekend. And I get to hear it all from others. Why don't you drop in on the Lisdoonvarna Bachelor Festival while you're there, David? It's only up the road and your timing is spot on. Just one twist of your ring finger and you'll meet all the other qualifications. Insular, self-serving bastard!

"Are you still there, Hannah? Um . . . I had Lily on the phone this morning."

"Yeah – I suppose she told you I went over to have it out with her about the letter to the Council. She admitted it straight away as bold as brass. No apologies to make to anybody, she said."

"She's really been under the cosh, though. These separations are traumatic – Erin going away at the same time hasn't helped. Cut her a bit of slack, Hannah – I'm sure she'll see in time that what she did was wrong."

That's the worst of suffering in silence, I thought. Split up with David and I'd have them coming round in droves, wine and chocolates at the ready. Stay in your own hell and people will think you're having it easy, even envy you. I should ask John to paint a sign on my forehead: *Broken Woman*. Yeah, that's about it.

Chapter Twenty-Five

"Come in."

Laura appeared at my office door, looking a little flustered.

"Laura, you don't need to knock – what's the matter?"

"There's a young lady at reception, Mrs Joyce, wants to speak with you. Won't give her name, says it is a private matter."

"Can you see her from where you're standing?"

"Yeah."

I got up and looked out at a dark-haired girl sitting in the foyer. "I don't recognise her at all . . . Maybe she's looking for a job, what do you think?"

"I asked her that – you get that all the time from people who think they can walk in and start work immediately, bypass the form filling and all that. Says no, it's not that."

"I'd better see her so or we'll both die of curiosity. Show

her in."

The phone interrupted me as I was about to greet the young lady coming through the door. "Yes, Giles, the food was wonderful, everything was great . . . I will, yes . . . our secret, thank you, Giles."

I stood and introduced myself but the girl ignored my extended hand. Mid-twenties, I guessed. Dark brown hair, no make-up, grey trouser suit, no visible jewellery except for a discreet pair of silver earrings. Demure, old-fashioned, perhaps.

"Mrs Joyce, my name is Sinéad Crowe and I want to speak with you regarding some hurtful things you have been saying about me. My partner, Vincent, was staying here recently and he told me what you said."

The pieces of the puzzle clicked together suddenly. Desperately, my mind raced as I sought to extricate myself from the situation.

She continued. "Seeing that you appear to be struggling with your memory, I'll give you some help." Her voice quivered just a little and her eyes were moist. "You said that I was an easy woman who preyed on older married men. I want you to tell me how you came to know that about me."

"I didn't . . . I was just repeating what was said to me . . . Lily is . . . was my friend. You're not the only loser – I've lost a good friend in all of this."

"This is not about friendship: it's about my character and the truth. They're more important. You don't know me and I'm not going to dignify your malicious gossip by saying whether it's true or not." Sinéad paused.

"Look, I'm really sorry –"

Sinéad stood up suddenly. "Save it, Mrs Joyce. I just came here to see you and let you know the hurt you have caused.

Vincent wanted me to go to a solicitor, but I wanted to keep this as private as I can. My real friends know the truth about me. Have you any real friends, Mrs Joyce?"

She paused at the doorway, composing herself as moistened eyes yielded to tears rolling down her face.

"You're a spiteful woman, Mrs Joyce . . . yes, spiteful, that's what I'd call you. I won't let you tarnish what me and Vincent have together."

* * *

"Laura, have you seen David this morning?" I asked.

"He was around earlier – I can page him for you."

"No, don't do that. Could you just tell him I've taken the rest of the day off?"

"I'll do that. Are you alright? There's nothing wrong, is there? You look like you've seen a ghost."

"I'll be okay – it's just a dizzy spell. I get them from time to time," I lied.

Take some deep breaths, Hannah, I mouthed wordlessly as my world started to spin out of control. Don't lose it – you've got to stay strong. Occupy yourself – this will pass.

I grabbed my bag, checked for my journal and made my way towards my retreat at the rear of the hotel. The door was slightly ajar. Puzzled, I stepped inside tentatively.

"Hannah, you've come down to see me, that's nice!" John Devery's voice came from behind me.

"What are you doing here?"

"What I'm always doing, painting," he smiled, mimicking brush strokes a little too close to my blouse.

"Well, keep at it, then," I replied, gritting my teeth.

I took temporary sanctuary in the Coffee Dock, five

minutes' walk from the hotel. Like the Castletown Arms, the Coffee Dock spanned generations of the same family down the years. That's where the similarity ended. The Murtaghs ran this little gem for over forty years – serving hot beverages, cakes, pastries, sandwiches and soups. All were homemade on the premises and the only concession to modernisation over the years was the introduction of specialty coffees and teas.

I sat drinking one of these, my third espresso, as I sought to quell the storm that raged inside me. A torn Danish pastry lay on the table beside me, the victim of my shaking hands.

"You'll go back on the cigarettes if you don't watch it, Hannah," I said to myself, counting the years back to my last inhalation.

"What was that?" Rhonda Murtagh was beside me with her scribbling pad and biro poised.

"Eh?"

"You said something just there – I thought you were ordering."

"No, but now that you're here, I'll take another espresso."

"Okay, anything with it?" she asked, eying the ravaged pastry.

"No, sorry about the pastry – it was fine. I'm just having a bad day."

"I know the feeling. With me it's beer mats. Rhonda the Ripper, that's what I'm called," she laughs. "I can't stand pubs – they bore me stupid but I tag along with my friends the odd time to avoid being labelled a killjoy."

She returned with my fourth espresso.

"How is your gran, Rhonda?"

"Still ruling the roost. Trying to ward off advancing years

and advancing technology. Did you hear her latest?" Rhonda pointed to a sign on the wall. *No Mobile Phones.* "She was watching a documentary about Japan the other night where they introduced mobile-free zones so that people can have a proper chinwag, face to face. Came straight down once it was finished and put up the sign. She's enforcing it too."

I laughed. "And Jenny?"

Jenny was Rhonda's twin sister.

"She's after getting a three-year extension to her contract at the tea-room in the castle. Sure, David would know that, being on the committee and all that. She's delighted. But put her and Gran in the same room and there's Holy War."

I was starting to laugh a little to myself. Rhonda was up and running full steam and it was hard to shut her up. I didn't want to.

"Wait till I tell you," she said, her voice dropping to a hush. "Last week, Jenny came to visit Gran, with her iPod dangling out of her. Within five minutes Gran had her on her bike, telling her that she was not going to compete with some drugged-up rocker for her attention. Etiquette, she's always using that word, young people have no etiquette."

It was always a tonic to listen to the Murtagh twins and I made an instant decision. I needed further distraction to help me get through this most awful of days.

Chapter Twenty-Six

Back in my dungeon there was a lot of work in my in-tray that needed my attention but I wasn't in the right frame of mind to attend to it. I needed to retreat, to be on my own, lose myself for a while, if that were possible in a small town like Castletown.

So I took myself off to the castle.

I should have known that David would see his pet project come to fruition. He was the leading force behind the committee that saw the restoration of the castle. As I walked into the building I felt a sudden sense of pride at our achievement. A handful of people had pulled this off. I had no real interest in history but it amazed me the number of tourists that came to the castle to look at estate records and mementos of times past. I noticed the American tourist that I had seen in the hotel foyer walking into the Visitors' Centre to see life-size models of peasants and soldiers from the 17th century. A new painting exhibition by a local artist had been launched in the tea-room of the castle. Of course David and myself had got invites to the opening night but we didn't get to go.

Jenny was bound to be there and there was always the possibility that she might cheer me up. I took a stroll around to look at the paintings. For a while I was lost in them and forgot my own troubles. I really should go back to painting – I had no more excuses. And I enjoyed it, though my own efforts were quite amateurish.

"Hello, there," a familiar face said.

I looked at the woman standing beside me. "Oh, Pauline," I said, relieved that her name had come to me. A fine line of perspiration moistened my upper lip. I hadn't expected to meet a local – I thought it was just visitors and employees that came here.

She was looking at a figure of a woman and child carved out of bog oak.

"This is lovely," she said with admiration. "Can you imagine the work that has gone into that?"

"Yes, it's beautiful." The graceful, fluid lines of the piece just made me feel sad. Gone were the days when I could make my son's world better by kissing his woes away. I no longer was a mother.

"How is the hotel going?" she inquired.

"Oh," I said, a little taken aback at her curiosity.

Her bright blue eyes settled on my flushed face.

Pauline had lost her husband a year ago. In school she was a few years ahead of me. Her life was pretty similar to mine. She married and raised a family. An ordinary couple just like David and myself. Was she still grieving for her dead husband? We hide so much of our pain in our ordinary lives.

"Fine, busy, you know the way," I replied off-handedly.

"You've stopped painting yourself?"

I shrugged. "Oh, you know how it is, busy with the hotel and . . ." I turned to look when I heard a commotion.

A guided tour had just descended on the tea-room. They were queuing and chatting amongst themselves.

"Doesn't it get busy here?" I remarked, glad of the distraction.

"Yes, but after September it quietens down a lot."

"I see."

"I love the gardens," Pauline said, her face brightening. "To me they are my great escape. I love to come here on a bad day and just walk in the gardens."

"You like gardening?"

Pauline shook her dark head. "Goodness no, I hate it, all that's in my garden is weeds – no, I love the peace of it here. I always come in the evenings – that way the guided tours are finishing up and sometimes I have the place to myself."

"That's really nice."

"It's been nice talking to you," she said.

"Yes – see you."

I ordered a glass of mineral water, in an effort to flush out some of the toxins that I had consumed all morning. A numbness was settling over me, weighing me down. I took out my journal and started to write a letter to my son.

Dear Timothy,

We used to be so close when you were growing up. We shared secrets. Remember you had that crush on a girl in school and we invited her to tea? Gosh, I just can't think of her name now. You must have been nine or ten because I remember us going for walks and you holding my hand. I loved our walks together. By the time you were eleven that had all stopped and I just felt so sad because I missed our walks so much. I know you were growing up and you had to move on to the next stage of your development but I wanted us to stay at that place for another while ~ it went too quickly for me. There I go drifting again, sorry.

Let's backtrack to when you had your first crush. I remember you didn't want any of your friends to know about it. (Boys can be horrible, spiteful little creatures.) I made chocolate brownies and we rented a video and invited the girl. Do you remember?

All those wonderful times are nothing but memories now and even they have become slightly distorted. I miss you ~ I miss my darling little boy that never left the house without giving me a kiss and a hug. I miss the lovely smell of your fresh skin. I feel saddened by the fact that I pour my heart out –

I closed my journal and decided to take a walk in the gardens to clear my head.

Chapter Twenty-Seven

I turned the key in the doorway, entering an eerily silent house. Thoughts of the night's sleeping arrangements sent shudders down my spine. I picked letters and junk mail off the hall floor and threw them nonchalantly on the kitchen table. They'd wait. The phone rang. It was Louise.

"Hiya, Hannah."

I stiffened immediately. Timid little Louise with the squeaky voice. Could she really be part of an international vice operation? "Louise . . . how're things?"

"They're okay. I just rang . . . sort of to apologise for dragging you across town the other night and thank you for bringing her to swimming also."

"Oh, that's alright, Louise. There is nothing you did the other night that needs an apology." I stressed "the other night" a little. "How is Jasmine?"

"She's in good form – her birthday is coming around in

two weeks' time. She'll be ten. We'd like you and David to come over for her party . . . Timothy also, of course."

Best I play along with this lady, I thought. She's either the coolest customer I've met or she is genuinely innocent. I'll keep my bullets in reserve for my brother.

"I'd love to, Louise . . . thanks . . . I'll let the men speak for themselves. Can you give me any hints on what she might like as a present?"

"Mmm . . . you'll have to leave that one with me. I'll have to prompt her. I'll get back to you on it."

"That's okay – tell her Auntie Hannah said hello and that I love her."

"Will do . . . There is another thing . . . Cormac was telling me that you discussed things the other night. Whatever you said seems to have had an effect on him."

"God, I'm surprised he even remembers. What's new with him?"

"Well, for a start he hasn't gone to the pub for the last two nights, hasn't drunk at all in fact."

"Well, that is a first." But why was she ignoring the huge crisis of last week which must have had a far greater "effect on him" than my few words?

"That's not all. He went in to see your David today about selling his ten per cent share. The way he put it himself, it's time to shake that hotel off his shoulders and move on."

"That's great, Louise. How do you feel about that?"

"Delighted, but nervous. I really hope he goes through with it. We need a fresh start, Hannah."

"And you deserve it. Well, bye, Louise . . ."

"I'll get back to you about Jasmine. Bye, Hannah."

So, all going to plan David and I would be full owners of the Castletown Arms. The irony of it, the exact opposite of what I wanted. Compose yourself, Hannah. I marvelled at Louise's shameless temerity. Poor downtrodden Louise . . . madam of the brothel . . . bizarre, surreal. Not so much as a word about last week's crisis – feelings of envy began to surface. I sat down, took out my journal and started writing.

Cedar Woods
Thursday 23/09/04

Dear Journal ~
I've been writing to you for over twenty-three years and this is my saddest day.

You look small right now but only part of you is here with me. The rest of you is locked upstairs. I have to thank you for keeping track of my life over the years. And my family's lives.

I used to show you to Timmy when he was a small boy. When I was explaining to him how he was born, he asked me a question only a child could ask – what did I do when I saw him coming? All I could do was pick the part of you that told about his birth. What were my first words? When did I first walk? Deliver on the potty? All these questions were answered by asking the part of you that would answer.

That's why I divide you up into separate books and separate you from your earlier thoughts on 1st January each year.

I know I am rambling but yet the light that was our marriage finally died yesterday ~ there you go ~ all the good things airbrushed into abstract history ~ don't count ~ end of story. You don't need the detail but David humiliated me yesterday ~ he took what was on offer and discarded me in the most brutal way. The spiritual link has been severed and there's no going back. I'd love to remove myself physically but I'm too afraid to go. All my life I've watched the relentless power of the

*Castletown Arms consume my life and the lives of my loved
ones. I'm telling you this because people wouldn't understand ~
they'd think I need psychiatric assessment if I wanted to walk
away from the riches that they covet. But I just can't walk out
~ I would hurt too many people. I went to the Coffee Dock today
and on to the castle ~ Rhonda, one of the Murtagh twins, was
great.*

Sinéad is very angry with me.

*I can't help wondering where David and Timothy went the
night the* Evening Herald *story broke. I've read some gruesome
stories about what happens to these foreign women when they
become surplus to requirements. Unsolvable crimes, Matthew
Kennedy said, given that the person doesn't exist in the first
place. Nothing except a wall of silence. Could David be in
cahoots with Cormac? Surely he wouldn't expose his own son
to that type of shady dealing?*

Bye for now,
Hannah

I struggled to suppress my rage at David's summary
dismissal of my needs and wants and lapsed into a state of
melancholy self-pity regarding the sacrifices that I'd made
for him.

I'm going to make out a list, show it to him, I thought.

My round-the-world trip with Brenda
My teaching career
My painting
My tennis
My horse-riding
My whole bloody life

Listlessly, I scanned through the day's post on the table,

separating junk mail for disposal and formal correspondence into a "to-do" folder. I opened a handwritten envelope. Don't get many of them these days, I reflected, and started reading.

20/09/04

Dear Hannah,

I cannot believe it after all these years that we have finally made contact. I have often thought about you and wondered were you still living in Castletown. Haven't the years flown by? That's what happens when you have children – they just absorb so much of your time.

I was so disappointed when you announced that you weren't coming travelling with me but were staying home to get married. I was determined to go ahead and do it anyway. Remember we were planning to go direct to Rosslare and take the ferry over to France – well, I did exactly that. I was so nervous, wondering how I was going to do this on my own. I remember leaving the boat and praying to God that I would get through it alive. I really was scared. Do you remember we were going to pick grapes in a vineyard? I had got some addresses for places that had cheap accommodation. Well, I didn't do that – instead I answered an advertisement for a chambermaid in a hotel in Cannes. A five-star hotel, even the chambermaids were snooty. I hated it. I was writing a few postcards home one day when this young man came up to me. He had heard me ask for stamps and he knew by my accent that I was Irish. He was also a student from Dublin. We were both on our own and we decided to go travelling together and we've been together ever since.

After that summer we both returned to college. Brendan

qualified as an architect and I finished my teaching. We have lived and worked in Sydney, New York, and we spent a crazy five months in Hong Kong and now we've decided that it's time to settle down. We have a little boy called Callum and we're expecting our second baby in January.

Brendan's family is from Galway, so we're hoping to buy a house and settle down there. I would love to meet you again. And I'm really sorry that I didn't go to your wedding. Looking back I was just so jealous that you had managed to catch such a good-looking man.

I hope everything is good for you. The reason I haven't put an address on this letter is because we're moving. So I'll write to you again when we get settled in Galway.

I can't believe that you've tracked me down! I'm so glad you did.

All the best for now,
Brenda

"Good to hear you're doing well, Brenda," I said out loud to the deserted kitchen. "I'm having a ball myself." A recall of Timothy as a young child flashed across my brain.

"I'm bored, Mammy, there's nothing to do," he would say as a launch-pad to suggesting the toddlers' playground, the bouncing castles, the five-a-side pitch or whatever else he felt he could wear me into submission on.

"What can I do now, Timothy?" I whispered softly in the dimmed lights of my kitchen. "Move to the spare room for a start, Hannah, and get it done before *he* comes home."

A manic energy came up through the soles of my feet and soon I was bundling all traces of me from our bedroom at a frantic pace. I fumbled for the key to my locker and was about to open it when I discovered that it was already slightly ajar. This is the home of my journals, my private haven.

"God, this has been prised open, we've had burglars!" I said out loud.

Hastily, I checked. My precious journals seemed to be all there. Then I saw that someone had ransacked a small wallet which had held some cash until now.

I reached for the bedside phone and dialled the Garda Station.

But . . . the bit of cash was all that was missing . . .

I thought of all the other valuables scattered throughout the house that remained untouched.

Surely not Timothy, surely not . . . David has sacked him . . . oh no . . .

"Castletown Garda Station, can I help you?"

I hung up quietly and slumped to the floor slowly.

* * *

I smiled grimly to myself when I reflected on how a life can disintegrate in a flash. Less than twenty-four hours back, I was making plans that would take me to the next phase with the man I loved and at least thought I knew. Now I sat with my body and dignity violated and my privacy intruded upon. Instantly, I decided to remove my journals to a safer place and I rolled down the Stira stairs that led to the attic. This will be safer, I mouthed silently to myself. My last will provided for my journals to be given to Timothy. It seemed the right thing to do with him being my sole birth-child. Occasionally, I felt that this was silly but, no, he was at least getting an opportunity to look back into his entire childhood at any point and choose what part of his life he wanted to go to.

I counted them again. "Twenty-two journals, that's about right," I said to myself as I arranged them on the laminated floor of the attic. All they will have for company up there is an old suitcase that David brought into our marriage and new home twenty-one years back. My musings, his past, I reflected.

"Old stuff from when I was young, nothing too interesting," he explained at the time.

Suddenly, I felt interest and temptation all at once. I had been blinded by my love for David from the day I met him and I had set aside most of my wants and needs in giving my love freely. Last night reality came home to roost, hitting me with hammer-blows to the very core of my being. I had spent my best years with a man who only entertained partnerships on his terms and it took me all these years to see that. A stranger. I descended the stairs with the suitcase under my arm and hid it in a wardrobe in the spare room, locking the room door as I went downstairs.

David was in the kitchen, making a toasted sandwich. I hoped he hadn't heard my manoeuvrings upstairs.

"Oh, it's you," I said curtly

"Yeah. Laura told me you went home today. Are you okay?"

I ignored his question. "I believe Cormac went in to see you yesterday."

"Yeah, it's strange after all the years he spent fighting off my, eh, our, efforts to buy him out and suddenly, out of the blue, he wants to sell."

"But it's not strange, David – you already said so yourself. Cormac cannot launder his ill-gotten gains so easily under the noses of the CAB. That's where you come in to give him a dig-out – to your own advantage, of course. *Your* contempt for *him* is looking a bit shallow now. I just hope you're not involving Timothy in your scam."

"That's out of order, Hannah. It's just good business – it's not a crime. I could have let your brother and sister-in-law sink in their own shit. Would you like to have a jailbird brother? Jasmine without parents, perhaps? This is a win-win result for us all."

"I'm glad things are falling into place for you. It's what you always wanted, your life's dream," I said with pure venom.

A long silence followed as I tidied up the kitchen counters.

Suddenly I was in his face, whacking him furiously with a wet dishcloth.

"That's right, David, say nothing! Protect your interests! Withdraw from the situation – tactics spot on as always – you bastard!"

David waited until I ran out of steam. He fixed me with his steely stare and the controlled, unemotional firmness of his voice pierced me like a dagger.

"Tactics don't come in to it, Hannah. I will not agree to the hotel being put on the market. There is nothing more that I can say on it."

I lashed out. *Crash!* David's coffee mug lands on the tiled floor, splashing on to his trouser legs.

"Fuck you, David, fuck you!"

"Hannah, you've lost control . . . stop it!"

"Don't you talk to me about control! That's rich coming from you. You've got where you are by controlling and manipulating people. You're a predator, completely amoral. See something you want and you just take it!"

175

The twitching of David's neck muscles betrayed his outward calm. "You didn't do too badly yourself now, Hannah. Daddy's little girl. What's that it was? Yes, a ninety/ten split in your favour. And from a man who believed that there were only two places where a woman functioned properly – the kitchen and the bedroom, that's what he used to say. Come to think of it, he wasn't too far wrong either, when I think back to last night . . . Aagh! Let go my hair, you bitch!"

Suddenly, Timothy was at the doorway. "Mum . . . Dad . . . what's going on?"

I shook with fury as I answered: "Oh, ask your father, I'm going over to see Alison."

* * *

I sat in tears on the road's hard shoulder as the uniformed Garda completed his inspection of David's Mercedes. I had taken the car purely for spite and now I was going to count the cost.

"Mrs Hannah Joyce and the car owner is your husband David Joyce. You'll need to produce your certificate of insurance *and* your husband's. I presume Castletown will be the most convenient . . . Okay, within the next ten days, that's not later than October 2nd. Here's your driving licence." He paused for a minute. "Now, do you realise what speed you were doing?"

"I don't know – we're in a thirty-mile zone. I'm sure I was over that."

"You were humming along at seventy-five an hour. Did you not see any of the signs – speed kills and all that? This is a very powerful machine you're driving, Mrs Joyce."

"I'm really sorry, officer. I don't usually go that fast."

"Yeah but, unfortunately, you're going to pick up some penalty points for your trouble."

Chapter Twenty-Eight

"Take it easy, now, Hannah, take it easy."

Alison was holding my hand as I sobbed convulsively.

On the way over I had run into a filling station and picked up two bottles of wine. "Could I have some cigarettes too, twenty Silk Cut, purple?"

Now I was in Alison's and on my third cigarette. I had smoked for the first eighteen months of my teacher training in Dublin and had built up to twenty a day. Nerves it was at the time, pure nerves, adapting to the freedom and the pressures of assignments and exams. I stopped quite suddenly after watching a TV documentary on the damage they can do. Now, the nerves were back and the fags had followed.

"No, Hannah, for the umpteenth time, I don't mind you smoking here in the conservatory – I can open a few windows later. It's you I'm worried about – the damage they can cause."

"It's just for tonight . . ."

"Let's hope it is, and we need to clear up one thing. You're staying here for the night, no arguments. I'll share a few glasses of wine with you, but I won't let you back out on the road. Deal?"

"Deal," I sobbed.

"Now, go through what happened with me, Hannah. I hate to see you like this."

Alison listened incredulously as I trawled over the events of the last few days. The wine and cigarettes were helping me to compose myself, but I could not turn these into crutches, an ongoing solution.

"Gosh, Hannah, this is the first time I've heard you speak like that – you've always been so caught up in the hotel."

"Believe me, the hotel is a lot of trouble and I am fed up with it."

"I'm at a loss, Hannah, I really am. It seems you've been keeping all this to yourself for so long. "

"I just got sucked in by events. I never thought I'd end up working in the hotel for so long. It's not just the hotel, Alison – it's the finality of his no. Dismissed. Not even considered . . . and after the evening we spent together . . . the meal . . . our bed . . ."

"Have you ever raised this with David before?"

"Well no, not really . . ."

"I'm not taking his side, Hannah, but think of the shock he must have got when you put this proposal to him. Here he is living in his dreams and ambitions for the past twenty years and allowed everything his way because you've not given him any reality checks during that time . . ."

I bristled at her suggestions. "But what about me? Where is Hannah Joyce in all of this?"

"Second, maybe even last . . . but it's where she put herself . . . and people have got used to it."

"Well, they better get used to something different soon," I said, uncorking the second bottle.

"And bravo to you, but give him a chance to get used to your idea. You probably scared him shitless."

"Good."

"Yeah, but you're not going to win this one from a different bedroom . . . You're playing into his hands. Tell us, David was talking to Eddie about the *Evening Herald* story. I believe he's getting crank calls from wannabe punters."

"I really don't care about the whole thing, Alison. Mammy and Louise are in denial and Cormac has gone to ground. I haven't seen him since – it's like it never happened."

"It'd be a nice way of making a quick buck . . . Legend has it that it's the oldest profession of all. Do you remember Jack the Ripper? They say he was one of the Royal Family who harboured a grudge against prostitutes."

I swayed drunkenly as I got up.

"Come on, Hannah, I'll take you down to your room. You are totally worn out."

* * *

Sitting in the kitchen with Eddie and Alison the following morning, I felt like an intruder. Alison had given me a nightdress and dressing-gown. My head was thumping violently with a hangover and I could taste the stale tobacco on my tongue.

"There you go now, coffee and warm rolls," said Alison.

"Thanks, were you out already?"

"No, the rolls are those part-baked ones that are all the rage these days. *Cuisine de France*. Pop them in a hot oven for eight minutes and away you go."

Eddie was tucking in to a fried Irish breakfast. The works.

I wondered how he felt about me being stuck in his face at the breakfast table. I needed to make some small talk. "You're not counting the calories, Eddie?"

"Nope, working on the buildings, you need to kick off the day with a good meal. You wouldn't last too long on muesli and orange juice," he said, eying Alison's food.

"If I ate like you, Eddie Byrne, I'd be waddling around and then you'd have something else to complain about."

A little later, food consumed, Eddie rose to his feet. "You know I'm off to Lahinch with David this evening, Alison. Could you pack a bag for me? I'll come by to collect it in the afternoon. Bye, Hannah."

"Bye, Eddie."

Alison and I sat quietly, eating.

"Thanks for last night, Alison. I just had to get away."

"Think nothing of it, girl . . . That's what friends are for."

"Were you talking to Lily since?"

"Yeah, last night on the phone after you went to bed. Erin is going to stay in Dublin with her aunt for a while."

"Get her away from my Timothy, I suppose. You'd think Erin took no part in the whole thing. It's not fair dumping all the blame on Timothy."

"Hannah, I didn't say that. It's just that Erin is very upset and so is Lily. It's a very emotional time for them right now. Erin adored her father and this one that he's going out with now is only a few years older than her. She's angry and the only person she can take it out on is Lily. They're fighting a lot and I guess they need a break from each other. And Lily thinks things were getting too serious between her and Timothy."

"Yeah, look, I should let go of it. Do you mind if I take a shower?"

"Not at all, I'll get you some towels. But I want you to do something for me first."

"What's that?"

"Come over and find out."

Alison stood at her pedal bin. Once beside her, she handed me my unfinished packet of cigarettes and stood on the lever.

"Remember me and my cancer, and I didn't even smoke – I don't want you going down that road," she said firmly.

I dropped the pack in the bin and we hugged tightly.

"You go and have that shower, Hannah Joyce," Alison said, a small tear glistening in her eye. "And come out fighting for yourself. You can do it. I did."

Chapter Twenty-Nine

I waved back at Alison as I departed down the driveway. My mobile phone rang.

"Yes, David. What is it?"

"You didn't come home last night."

"That's right. I stayed over with Alison. We had a few glasses of wine, better not to drive."

"Alison rang the house. Timothy took the call. He's upset. He's never seen you breaking things before."

"He's upset at more than that. I mean, isn't it you that turfed him out of his job? He needs that money to give him his own sense of independence."

"I thought we decided that together?"

"No, David, we didn't. You took the situation over completely. Nobody else ever gets a word in. And you don't think, you assume – there's a difference."

"Okay, look, maybe you're right . . . I may have

overreacted, been a bit harsh. He was a good worker. I'll talk to him, come to some understanding. Are you coming in today?"

"No, I don't feel up to it."

"That's okay. I've taken on a new assistant manager, actually manageress, on a trial basis. Juliet Barnes – she's starting this morning. I see you've moved your stuff from the bedroom . . . Come back, Hannah."

I thought of Alison's advice the previous night. "Give me a few days – there's things we need to talk about."

"Okay. I see you've taken my car – I'll need it for this evening. Can you drop it in at the hotel?"

Thoughts of my imminent penalty points surfaced again. Isn't it an unfair world, I reflected self-pityingly. People are pocketing millions from organised crime rackets and getting away with it. Put your foot on the pedal just once and the law flexes its muscles immediately. Easy targets – keep building up the statistics so the minister can lay claim to cleansing Ireland of its roguery.

* * *

"Mrs Joyce, you rang earlier. Marguerite is just finishing up another appointment. It'll be about ten minutes. Would you like a cup of coffee while you wait?" The young assistant was a slim girl, dressed in black with orange streaks through her blonde hair. It looked like she was doing everything possible to make herself look unattractive.

"That would be nice. Milk, no sugar."

I thumbed my way listlessly through the latest issue of *Hello* magazine.

"Nothing but photographs of famous people in that one," said an old lady seated beside me. "They get paid a fortune just for letting someone take photos of them and their houses. You'd get a good paperback novel for a few cents more than the price of one of them. Me, I'd prefer Oprah Winfrey's magazine. At least there are some stories and features in it."

I smiled in agreement. Marguerite was now beside me. I had been coming to her over the past few years. Alison had recommended her. "She's brilliant," she'd said as she fingered her newly styled hair. The salon was fitted out with leather seating and chrome fittings, recessed lighting and display shelves filled with salon products. I always sympathised with the young trainees that had to spend time dusting shelves just so they looked busy.

"Can you go to the last basin? Colour, wash, cut and blow-dry."

Marguerite was the owner of Cutz hair salon. Dark-haired, slim and elegant, she would proudly tell you that she stands six feet tall "in her stocking-feet". She'd had her wedding in the Castletown Arms earlier that year.

"How is Chloe?" I asked.

"She's great . . . she's twenty months now and walking. She threw terrible tantrums with Mammy when Derek and me were on honeymoon in Majorca. We really couldn't bring her out there. We hadn't planned on having children before we married – it was a right shock for us. Still, we wouldn't be without her now."

"Are you still living at home?"

"Yeah, but we've a deposit paid on a house at Oakland, the new estate. Your friend Alison's husband is building them. We should be moving in before Christmas. I really hope so. Mammy has been absolutely brilliant, but you need your own space."

Marguerite continued applying the colours to my hair. I closed my eyes and thought of my parents' sprawling Georgian house that I had grown up in. Somehow, I couldn't imagine David, Sammi, myself and Timothy moving in with her until we got our own place. In our family we didn't need to shuffle ourselves around to make space for each other. This was a skill we never had to learn. Thanks to the hotel we were always cushioned by money. I tutted in disgust – everything revolved around that place.

"What prompted the call this morning? I wasn't expecting you for another couple of weeks." Marguerite asked, breaking into my thoughts.

I opened my eyes and looked in the mirror. I was wearing a black cloak and my hair was pasted with hair colour.

"Looking in the mirror, I guess."

*　*　*

Loud music was blaring upstairs when I got home. The breakfast dishes were still on the kitchen table. I felt my chest tightening – I had to take a few quick gulps of air to stop myself from getting all worked up. I had learned it never did me any good to lose my temper with Timothy – he just carried on as normal. His brown eyes mocking me while he said nothing. My new hair-do had lifted my mood and I would be damned if I was going to let myself slide back down to that pit of despair that I had felt last night while I lay in Alison's guestroom. I quickly set about rustling up a chicken curry, rice and home-made chips. I knocked loudly on Timothy's door.

"I'm making us lunch downstairs – it'll be ready in fifteen minutes. Come on down now – it'll give you time to clean up the mess in the kitchen."

Minutes later he sauntered in. He was wearing a crisp white cotton shirt and black chinos. He stood awkwardly inside the kitchen door and scratched his dark curly head.

"Clear them away, Timothy – I'm not sitting down to eat amongst that mess."

Within minutes, my kitchen was restored to showroom condition. There, you can do it if you want to, my lad – dip into female chores. A little victory against the male chauvinism of the Joyces. Don't get too smug, Hannah – you never know what's waiting around the corner for you.

We sat down to my son's favourite childhood meal – "Brilliant!" he would exclaim when he heard what was waiting for him at home – first, though, Timothy, you're going to take off those filthy school clothes and wash your hands – no, Colm and Killian cannot come over to play this evening – last time I ended up writing notes about unfinished homework for your teacher . . .

I never predicted that I would feel so sorrowful when that stage of my life was over – that I would be in mourning, grieving for the death of childhood, the loss of innocence.

We sat quietly at the kitchen table, Timothy munching away. Chicken Curry Day was treated as a serious matter in the Joyce family and there were rules – no talking until second helpings were polished off, little appetites sated. Eventually, he wiped his mouth with kitchen paper and looked at me smilingly.

"Yourself and Dad were certainly going hammer and tongs at each other last night – I never knew you had such a temper."

"We were. I'm not sorry it happened – I'm just sorry you had to see it and that I didn't phone you myself from Alison's."

"Hair-pulling, though, that was a pocket-money forfeit whenever I finished a row that Sammi started. I don't know what we're going to do with you, Mum – you had poor Dad examining his head for bald patches."

This fellow is enjoying this, I thought. "Less of your flippancy, young man! Now, what's with the neat dress today? Going somewhere important?"

"Important enough – Dad's given me my job back."

I stifled a sense of disapproval. Secretly, I wanted my son to build a future for himself away from the hotel despite my self-righteous indignation at David for sacking him. "I see, and what are the conditions?"

"Very few." Timothy stopped eating, his face turning sombre. He spoke in a staccato voice, imitating his father. "*Timothy – report back for duty at one o'clock tomorrow – one rule: do not even put a foot on the stairs – thank your mother.*' I was tempted to put a word in for Erin, met her in Dublin after the match, but I thought better of it. No point pushing your luck."

Erin . . . I felt a surge of concern rising. "I thought you had burned your bridges with her, Timothy. I'll have Lily around breathing fire like a dragon. Surely you don't need to keep it so close to home – there's bound to be other girls."

Timothy glared obstinately at me. "I like her, no crime in that. Maybe you should change your friends if you're so hung up about it."

Better let this one pass, I thought.

"When you were here yesterday evening, did he tell you

what we were arguing about?"

"Yeah, said you wanted to sell the hotel, couldn't get his head around why you'd want that."

"And what do you think?"

"Well, I told him that he should think about it. Like, we're not scarce or anything. If I was in his shoes, I think I'd chill out. He's over fifty now, isn't he?"

Chill was one of Timothy's favourite words. Sometimes it was hard for me to believe that he was David's son, they were so different.

"Mum, that was the best curry I have ever eaten."

"Thank you, Timothy." I eyed the plates, hoping he'd remember his part in the deal. "I'll teach you how to make it," I added.

"Yeah, that would be great – then I can have friends round and cook for them."

"Timothy, there's something I need to ask you. I found my little cabinet in my bedroom prised open yesterday. Some money is missing. Do you know anything about it?"

I felt instant relief as he looked at me completely puzzled and indignant.

"Mum, you surely don't think . . . Mum . . . no, I never went near it."

"Gosh, I don't know whether to feel good or bad about it now. It means we had a burglar."

"What else is missing?"

"Well, nothing. I have my journals locked upstairs. The lock was prised open and the money that was in the wallet was taken."

"Mum, I did have a few lads in the house Wednesday before we travelled up to the match. We had takeaways in the kitchen before we went. If one of them . . ."

I sipped some coffee. "Leave it for now, Timothy. I'll talk to your dad about it first. It looks like we'll have to report it."

"Can I take your car into town, Mum? We're playing a five-a-side challenge later on."

"You're still hoping to make it with Arsenal, are you? Yes, but make sure you don't drink. And don't say anything to your friends about the missing money. And just one more thing . . ."

He was on his feet already. "Yeah, what's that?"

"Do I have to ask for a hug before you go or do I just get one?"

"Mum," he said, red-faced. "You really . . . come here."

A screech of tyres on the driveway and Timothy was gone. I could not bring myself to ask about his late night expedition with his father – I felt that I might not be able to handle the answers. David wasn't one for doing about-turns on his decisions, yet he had surrendered so easily on reinstating his son at the hotel. It was as if the father and son bond had been restored and cemented since that night and I felt strangely ill at ease about it. Was this the beginning of my son's reincarnation in his father's image . . . his grandfather's . . . his ceremonial initiation into the devil's den that was the Castletown Arms?

Chapter Thirty

Over the course of the day, I quarrelled with myself as to what I should do with David's old suitcase. Now, it sat on my bed. A shaft of late autumn sunlight permeated the room, highlighting the aging faded leather. Could I capture this on a canvas? I could imagine myself viewing it in the National Art Gallery with an artist's explanatory inscription: *Hannah Joyce – Woman on the Edge of Departure* – edge of sanity more like. The crowds gathering around – looking and taking their own meaning. What was the artist trying to tell us? I could visualise Barbara Joyner summoning Fred to attention. "Take a look at this, Fred – it's one of my grandmother preparing to leave home, contemplating that big decision, the one that was to bring us together . . . Fred, could you ask if this is for sale?"

It was a long time since I had felt a compulsion to draw, to lose myself in the moment and blank out everything around me. What could I possibly expect to find inside? Stop examining your conscience, Hannah Joyce. Love can blind you in so many ways. When I was growing up, I was part of a large extended family that was laden with grandparents, uncles, aunts and cousins. Not all of them visited regularly, but I was always conscious of their presence and could recite their names off at the drop of a hat. Thirty-four cousins in total and I could tell where they all were now. Sadly, two of them were in a place they would not be moving from. I closed my eyes and tears flowed as memories surfaced . . .

Therese – she lived in Tralee and we holidayed there every second summer. Mammy and Dad would bring us down. Cannot stay, duty calls, Dad would say. They'd come back for us at the end of the week. Therese was the same age as me and we started secondary school at the same time. Two weeks into her first term, she was knocked down running for the school bus. Her funeral was an awful experience. I cried every morning for two weeks going to school, but Dad was so stoic. "Keep going, girl!" No hugs or comforting words. I winced.

Quentin – I never met Quentin. He lived in New Zealand but there were photos of him at Mammy's house. He was born with a hole in his heart and died when I was five.

We always went to see our grandmothers – Dad's mother outlived him, passing away at the grand old age of ninety-four. She even got to feed Timothy his bottle and enjoyed tending to him. She would say both joyously and sadly, "Who would have thought that I'd get to feed my son's grandson . . . me a great-gran!"

David was the man from nowhere. He had a sister Judy in Scotland and she had two young boys. We went over there twice when Sammi and Timothy were younger and they came to see us once. There was always an air of tension, though, and they stopped sending Christmas cards several years ago. His mother was dead and his father was in a nursing home in Kilkenny. Alzheimer's disease, David would say, doesn't even know me. He would travel down to see him roughly four times a year to pay his bills and sit with him awhile. If you didn't want relations calling, David Joyce was your man.

I reached first for an old photograph album, carefully observing how the case was packed. I hoped to have this task completed and the case back in the attic by night. This felt seedy and sordid. I flicked through the album, smiling as I identified several snaps of David as a child. His curls were unmistakeable. I paused at one photo and looked at the back – *David and Frances, October 1973* it read. First real girlfriend, maybe – who knows with David? *David, Claire and Sammi, November 1978*. I thought of Sammi: she kept a single portrait photo of Claire and herself, aged four, at her bedside always and took that with her when she moved out. It was their last photo together, David told me. A single black and white photo of a newborn baby, no name on the back – maybe Judy's son Aaron in Scotland. I shut the album and clasped it tightly to my chest.

I was fascinated by my search. It was becoming addictive and my feelings of guilt were being cast away. A small teddy bear. What can you tell me about David Joyce, little fella? Come on, you knew him as a child before self-preservation took a grip. He won't be a mystery to you – you can tell me – it'll be our little secret. You look very, very old. Did you sleep in his bed with him when he was a little boy? Why is he keeping you? I can't ask him – he doesn't know I've found you. I would love to have you out in the open, take some ornament from the bedroom and replace it with you – watch for his reaction. Hold on, I might have a name for you – back to the photo album – yeah, there's the one that caught my eye – that's you – *David and Bugsy, March 1961*. Bugsy, that's you. You're at least forty-five, older than me, you are.

I smiled as I picked up a toy gun. Cormac had one of these, often came up behind me and frightened the life out of me. Used to buy "caps" at the local toyshop. They would make a resounding noise when you pulled the trigger and yield a small puff of smoke. Just like the Wild West. I laughed as I picked out a child's cowboy suit – didn't I see this in the album, yes, there it is – *David "Billy the Kid"*, *Christmas 1965*. I created a mental picture of David rampaging around the hotel today in this outfit, smoking gun in hand. The world can be a beautiful place through the eyes of a child – uncomplicated, simple and loving. The changeover is instant, almost occurs overnight. The loss of innocence, I reflected wistfully, as I recall Timothy turning away from me, aged thirteen, when I went to kiss him goodnight in his bed. "*Mum!*" he said in a scolding voice, as if I should know better. Up to the previous night, it was ritual, normal procedure, not to be overlooked. "When did it happen for you, David?" I asked, as memories came flooding back.

"David was born an adult," his mother once told me on one of our rare visits to Kilkenny, where his parents lived. "He was about ten when he developed an obsession with money. He was a godsend to people organising raffles in the town. Top seller always, he would traipse the estates knocking on doors until his father came looking for him. He would pocket his commission money gleefully and it would be in the post office by the following day." But he was a child too, Grandma Joyce, this suitcase proves it. How many men hold onto their childhood toys?

Before our wedding in Mauritius, David had brought me down to Kilkenny on an overnight stay to meet his parents. Sammi came with us. They lived in a neat, spotlessly clean bungalow at the edge of town. I recall overhearing his mother crying in the kitchen as she tried to reason with him.

"It's so inconsiderate of you, David. You promised to come for a full weekend and now you tell me you're going back in the morning. Your dad and me have been looking forward to this. We never get to see Sammi – when was the last Christmas you spent here?"

David just stood there awkwardly, making no attempt to console his mother. "I'm sorry, Mum – it's just that this place holds bad memories for me – the car crash. I just can't handle bumping into her parents . . ."

"Claire is dead, David, there's nothing you can do for her. Think of the living. Us. Me. The Maloneys. They lost their daughter. I do meet Mrs Maloney in town – it's so embarrassing. She'd love to see Sammi – it's her only link with Claire. You're so cruel. Judy is going to live in Scotland – you might as well be in Africa for all we see of you."

I paused to pick up a bundle of letters, removing an elastic band from around them. One was from David's mother.

Sycamore Drive
Kilkenny
05/10/82

Dear David,

195

I am so worried about you. I would love for you and Sammi to come and stay with us for a while. We could take care of Sammi and it would give you a chance to get back on your feet again.

I don't want to worry you but I have to tell you that your father isn't well. The doctor says he is showing signs of the first stages of Alzheimer's disease. He is sending him for tests. Your dad insists on going out every morning to get the paper and then comes back without it. You have always got on so well with your father. Last night he was talking about you, reminiscing about when you two went fishing. He knows that there's something wrong with him. He cried the other day when he came back without the messages I sent him for. The list was still in his pocket. He dreads going into a nursing home – he said he'd rather die than go in there.

Bridie Smith is getting married next week. We were invited to the wedding but we're not going. Only for your sister Judy, I don't know what I'd do. She stays with me every night and then goes home in the morning. It's not easy with two young children of her own. She and Mark are talking about going to Scotland. The company he works for have a factory over there and they've offered him a job with much better money. Mark thinks he has no choice but to go. He suspects that they will move the whole thing out of Kilkenny any day soon.

Please, son, come home, even for a visit – we're so lonely. You can't go on blaming yourself for Claire dying. It was nobody's fault. We're all losing out, even Sammi. Her little friend Rebecca came around yesterday asking where she was and would we be having a birthday party this year. You really shouldn't have left your job here. Sammi should be here, with friends and family, after losing her mother. Not with strangers. I am enclosing five pounds for her. Treat her to something nice.

God bless you, David,
Love, Mammy.

God, this suitcase was turning out to be a right Pandora's Box!

Why does his mother say that Claire's death is not his fault? I asked myself silently as a sense of unease came over me like a shroud. David and I got married ten months after we met. What with Dad's death, inheriting the hotel and getting an instant family in Sammi, I had never paused long enough to reflect on his life before he came to Castletown. I would have seen that something was wrong, missing. We were too busy. I never got round to asking the obvious or seeing the obvious. The gaps.

My head began to spin and I went downstairs for coffee, tears welling in my eyes. Poor Mrs Joyce died suddenly six years ago, most likely of a broken heart. A husband in a nursing home who had stopped recognising her, a daughter moved abroad and a son who just removed himself from her life. Bastard.

But you could have done more too, Hannah. How often did you take Timothy down to see his grandmother?

I tried to excuse myself by remembering her dislike of me.

Maybe I should stop this – it's too painful, I reasoned with myself.

I felt myself crumbling inside, breaking down into smaller particles as if I was turning to liquid and becoming insubstantial. I stared out the kitchen window at the view that had held me captive for so many years. I roughly wiped away the tears as I looked out at the carefully manicured lawns, the tended rose bushes. Tears trickled down my cheeks. The kettle switched off as I stormed back upstairs, my breath coming in ragged gasps as I started replacing David's past in the suitcase. The teddy, the cowboy outfit, the gun, the photo album. Where's the elastic band? As I bundled up the contents, the corner of my eye zoomed in on a letter addressed to David. I froze as my eyes became locked on the words *"your son Jason"*.

Chapter Thirty-One

McCourt Solicitors
Morehampton Road
Waterford

Mr David Joyce
Sycamore Drive
Kilkenny

24/09/74

Dear Mr Joyce,
We are instructed by our client Miss Frances Devlin to write
to you regarding the matter of maintenance payments for your
son Jason. Miss Devlin advises us that you had an informal
arrangement whereby you were to make regular weekly

payments for his upkeep. She further advises us that these
payments have become irregular and are considerably in
arrears.

Our instructions from Miss Devlin are to formalise this
arrangement and have these payments sent directly to this
office. Failing your co-operation or a reply to this letter,
proceedings for the maintenance of your son will be taken at the
local District Court.

I would be grateful if you might contact this office
immediately to discuss this matter.

Thanking you,
Yours sincerely,
Patrick Mc Court
Mc Court Solicitors

I sat for a moment, blinked my eyes and read the letter
all over again. A third time. Yes, there was no room for
denial, no escape. David had another son, older than
Timothy and Sammi. My hands were sweating profusely as
I fumbled frantically through the suitcase, emptying all of its
contents onto the bed. All thoughts of secrecy were gone. I
no longer cared if he knew I'd been prying into his past. I
picked up a small bundle of receipts and saw that they
spanned a period between the mid-seventies and early
nineties. Until Jason was eighteen, I guessed, my mind
racing. Gosh, this is unreal, I thought. David was making
regular payments for another son during our marriage. What
would Timothy think if he got to know that he was not
David's only son? What would it do to him? Earlier tears
gave way to cold, unemotional shock. I read on, a dull
thudding ache in my head. I felt suspended – the bottom
had collapsed out of my world. Nothing would ever be the

same again. My hands shook as I picked up another letter and started to read.

Strand Road
Dunmore East
Waterford

18/12/73

Dear David,

I am just writing to tell you that you that I went through with the pregnancy and I now have a son. His name is Jason. He was born on October 5th. I hope you like the name. He is just the most wonderful baby – he sleeps through the night and seldom cries.

He's got your eyes and he lost the hair that he was born with. Now, his hair is blonde. He looks like a little angel.

I feel sad that you don't want to be with us. I'm hoping you'll get this letter before Christmas. I'd just love you to come down here to see us, even if it's only for Jason. My brother says he saw you at a disco in Kilkenny with another girl – he wanted to go back up with his brothers to fight with you, but I don't want that. I am sending you a photo of Jason with this letter. It might make you want to come and see him. Maybe we could be a family. I'm waiting for the unmarried mother's money to come through and things are very tight, and Jason needs stuff. Can you send some money?

I will always love you, David. I know that I can't make you love me. I'm so hurt, but I've got Jason to remember you by.

With all my love,

Frances

PS The photo of Jason was taken last week. Isn't he

adorable? Please don't leave your son without a father.
I love you, David, and I talk to Jason about you all the time.
I will always be here for you,
Frances

I read through some more letters from Frances and could see that they were getting more urgent, that she was getting angry with David for his neglect of Jason. She mentioned at one point that she knew he was working as assistant manager now and surely he could afford to send a few pounds for his son. I focused in on a piece of one really long letter from her.

How can you do this to Jason and me? I've only got four postal orders from you and Jason is now six months old. I now can see it, I was your bit on the side, nobody would know. You were going out with this Claire at home all along. I'll tell her about Jason if you don't start treating us right. Go into any shop and check the price of cots and prams, David. I trusted you – you said you knew all about safe sex and look at me now. Mammy and Daddy won't even talk to me – you'd think I had killed someone. Only for the fact that my sister gave me a place to stay, I'd be on the street with our baby. And then I hear you're at discos in Kilkenny. I'm going to a solicitor – you can't do this to us.

I returned to the photo album, skipping frantically through the pages. I removed the photo of David and Frances together and the photo of the unnamed baby . . . yes, blonde hair like she said in her letter . . . Jason. I looked for an age at the photo. Where are you now, Jason? You'd be thirty-one . . . maybe married, your own children . . . a half-brother to my Timothy. Impulsively, I turned over the photo and wrote Jason on the back.

How could David be so selfish? How could he abandon his girlfriend and baby? It was heartless. I was snooping into David's past but I no longer felt that it was wrong to do it. This suitcase was yielding the grim truth of David's history with each item I picked up – it was ghastly, macabre. Had he forgotten about those old letters? Maybe he was hoping I would find them. Why else would he keep them? He could have destroyed them. That letter from Frances was written from her heart and I wondered if he had even replied to it.

I read through a letter from the South Eastern Health Board from nineteen seventy-five asking David to come to its Waterford office so as to register himself as Jason's father. It said that Frances Devlin requested that he be entered as the baby's father and they needed his consent. He was to bring his own identification papers, preferably a passport. The registration was being completed with each partner present – procedure for children born out of wedlock, the letter said. I checked the birth certificate that lay in this gruesome bundle and, yes – David Joyce had gone ahead and registered himself as father to Jason Devlin. Official – no doubt involved.

I pondered this letter and created a mental picture of David and Frances meeting to complete the formalities. Did she bring Jason with her that day – he would have been about six months old? Questions, questions . . .

I carried on towards the end of my sordid investigation, my sense of rancour and estrangement towards my husband increasing as I went along. Unconditional and unquestioning trust and love – that's what I gave to David and he had raped it mercilessly and violently.

I stiffened as I saw the date *20/09/2003*. Recent history.

85 Sullivan Way
Islington
London
20/09/2003

Dear David,
It feels a bit weird writing to you. Every time I have started a letter I have ended by ripping it up. At this rate I am never going to get one written to you. Anyway, here goes. Mum tells me that you're my father. She was home last summer and she found out your address and gave it to me. Now that I have kids of my own I would like to meet you. Just to see you, ease my curiosity. My mother used to tell me that I looked like you. I don't know if that's still the case.

Every summer Mum used to take me back to Ireland on holidays. I loved the freedom after being cooped up in London. Now, I take the kids to France on their summer holidays – Keycamp – I think they're in Ireland too. My daughter Nicki has started asking for a photograph of her daddy's daddy, as she puts it. It would be nice for us to meet and I'd like my daughters to see you. Nicki is five, Aoife is three and I'm married to Gwen. Maybe I am hoping for too much. You mightn't answer this letter and that's okay.

Best wishes,
Jason.
PS I was tempted to send you photographs of your grandchildren and myself but I thought they might upset you. I'll wait to see if I hear from you.

I felt that I could stomach no more of this and sat silently on the floor contemplating what to do next. Did David go to meet Jason? Even answer this letter? A frisson of cold dread raced swiftly through my body and pierced my soul. I shuddered at the thought of confronting David, hurling accusations, showing him my evidence. Somehow I didn't feel up to it. I found my thoughts straying to Cormac and Louise and David's barbed comments about their marathon courtship.

"Fourteen years," he would snort cynically. "Are they holding out until they get to know each other?"

"I would have been wise to wait a while longer myself, David, wouldn't I?" I whispered now. Somehow, it seemed that Louise had got the better deal.

Chapter Thirty-Two

My mobile phone rang as I sat on my bed, brooding over the suitcase that had exposed my marriage of twenty-one years as a lie. It was almost like it was bigamy, though not quite.

"Hannah?"

"Yes, David."

"Did I tell you that I am going to the Irish Amateur Open this weekend? They're holding it in Lahinch."

"No, David," but Alison did. In another situation I would give his ear a roasting for not telling me, but it seemed incidental now.

"We're really going down to continue our lobbying for it to be held in Castletown in 2006. It's important to be there in person, pick up some support."

"Fine."

"Eh, okay, that has me gone tonight and Saturday night. See you Sunday. I've arranged cover for the weekend. Juliet and Timothy will keep an eye on things. You needn't go in if you don't feel up to it."

How thoughtful of you, David, how thoughtful, I reflected bitterly.

I set aside some things from the suitcase and threw the "trivia" back in. I had lost interest in whether David noticed I'd been snooping. Wearily, I returned it to the attic.

A plan of sorts began to form in my mind, and I began to pack a large suitcase from my wardrobe. Using a pocket folder taken from the study downstairs, I crammed in the important letters, photographs and bits retrieved from David's Pandora's Box.

I rang Timothy on his mobile.

"Are you coming home this evening, pet?"

"No, Mum – actually Dad has asked me to stay in the hotel over the weekend. Needs to have someone reliable there. What a turnaround!"

"No messing now, Timothy, you hear me. Is Cormac at the bar?"

"Not right now. He was here earlier, though. Has taken to the coffee the last few days, seems to be brooding over something – not like a man with a big stash if you were to believe the *Evening Herald*, at least. See you later, Mum, gotta go."

Laura was at reception when I dropped in David's car keys in the afternoon. She looked fit to explode.

"Have you met this Juliet Barnes that David took on yesterday? Sent me home to change my uniform, she did, this morning. Five minutes into her new job," she fumed. "Crumpled and stale-smelling, that's how she described it. Obviously, she doesn't have any babies. Straight from the School of Catering classroom, I suppose."

* * *

I slept fitfully throughout the night, waking in a sweat a couple of times. I dreamt that I was Pandora from the Greek myth, reaching in and plucking out a little boy with a gun and a teddy bear.

"Leave me alone or I will shoot you," he said. "Put me down, put me down . . . Bugsy, help me!"

"Let go," Pandora said. "Let go and I will release you from all the ills that beset man – you will only have hope within."

Flashes of Jason burned across my brain, wrestling as a child with Timothy. He was screaming. "I am the first one, I am the first . . . Give me back my dad, you can't have him, he's not yours!" Timothy had removed his mattress to the garden shed and was lying in his Boy Scout sleeping bag. "I'm 'a scared' of my big brother, Mammy – he's torn down my Arsenal posters and covered the walls with racing drivers. I'm not going back in until he goes."

I woke with a blinding headache. Soon I was in the kitchen, downing aspirin and coffee. Later, showered, dressed and changed, I closed the front door softly, dragging my suitcase to the car.

I glanced backwards at the home we shared for over twenty years – reminiscing with irony on the day David carried me across the threshold. Now I had stepped back across it, perhaps not to return. In the bedroom we shared for over twenty years sat a teddy bear, propped up against the pillows with a photograph of a baby pinned to his chest. Awaiting David's return on Sunday evening.

Chapter Thirty-Three

I felt a great stab of annoyance when my mobile rang, my mother's number flashing on the screen. "Not today, please not today," I gritted through clenched teeth before answering.

"Hannah, I was wondering, dear, would you mind bringing me some tea bags, I forgot to get some."

"I can't right now, Mammy – could you phone Cormac?"

"Hannah what's got into you? Surely you can bring me a few tea bags and boxes full of them in the kitchen."

"That's not the point. Cormac will be just getting up now – he'll get them for you."

"Hannah, you shouldn't talk to me like that!"

"I'm sorry, Mother, I know I shouldn't." I felt overwhelmed by it all. "I'm just tired, that's all."

"Aren't we all?" she said haughtily.

"Look, I'm in the hotel right now. David's gone off

golfing for the weekend. I can't really leave."

Briefly I closed my eyes and reopened them. I had to get her off the phone – any minute now I would surrender, the weight of these domestics pinning me down. I had to do it, goodness knows I had threatened often enough. I massaged my forehead and before I knew it I was organising a family get-together. "Sunday lunch," I heard myself say. And I wasn't going to be around for it. Since childhood, Cormac and I had to be on our best behaviour in the hotel dining room. In those days I saw more of my mother's back than her face as she tended to every whim from guests, whilst we were ignored. Back then I swore I would never work in the hotel and look at me now! I still hold a vivid picture of my mother smiling serenely at guests while she made pleasant inquires about family members. If we got troublesome she'd turn to us wearing that "What now?" look on her face. She had an inbuilt elegance that was enviable, which I never could nor ever wanted to imitate. A wry smile came to my lips as I pictured her thin, sinewy hands fluttering around the place as she gave directions to the staff. My father leaning against the bar talking about politics or golf, his two favourite subjects. This pull of guilt had always taken me homeward. I had always surrendered to it. But this time I was leaving and nothing was going to stop me.

"Where are you going to have Sunday lunch, at your house or in the hotel?" my mother asked quite reasonably and the question brought me back to earth with a jolt. Oh, what was I doing? I hadn't the courage to tell her that I mightn't be there, that I was running away from home. Coward, I chided myself. What was I to do? She wouldn't understand anyway. My efforts would be wasted on her just like they would be on David. I hadn't left and already I felt myself being drawn back into the family web. Leaving home was really tiring stuff.

"Oh, I haven't thought about that," I admitted.

"Did you ever cook in that new oven?"

"Well, as a matter of fact I did. I roasted a chicken last Sunday in it."

"And was it any better than the old one?"

She had sided with David and was opposed to me getting the new Neff cooker. I knew if one was good enough for Alison it was good enough for me. I could picture my revamped kitchen and I could imagine how messy it would get after a few days with no one to polish every surface and remove the debris from the worktop. Really, the best thing that I could do was to detach from everything.

"We'll eat in the restaurant," I announced.

I knew my mother was disappointed – she had this way of going really quiet and saying nothing when she was disappointed with me. Dignified silences are torturous. I just can't bear them and she knew it. Usually, David adopted the same method when dealing with me. He'd go really quiet and that made me just so angry. What do you do when someone won't engage in a conversation, when they won't try and discuss what's going on? I had given up trying with David. I had to surrender to the fact that he didn't really care.

Eventually she said, "That would be lovely, dear."

"Good – I'm afraid I won't be able to drop out with the tea bags," I hastily added.

"Oh, I'll phone Liz – she'll bring some over when she's coming."

"Great."

I walked down to David's empty office. I let my rage ravage me, I was no longer going to suppress it or reason with it. This time I was taking action. My limbs felt heavy so I sat down at his desk. Every cell in my body tingled nervously. I can't do this, I thought. The coward in me came to the forefront. My stomach rumbled nervously, fearing that any moment he'd open the door and catch me.

We had come to this. I opened the drawer of his desk and saw the keys for the safe. I was already doing it. I was seeing myself taking action, no longer passive. I opened the safe and bundled some money into my bag. An impulse made me also grab a bunch of personal letters stored there, belonging to David.

I stopped at my office to pick up my own mini-directory, which I started maintaining when I started teacher training all these years back. Oh, it wasn't the same one. Every few years, I would make a clean start, switching still-used names, addresses and phone numbers over. Some older names made my new book for the sake of sentiment and nostalgia. "You'd never know, Hannah, you might get to call on them some day," I would say.

I avoided looking at the family photographs that were on my desk. I took a breath, smoothed back my tossed hair and then walked calmly towards the back exit.

I will always remember that day. The air was heavy with the scent of furniture polish, then it became mingled with the appetising smells from the kitchen. Once outside it tasted fresh and calming. Rain drizzled quietly from a grey sky, shrouding the place in gossamer light. The sun hadn't broken through after all. I felt lighter than I had in a long time.

"David, these are my reasons for leaving . . ."

I sighed heavily at the very thought. I really didn't know my reasons for leaving.

"I've had enough!" I played the words with a slight touch of drama in my head. I sneered at my own stupidity.

I had plenty of reasons. I felt justified in what I was doing. How dare he keep his son a secret from me? Past hurts started to string themselves together. Knot themselves into a web of justification. I felt entitled to my anger. I'd earned it. My dislike for David swelled inside me, turning over into something more like hate and that scared me. I didn't want to hate him – he was the father of my son. There was no point talking to him about this. Once composed from the shock that I knew, he'd sit wearing that detached air, his tie loosened, shirt sleeves rolled up, looking like he was really there to participate. I knew the procedure so well, and right now it made me want to puke. A part of him would be somewhere else. In the latter days of our marriage I fantasized about getting a male mannequin, dressing it in his clothes and putting it sitting at the table to see if I could bring the point home. There was never any live response, just conciliatory words spoken, agreements made. And as quickly forgotten.

"Hannah, I didn't want to upset you," was a favourite line. Once upon a time his words were touching and could reach me – now I felt they were a joke. I couldn't bear to sit down at our kitchen table and discuss his secret. What else had he hidden from me?

He was going to spend the weekend playing golf with that scoundrel Vincent. I drew strength from my self-righteous position. Shouldn't he be spending the weekend with me? More ammunition for me, I thought sourly. This was a matter of survival. My survival. Look at what had happened to Lily. I didn't want the same thing to happen to me. From now on I was going to do what was right for me – only trouble was I wasn't quite sure what that was, yet. I had to stay focused. I was going to take myself out of the picture. I had visualised it and now I was doing it. Later I could list out reasons for leaving, once I had reached my destination. In a matter of hours I could be somewhere else, anywhere, it really didn't matter. From that safe distance I could look back. I was going to look my reality straight in the face and see it for what it was. For years I had fooled myself, pretending that everything was okay when it really wasn't.

I had all I needed in my bag. My wallet with credit cards and bankcards. The bundles of cash and, tucked in beside them, the letters that David had kept in the safe. I had never ventured to read those letters before.

I had to keep going – there was no turning back now.

At the car I suddenly felt dizzy and leant against it for a minute or two. The aspirin I had taken earlier seemed to be gnawing at my stomach. I realised I couldn't remember when I had last eaten. Not a good idea setting out on a long drive. I decided I would grab a takeaway coffee and Danish somewhere to get my blood sugar up. Later, when I had Castletown behind me, I could have a proper breakfast.

The main street of Castletown was all but empty. I hurried off down it, praying I wouldn't bump into anyone I knew. Thankfully I was wearing flat shoes.

"Hannah!" Alison called and crossed the road to stop me. "You look like you're in a hurry."

"Oh, Alison," I said. Right then I felt totally disorientated.

"What are you up to?" she inquired leisurely.

"Nothing," I snapped defensively. "Why, do I look like I'm up to something?"

"Hannah, relax! You should see the look on your face."

214

Beads of perspiration dampened my shirt collar and under my armpits. I heard myself laugh and babble on. "Ah, it's just one or two problems at the 'big house' – if it's not one crisis in the hotel it's another."

"I've seen this really nice outfit that I'm thinking about buying, I'm really not sure about it. I guess you don't have time to have a look at it with me?"

A hot guilty flush rose up from my neck. For a fleeting moment I thought she knew what I was up to. I stood motionless and felt the pulsating urge in my chest, urging me to hurry on. I took a breath and slowly exhaled, trying to calm myself. Alison went on to describe the outfit, while I feigned interest. I had no luggage, so she couldn't possibly know that I was leaving. There I stood, wearing a fashionable blue tailored trouser suit. Perhaps I looked frazzled. I should have paid more attention to my appearance, glossed my lips, those little touches could have concealed a lot. I had to get rid of her. I couldn't explain what I was about to do. She might try to persuade me to stay and think about what I was doing, sleep on it, that's what she'd most likely say. I needed to keep going, standing was making me lose momentum. In the shop window I saw us reflected. I didn't like the way I looked. Somehow the image wasn't me. My trouser suit looked hideous and was my hair that brassy shade of blonde?

"Alison, I'm really sorry –" I started to apologise and wondered what for. I felt I was sagging under the weight of it all.

"And imagine Vincent moving in with that bitch!" Alison went on regardless. "Flaunting her about the place . . ."

I felt agitated and was desperately searching for ways to

get away from her. She always seemed to have all the time in the world to talk while I was on a mental treadmill. A breeze stirred around us, lifting the scent of her perfume and whirling it around; a café door opened blending in the smell of fresh coffee. I was tempted to step inside and forget about it all.

"You'd think they'd have the decency to put a bit of distance between themselves and Lily," Alison was saying, "but no, that harlot has got him in her grip."

I had to resist the temptation to mention that Sinéad had dropped in on me or I'd be in the Coffee Dock in next to no time, going through the finer points. Then Rhonda Murtagh would start. This was claustrophobia in an open street.

She moved slightly back from me and continued. "And we have to plan our next shopping trip. Where will we go next – Galway?" She giggled. "Or maybe London, New York, Paris?"

"Oh, I don't know, I haven't thought about it since. We'll do it though, soon." After a moment of private deliberation I then added, "I hope the boys enjoy their golfing trip this weekend."

In the background a tour bus drove down the main street. I knew it was stopping at the hotel. I quickly glanced at my wristwatch. My stomach muscles contracted into a tight ball. Did someone call my name just there? I turned my head in the direction of the hotel.

"Did you hear someone call my name?" I said, panicked.

Alison smiled with amusement. "You're imagining things." She gently touched my arm.

"Yes," I said in agreement. I heard the familiar sound of the train coming into the station.

The expression on my face must have told her

something, for she smiled sympathetically at me. "See you later," she said.

The steady boom of my heart against my chest made me aware of just how panicked I was. I abandoned the coffee and Danish venture. My shaky legs were taking me round the back of the hotel to the car park. It was like some force stronger than myself was carrying me forward, propelling me out of town. From cradle to the departure lounge, forty-one years on. Goodbye or was it au revoir – I didn't know yet.

I pulled jerkily out of the car park. A lorry was holding up traffic as it tried to manoeuvre its way down the narrow side street. I waited until it passed, tapping the steering wheel impatiently. I turned right onto the main street and headed south out of Castletown.

Chapter Thirty-Four

Kilkenny
29/09/04

Dear Journal ~
It's me again. I see it's been a few days since I talked to you.
My life has changed completely since I last sat with you. I've
discovered I've been married to a stranger for the past twenty-
one years and it's not a nice feeling at all. I'm here in Kilkenny,
David's hometown, and I plan on doing some investigating
tomorrow.

Remember when I told you about our first son Timothy's
birth? Well, I've just found out I was wrong ~ he wasn't the first
son. David has another son, Jason ~ he's thirty-one now.

I've left Castletown, don't know if I could ever face going
back, not right now anyway. I'm so afraid for my future and
have a burning desire for revenge. I read a story in Woman's

Way *once about a woman who got an annulment because her husband hadn't told her he was gay when they were getting married. Wouldn't that be sweet? I would get to take back the hotel for myself and I would become Hannah Duignan again and David would be on the street. I'd have to ask Timothy, though, he wouldn't want to risk people calling him a b~ you see, I can say it, but I can't bring myself to write it down. I've brought my address book with me but I don't have any entries for old friends in Kilkenny. I have a sort of a plan about finding out a few things, but it's more than that ~ I want to decide what's best for Hannah from here on. I've told nobody but you where I am. I really should have told Timothy and Mammy. Anyway nobody will notice I'm gone until tomorrow evening. David's gone to a golf do and Timothy is staying at the hotel ~ I'll ring him tomorrow ~ he's still just a boy.*

Bye for now,
Hannah

I look at the menu in Langton's pub and decide on the Irish Stew. Langton's scooped up the Irish Pub of the Year Award several times during the nineties. Invariably, David would bring me here on the few occasions he visited his parents in years past. I used to look forward to these family days out, just our two children and us. We would generally pack up on a Sunday to "get away from it all", in his words. McNean's Bistro in Blacklion, Smuggler's Creek in Rossnowlagh and Patrick Guilbaud's in Dublin were among the many places we lunched as part of these relaxed Sundays off. Eventually, it came home to me that all of these places we visited had a common trend – they were award-winning and were being "hit on" as part of David's relentless quest to get the Castletown Arms on the same exalted platform. I was furious, but I got my revenge by taking over one Sunday and driving over one hundred miles to plant him on his backside in Burger King in Galway. Timothy and Sammi were delighted. We went on to Leisureland in Salthill afterwards. David was outvoted on where we'd have our tea that evening – more burgers, chicken nuggets and chips at McDonald's in Salthill. I almost collapsed with laughter when Timothy asked, "Are you not going to ask for a copy of the menu, Dad? You always do."

"Your meal, madam." The waiter returned with a large bowl of steaming hot food and home-made brown bread.

I sat alone, eating away, savouring the lamb, carrots, celery and soft potatoes. Mopping up the last of the juices with the brown bread, I paid up and left.

I found a really nice B&B to spend the night. I strolled around for over an hour looking at different ones. Funny, I came full circle, returning to the first one I saw. The reason I picked it was it reminded me of Lily's garden and home. The garden was so well tended – the contrast of flowers, the different textures and shades of shrubs. I knew Lily would love it and it made me feel at home.

The lady of the house didn't look like a gardener at all. Long manicured nails, coiffeured hair and lips glossed with a tasteful pink lipstick.

There was only one word to describe the bedroom: beautiful. Delicately embroidered linen curtains with matching bed linen. An antique chest of drawers – a vase full of fresh flowers. If Lily could see me now . . .

I had nothing planned. Was this what they call living in the moment? Perhaps I would go for a walk. Reacquaint myself with the area. I should count my cash – see how much I'd scooped. Perhaps not.

"Are you going out, dear?"

"Yeah, just for a walk, I won't be long."

"Well, I'd better give you a key then. I go to bed early."

"Okay, thanks."

My walk about Kilkenny took me through its narrow winding streets, past Kilkenny Castle. I dismissed the thought of going in – I'd had enough of castles lately. Evening Mass was about to start in St John's Church and soon I was sitting near the front as the priest and his young altar boys emerged on the altar to the sounds of choir music. The sermon spoke of age, loneliness and fear and the priest was exhorting his congregation to look out for our senior citizens – call in on them, you'll reap the rewards. I felt a pang of guilt when I thought of my own mother, defiant in her declining years. I'd just have to ring her later. I didn't need to say I was gone away. Before leaving, I lit some candles and silently asked God to look over my loved ones and give me guidance. Outside, people were gathered together, laughing, talking. I got a sensation that I was being followed and I turned to look around. Nothing except an old lady shuffling along, looking downward at the road. Hardly a handbag snatcher, I thought, easing my grip on my bag and walking on. Suddenly, I heard a voice behind me.

"Hello, I'm sorry . . . can I walk with you?"

The old lady caught up, wheezing heavily. Little more than five foot, painfully thin, her wizened face was further narrowed by the scarf she wore.

"Yes, that's okay."

"You're a visitor?"

"Yes, I'm staying in town overnight." She looked agitated and frightened, I thought, remembering the priest's sermon. "I can walk you to your home – that's if you like?"

"Would you do that? It's only five minutes' walk."

"That's no problem at all," I said, linking my arm in hers.

"I saw you lighting candles after Mass. I light two for my husband and daughter every time. Never miss – it's my way of keeping in touch. Do you mind if I sit on the wall for a minute. I'm beaten."

Eventually, we got to the door of her house, a small cottage near the Health Board building on the Lacken Road.

"You must come in for tea," she said.

I started to decline, but the words got stuck in my throat. She's lonely, Hannah, don't be selfish. Probably frightened by the sermon where the priest spoke graphically about violence against the elderly.

"Okay, I will."

Inside, the fire was burning. "I make sure to fill it before I go out – it's nice to come back to a warm fire. I'll go make the tea."

Nice and cosy, I thought, standing up to look at family photographs on the wall. "Do you live here alone, Mrs –" I stop suddenly, reeling back from the fireplace, staring in surprise . . . Sammi . . . her mum Claire . . . what . . .?

"Maloney," said a voice behind me. "Mrs Maloney, Claire's mum, Sammi's grandmother. You can call me Bessie, if you like."

I froze. My instinct was to run out the door.

"Sit down here, Hannah. Would you like a fruit scone with your tea?"

We sat quietly drinking our tea.

"God, you gave me the most awful fright. Seeing Sammi and her mother like that knocked the wind out of me completely. You should have told me who you were."

"I'm sorry – I really didn't mean to frighten you. I saw

you walking up the aisle. I always get in early to Mass – sit at the back. Get to see nearly everyone that way. It's just a pastime – see how many I can recognise."

"But I've never met you before. How did you know me?"

"Through Sammi. She's shown me no end of photos of you over the years. You on your own, you and *him* at various dos. She also had a video of a house party for Baby Dan's christening . . . no Maloneys present of course."

"So you were following me . . ."

"No, it wasn't exactly like that. We were going the same way and I was curious. I knew David's mother had passed on and his father is in St Canice's Nursing Home down the road."

"Sammi is married now and has her own baby, Mrs Maloney – Bessie."

She laughed. "You've neither been listening nor looking closely enough, Hannah. I know that. Sammi was here only last week. There's Baby Dan up there on the wall. Your grandson, sort of, and my great-grandson."

Over several cups of tea, Bessie talked away – at the same time peeling away the layers of deceit that David had shrouded himself in over the years. The word mystery or enigma could no longer apply to him as his secrets, when bared, were sordid and sad. Quite simply, David had harmed the lives of many and left a trail of broken people behind him.

Claire was a year older than David and started going out with him when she was sixteen.

"We were very pleased at first. David was clean-cut and ambitious, had his eyes fixed on going places. At first I thought he was just shy but as time wore on I saw it as more of a coldness – an indifference to other people's feelings and

223

needs. Claire couldn't see it – she was absolutely besotted with him. They'd go to the pictures twice a week, rarely went to the pubs. David had trained in hotel management and was completing his training at the Newpark Hotel in town here. He got an offer to manage a small hotel in Waterford and he was down there for two years. I thought it strange at the time that he never invited Claire down, but she didn't seem to notice."

She faltered occasionally as if going down Memory Lane was too upsetting for her. Now, she was looking towards a portrait photograph of Claire above her fireplace.

"You don't need to go on with this if you don't want to talk about it," I said. "It must be hard for you." But I was desperate for her to continue.

"No, no, not at all. I love talking it through, sort of brings Claire alive. Anyway, he came back as assistant manager of the Newpark two years later. They got married and even though I didn't like him, things were going great for them, so we thought. He was manager of the Newpark at twenty-two and Sammi was born the year after. Look, I'm sorry, I'm forgetting that you're his wife when I say I don't like him . . ."

"It's okay, Bessie," I said, fearing that I was losing her. "You see, my reason for being in Kilkenny is that I was going to look you up tomorrow. It's amazing that you caught up with me first. I've found out some things about David lately and I just need to –"

"Do you mean Jason?"

"Yes."

"Ah, well. I can talk freely so. Poor Claire got to know about Jason when his mother turned up on her doorstep, demanding to see David, threatening all sorts. She was very unbalanced and seemingly had just left a psychiatric hospital. Anyway, the long and short of it was that Claire got to know about his love-child in the same way as you did – out of the blue. It was bad enough but Frances made it worse by claiming that she and David were married – she actually believed it – she was supposed to be taking anti-psychotic drugs at the time. She had a stand-up row with David when he came home. Claire rang me up, hysterical she was, not just about Jason but the betrayal, as she was David's fiancée at the time Jason was born. She was coming over, was leaving him, but first she had to pick up Sammi from a friend's house where she was playing. She never got there – her car hit a tree."

"How much of this does Sammi know?"

"None of it, as far as I know. She loved her mother, still does. Rings me twice every week, she does, and rarely would a month pass that she does not visit me. I've gone to see them also – I have the free travel pass, but I'm finding it harder to get about these days." She sighed. "I could almost forgive your husband for the way Claire died but to keep our granddaughter – our link to Claire – away from us for twelve years was the most painful thing I've ever had to endure. Poor Jack, my husband, died during that time. He is a mean, callous man, your husband."

"Mrs Maloney, I don't know what to say . . . I'm so sorry . . . I should . . ."

"There's no need to be. You were in the dark. I thank God every day for bringing Sammi back into my life. I would have died a very lonely and broken woman had that not happened. You won't tell David? Please don't . . . I don't think he knows . . . I'd hate him to take Sammi away from me again."

"There's no need to worry about that, Bessie. Anyway, I'd say Sammi would tell him where to go if he tried to interfere."

As I left Bessie Maloney's house we hugged tightly and I promised to call again soon.

* * *

The next morning I took myself down to the main reception room. We had agreed the previous evening that I would have breakfast at ten. The house exulted in luxury. Liberal taffeta curtains hung from the sash windows. Unusual curved console tables flanked the fireplace. It was a beautiful room, one that I would love to copy, as I would never be able to put the pieces together myself. I imagined sitting there, with the fire lit, the flames dancing merrily in the grate. The wind howling outside and me cosy on the inside. I heard the click of her heels on the hall floor. My hostess entered the room smiling.

"Did you sleep well?" she politely asked.

"Yes, thank you."

"Would you like to have your breakfast in the conservatory?"

"Yes, that would be lovely."

She blessed me with another gracious smile, then turned and led the way.

"You have a beautiful house," I said.

"Thank you," she replied. There was no chink in her hostess armour. This was as friendly as she was going to get. I didn't mind, for I was basking in the luxury of it all. Delighted to be the guest for a change. And this beautiful house was just what I needed to ease me into the next step. Whatever that was going to be.

"It looks like it's going to be a nice day," she commented as she placed a bowl of porridge in front of me. "There you go, Flahavan's organic."

"Mmm, this is just right and full-cream milk at that. I'm not sure Weight Watchers would approve, though."

It would have been nice if we could have had breakfast together, talked about things that mattered to us. But then I was okay with that – in fact I preferred silence to laboured small talk. I wanted her to think of me as just a tourist. Someone passing through. It also suited me to target Bed and Breakfasts – I risked being recognised by our trade colleagues at the larger hotels and I did not want David tipped off.

"Here's my card if you should like to book a room again," she said courteously to me at her front door as I was leaving.

"Thank you," I said, slipping her card into my bag.

Armed with directions for St Canice's Nursing Home, I picked up my holdall and walked down her cobbled path towards the gate.

Chapter Thirty-Five

Sitting in my Renault Clio in the grounds of St Canice's Nursing Home, I dialled my mother's number.

"Hannah, where are you?"

"Over at the house," I lied guiltily. I'd only get away with this until David came home that evening. When he saw the calling card I left in the bedroom, he'd be on to Mammy pronto, then Alison, Lily . . . He'll have me on the RTÉ News within twenty-four hours . . . "*wife of one of Ireland's leading hoteliers goes missing*" . . . get a bit of publicity at the same time. I cringed inwardly at my cynicism towards him.

"Sammi rang to apologise . . . She's not able to make it this weekend. She sent a text to your mobile as she could not get you at the house."

"Oh, yeah . . . I got that, maybe we'll hold over the lunch until she comes."

"Well, that actually suits me. Cormac and Louise came

228

over last night with Jasmine. He's not drinking and they asked me over for lunch today. I felt I couldn't refuse. I asked him had he taken The Pledge and he just laughed. Didn't answer me, though, but they all seemed very relaxed and happy."

"That's great – did he say anything about the hotel?"

"No, should he? Are you holding back something on me, Hannah?"

"Ah, no. Listen, I'll leave you alone for today so. Take care."

I was mightily relieved that my foolishness in setting up the Sunday family occasion was going unpunished for the moment. I wanted David to be the first to know of my departure and to know the reason at the same instant. "You're going to do that for me, Bugsy, aren't you?" I said aloud in the safe privacy of my car.

* * *

Inside St Canice's, the assistant matron directed me towards David's father.

"He'll be delighted to see you – he rarely gets visitors," she said a little acidly. "Your husband calls at intervals – he's a terribly busy man."

I ignored her barbs. "Will he know me?"

"It depends on what type of day he's having. It's amazing really. He's had it for so long, you'd expect him to be in the final stages. But he gets days when he's aware of his surroundings. He doesn't talk, though."

Joe Joyce was sitting up in a wheelchair looking out the window.

"You have a visitor, Joe. Do you want your photograph album?"

Joe looked vacantly at both of us, suddenly breaking into a smile. He began to point and stare at me.

"I think he recognises you," she said, sensing my unease. "Here are your photos, Joe."

My thoughts drifted back some twenty years to when David introduced me to his parents. Joe was in his sixties then and had just retired from his job as sports reporter for the *Kilkenny People*. It was around this time that the first symptoms of his disease were emerging. He was a shy, reticent type of character and had an encyclopaedic knowledge of Kilkenny sports. I recall Timothy looking confusedly at the hurley and sliotar he got from Joe for his fifth birthday. Joe claimed that he had been given them by Eddie Keher, "Ireland's greatest ever," as he put it. It was to remain untouched in the garden shed for three years. After that, it was a case of broken conservatory windows and endless lost balls as Timothy whacked relentlessly outside until it was too dark to see anything. Joe always supported his children in doing their own thing but it wasn't hard to pick up on his disappointment at David's apathy towards sport. On one particular day, they went off to play golf while Patricia, Joe's wife, and I went off with Sammi to Kilkenny Shopping Centre. I was pregnant at the time. I overheard them arguing when I got back.

"You know I'm not a big fan of golf, son, but I'm prepared to *play* it, just to please. But I'm not prepared to be left standing there waiting while you abuse the situation by using it as an opening to make business contacts."

"They're at it again – one lives for sport, the other for money," Patricia whispered.

Joe sat with the photo album on his lap, gazing blankly over many of the pictures. I watched his eyes, vacuous as he trawled over the pages – suddenly flickering towards recognition, frustration – then vacuous again – fighting the dying of the light. Occasionally, he became animated, jabbing furiously at a particular snap and looking frantically at me, trying to say something. He was now looking at his wife and tears came to his eyes as he stroked her face gently and then looked up despairingly at me.

"I know, Joe, I know," I whispered gently. "You still can feel, you still can feel . . ." I hugged him tightly but he was lost to the world as nature catapulted him once more to the wrong side of life's cruel see-saw.

Outside, I pondered awhile over the next stage of my journey. It was to be Waterford to see if I could connect with Frances Devlin's family. It seemed pointless at this stage. Pandora's Box had opened the door on David's secret world and Bessie Maloney had filled in the gaps. I had no invitation to look in on Jason's life or that of his family. It was not my affair. It was down to David to let Timothy and Sammi know they had a half-brother, I thought, pleased with myself at this inspiration. "You're letting go, Hannah," I whispered to myself.

I looked through my address book and asked it to bring me somewhere for me, nobody else. Just me.

Chapter Thirty-Six

I pulled up on the hard shoulder of the road on seeing a young hitchhiker with a sign for Galway.

"You're going the whole way – that's great," he said.

"Seat belt, please," I said to the young man sitting in my car. I felt a sense of abandon, a free spirit rising powerfully above the fraudulent "kindred spirits" that were David and me. "So, who's going to lead the conversation, me or you?"

He looked at me, startled for a moment. "Well, my name is Chris and I'm on my way back to Galway to finalise my accommodation for the coming year. I'm a second-year student – I'm going to be an architect. I like having a good time so I have to save on bus fares. I like getting picked up by lady drivers . . . even if they're inquisitive." A boyish smile sat broadly on his face.

"I see, and cheeky to boot. So, you live in Kilkenny then?"

"No, Cavan. Came down here to my girlfriend and I'm

going back with no girlfriend."

"Falling out?"

"You could say that . . . . sort of. Looking for commitment and all that nonsense. Me, I'm off to the Big Apple once I get my qualifications. Went there this summer to save money for the coming year. Didn't work out that way though – I'm as skint as I ever was. Still though, the crack was great."

"I'd say it was. Does the Regional College in Cavan not do your subjects?"

"It does, but I wanted to get away from the place, not have my parents looking down my neck all the time. You get a bigger grant if you live away from home, too."

"I bet it costs more, though."

"It does, but I do two night shifts a week at a twenty-four-hour petrol station. Seventy euros a night, cash in hand. I get to do most of my assignments during this time. Works out well, apart from when I get caught sleeping during lectures."

"I bet you don't tell your parents about your little 'nixer', do you?"

"Can't answer that, you might run into them one day."

The journey to Galway passed quickly. Chris gleefully accepted my offer to stop en route for a bite to eat and tucked into a large Irish breakfast while I sat there watching and drinking coffee.

"Well, thanks very much for that," he said, wiping his mouth with a tissue.

No doubt who's paying the bill then, I thought. Still, Chris's openness appealed to me. Timothy should really be looking at his options. There was something engaging about the way this lad lived his life – he wasn't living in anybody's shadow.

I waved him off in Eyre Square and turned into the Roche's Stores car park. I spent a while browsing the shops and asked a man in a busman's uniform for directions to the Great Outdoors.

He looked at me quizzically. "I'm not sure it's called that but if I'm guessing right that you're looking for stuff for walking the islands or maybe Connemara, try out Shop Street. There are a few of them down there."

* * *

"Can I do anything for you?" said the young girl hovering behind me.

"Well, you can," I said, feeling a further surge of gay abandon. "I'm putting myself entirely in your hands. I want you to equip me head to toe for walks around Connemara and the Aran Islands." The wad of notes from David's safe was considerably smaller as I left the shop with mountain boots by Timberland, waterproof, breathable suit by Gore-Tex, scarf and wool hat by Lacoste and thermal underwear by Canterbury of New Zealand. The young lady, God, she was a ringer for Lily's Erin, was up and running, even coaxing me to buy oils, scented candles, incense. Treat yourself, she said, the chill-out at the end of the day is the best part. Her enthusiasm was infectious despite the fact that her dress and demeanour suggested that she rarely ventured beyond the trendy discos of the city.

Back in the car, I took out a small *Fáilte Ireland* booklet. Soon I was on the phone.

"Good afternoon, Abbeyglen Castle Hotel . . . Yes, we do have single rooms available . . . You expect to be here about

234

six o'clock and you'd like to book dinner for one as well. Dinner, bed and breakfast for one night . . . that's one hundred and thirty euros . . . You'll be paying cash when you come. That's fine. We'll see you at six then, Mrs Joyce, dinner at seven thirty."

Two hours later, I was unpacking in my room in the Abbeyglen. Outside, I paused to admire its beautifully tended gardens and the little stream coursing through them. Clifden Bay shimmered in the late evening sun and in the background the Twelve Bens mountain range seemed to closet this particular piece of heaven in a comforting embrace.

I decided to ring Timothy. "Well, young man, how are you getting on as lord of the manor at the Castletown for the weekend?"

"Fine, I thought you'd be around, but everything is fine, it's under control. I think I'll vote with you about Dad retiring. I'm ready to assume control."

"Timothy, don't get carried away on the euphoria of one weekend – it's not an easy life."

"Take it easy, Mum. I'm joking . . . sort of . . . Oh, listen, I've got something to tell you. I heard that Lily confessed that she wrote that anonymous letter to the County Council about Dad and the planning permission thing?"

I bit my lip silently. I could come to terms with an impulsive telephone call, put it down to a fit of irrational rage . . . but a letter, so formal, so calculated . . .

"Lily didn't do it. Erin did. Revenge against Dad for sacking her. We spoke about it – she was sorry her mum and you fell out about it. Wanted to put it right between you two."

I listened in resigned silence. What is it about the

235

psychology of women that alters the way they look at the world once they conceive? The child remains eternally ensconced in the emotional womb to be protected at all costs. The risk of personal sacrifice is no match when pitted against the parental instinct. I thought of the Arctic penguins shrouding their newborns while standing bolt upright in sub-zero conditions for several months, not surrendering until the chick can assume its own care.

Timothy broke into my thoughts. "Erin felt it was an 'eye for an eye' situation. After all, Dad had sacked her for romping with me while her dad romped upstairs. She's spirited, is Erin . . . That's what I like about her."

"Timothy, you've noticed that things have been bad with me and your dad lately, yes?"

"I was getting suspicious by the time you smashed your sixth piece of Denby on the kitchen floor. Yeah, I've seen the friction, the bad vibes, for a little while."

"I've gone away for a few days, Timothy. He'll get to find out when he comes home tonight. If he asks, you can tell him I've gone away somewhere to . . . de-stress, yeah, you tell him that."

"Okay, and where would you be doing this de-stressing?"

"Well, you must promise not to tell . . ."

"Done."

* * *

The hotel restaurant was half-full, mainly with middle-to late-age couples and groups. I reflected on how the hotel trade has adapted to the economic boom with inflated prices Thursday to Saturday for the Beemers and Mercs while from Sunday to Thursday you get the special offers. I got a few curious glances when I sat alone at a small corner table.

"I'll have the seafood chowder and the monkfish with peppers and prawns in champagne sauce, please."

"Thank you, madam," said the probably-Spanish waiter, removing the setting opposite me.

Wouldn't want anyone joining me now . . . I've got claws, you see.

I had dressed up a little for my meal – it didn't matter that I wasn't meeting anybody – a woman's gotta look her best, as Alison would say. With the help of an iron from room service, I'd transformed some crumpled choices from my suitcase. White cotton short-sleeved shirt, pure wool black trousers with a discreet stripe. Simple black shoes. Gold necklace, matching earrings and bangle. My engagement and wedding rings were sitting safely in a purse upstairs. I was not on a get-a-man expedition but, just for today, I needed to wash away all traces of my turbulent past.

"Your seafood chowder, madam."

I examined the soup carefully with my spoon. There are so many interpretations of this famous dish. This one had all the right ingredients: salmon, cod, mussels, smoked fish and celery, carrot and potato. All in the right proportions. It tasted heavenly. The assorted breads that came with it were warm and tasty.

Suddenly, an elderly lady sat down next to me – her husband had left their table temporarily.

"Did you come here alone, dear?" she asked, eying me inquisitively.

"I did, yes," I replied, somewhat startled. Normally, I would have been annoyed at such an intrusion but what the hell . . . "My daughter was due to come along but cancelled at the last minute. I said, no matter, I'll go myself." I cringed inwardly at my deceit. Why is it that women have to make excuses for being alone?

"Harry and me, it's our fiftieth wedding anniversary. Well, it's not until next weekend but we suspect there's a surprise party organised for us. We have eight children, we wouldn't want to disappoint them – but we were determined to mark the occasion with our own personal celebration. We're from Limerick, we are."

"Oh, that's nice."

She seemed a little disappointed that I didn't reciprocate further. Then Harry returned and she stood up to go back to her table.

"Listen, would you mind taking a photograph of me and Harry?" she asked, offering me a camera.

"I'd be delighted to. Okay. Move in a little closer there – raise your glasses. That's it."

The chowder and bread had taken the edge off my appetite and I struggled with my main course. My waiter eyed my plate quizzically.

"Is there a problem with your food, madam?"

"Oh, no – it's fine. My first course was very filling and I just cannot eat any more."

"I understand. In Spain our soup is Gazpacho. You serve it cold. If you eat it with bread, you do not need a main course. Dessert? Coffee?"

"No, thank you."

Returning to my room, I retrieved my phone book and thumbed through the pages to see if there was anyone I could contact in the area. It's not looking too good, I mused, as I went through the book.

Then I blushed as I saw Murdoch Goodman's name. "Gosh, he lives in Leenaun," I murmured. That wasn't too far from here.

Then I spotted it: *Eunice Jones C/O Vera O'Malley, Sky Road, Clifden.*

Picking up courage, I dialled the number.

"Good evening, O'Malleys' Bed and Breakfast. How can I help you?"

"Eh, my name is Hannah, Hannah Joyce. I was friendly with Eunice Jones – she taught me how to paint many years ago. I was in the area and had your name in my phone book. I was hoping to meet up with Eunice."

"Eunice is in bed right now. She goes early. You could call up and see her tomorrow if you wish."

"That's great. What time is suitable?"

"Anytime after nine o'clock. Just take the Sky Road and keep going until you see our B&B sign. If you're on foot, it's about a fifteen minute walk."

Chapter Thirty-Seven

I was awake at half seven the following morning. My first thought was, oddly, of Murdoch Goodman and I experienced that wave of embarrassment all over again.

I got up and showered. Pausing naked before the mirror, I reassured myself: "Hannah Joyce, you're all woman, as good as anyone – I bet Murdoch Goodman has never seen better." I laid my purchases of the previous day out on the bed. Gosh, that Canterbury underwear, it seems stretchy, I thought – any spare tyres or cellulite would show up with these on. How can they make something that is both warming and cooling at the same time? I think I'll go down to breakfast first, wear yesterday's clothes.

"Will you be staying tonight, Mrs Joyce?" asked the receptionist as I passed by.

"Eh, I doubt it. What's the latest I can let you know?"

"Well, you need to check out by two o clock at the latest."

Back in my room after eating, I was soon suited, booted, scarved and capped. A walking advertisement for designer gear. Unusually strong winds for September were blowing and there were gale warnings on the weather forecast. I had gone for broke at breakfast: fresh grapefruit, porridge and a full Irish with toast and brown bread.

The Sky Road circuit was about eleven kilometres, the Spanish waiter had told me. Could I manage it? That would be about seven miles Irish-speak. Charged with euphoric energy, I set out. One mile out, I saw the sign for O'Malleys' Bed and Breakfast. It was just nine o'clock. I decided to pass it by – I should be round again by eleven, I estimated.

Quite soon I was bathed in a pleasant sweat as the last vestiges of the early morning fog faded. The views were spectacular – of mountains, cliff formations, water, coastline and islands dotted in the distance. Just beyond the entrance to the old castle, the vast Atlantic Ocean came into view. This was not a walk for the faint-hearted and there were points at which I could almost touch the road, so steep were the climbs. The freedom of it all, though, a sort of sensuous, moist exertion that contrasted sharply with the cold, stale wetness of street clothes as I hauled shopping bags through the capital, weaving, bumping and colliding . . .

When I at last reached O'Malleys' for the second time, boy, was I glad to see it! You'll be a while building up to the Inis Mór Way, Hannah, I thought. I'd overheard some tourists talking about it at breakfast: "It's on the Aran Islands, fifty kilometres," boomed a small man with an Australian accent. "We're going to have a crack at doing it today, the whole works!"

The front door of O'Malleys' was ajar and I knocked lightly on it. "Hello, is there anybody at home?"

"I don't have to ask who that is. Your voice is unmistakable. Come in here, Hannah Duignan."

I walked through the door and there she was, sitting propped up in an armchair beside the fire. We hugged wordlessly for a long time. As a child, particularly when I felt neglected by my parents, I would find escape in my paintings. Eunice had spent many long hours teaching me, encouraging me and was very proud when I had a launch of my works at the Backstage Theatre some fifteen years ago.

"Eunice, you look great! What are you now – ninety-one?"

"Almost ninety-three, dear, you're losing count. I came up here from Castletown to Vera seven years ago. I was very ill, certain my time was up. The priest came to anoint me. I sent him packing – told him I was having my own private conversation with God and I did. I can remember the night well. I lay in my bed here. I wanted to die in a place I loved and where I was loved. I thanked him for allowing me to do that – thanked him for my life, for my parents, for Ernest, God rest him, for Vera, for giving me the gift . . . then I drifted off peacefully. I got the shock of my life when I woke up!" She laughed infectiously.

"Well, you look like you never looked back since. Were you afraid?"

"No, not afraid, but sad in a peaceful sort of way. Anyway, it looks like he wants me around for a little longer . . . Is that you, Vera? I want you to meet someone."

Eunice did the introductions. Vera is her sister's daughter and is widowed. We chatted over tea and hot buttered scones.

"I saw you doing the Sky walk earlier. You must have gone right around?"

"One circuit and a bit. I was glad to see your house second time around. I haven't walked that far in a long time. Have you been busy this year?"

"Gosh, we were full most nights between May and now. We can take eight people – if you include the caravans, twelve. It starts to slow down from here on in, though."

"Is there a caravan available right now?" I found myself asking without even thinking.

"There is. Are you interested?"

"Yes."

"For how long?"

"Well, today is Monday . . . say until next Monday . . . I stayed in Clifden last night, the Abbeyglen Castle Hotel. My car and belongings are down there."

"It would be two hundred and fifty euros for the week."

"That's fine." Not bad at all.

"I'll go out and get it ready so."

Eunice was looking at me thoughtfully. I felt that she was deciding in her own mind why I was there. But when she spoke I was taken by surprise. "How long is it since you painted, Hannah?"

"Fifteen years . . . you remember the exhibition. I sort of lost touch . . ."

"Well, sure, we can put that right this week."

"Oh, I don't know."

"I do. I can no longer paint myself owing to shakes in my hands. Had to stop about three years ago. We'll go up the Sky Road in the morning and stop at one of the viewing points. This is what you need. Write these down. You'll get them at Ruanes' in the village."

"I hope I don't embarrass myself . . . and you."

"Nonsense, I'll be your eyes and you'll be my hands. I'll

get Vera to prepare us a picnic."

* * *

Dizzily, I skipped on down the road to Clifden. I had time to have a shower.

In the hotel foyer, my attention was drawn to a painting while the receptionist prepared my bill. It was a castle, surrounded by mountains, trees, lakes and rivers. A look at the bottom right corner confirmed my suspicions: *Ballynahinch Castle ~ Eunice Jones 2001*. That must be one of her last paintings, I thought wistfully. Eunice always claimed that an ability to see and appreciate colours was *the* essential ingredient to painting successfully. "If you haven't got that, you're wasting your time. Go and buy yourself a good camera, do something else," she would say.

My mind skipped back to Castletown almost thirty years ago. Eunice had set up a summer painting school for children. My parents housed the summer school at a room in the hotel in payment for her magnificent depiction of the Castletown Arms. Eunice would not accept money – quite simply, she used art to further art. I must get that painting back out in the foyer or the bar where it can be appreciated, I mused. David had moved it from the bar following renovations. Doesn't "sit well" in its new surrounds, he had said. I smiled as I recalled our first day and week at the school – we arrived with our pads, crayons, paints and paintbrushes all ready to blitz the place. We were in for a shock, as we never lifted a brush or a crayon the first week. Eunice sat us all down and switched on a small tape recorder. We listed as the song "Forty Shades of Green" blared out.

"Does anyone know who sang that song?" she asked

Silence.

"That's Tom Jones. He's from Wales where I was born and he's a fool. And whoever wrote the song is a fool. Every colour has its own tonal range from full strength to the palest tint. He'll never be an artist if he can only see forty shades. There are so many more. For the first week, I've hired a small bus to take us in the mornings to the castle, the lakes, rivers and forests surrounding Castletown. I will be asking you to take in the colours and the wildlife and you will be coming back here in the afternoons to write essays on what you've seen."

The collective groans of her young audience told her what they thought of that. The class size was halved by the end of the week, but the torch Eunice carried for her work continued undimmed. "Now I'll be able to give each of you a little more attention," she smiled.

"Your bill, Ms Joyce?" came the voice from reception.

"Oh! Sorry! I got lost in the painting . . ."

"Many do – an old lady up on the Sky Road did it."

I smiled to myself – didn't I just know . . . "Is the place, Ballynahinch Castle, near here?"

"Yes, it's down at Recess, just a short drive. Here, I'll get you some pamphlets about the region and the islands. There's no end of places to visit."

Soon, I was back at O'Malleys'.

Vera greeted me. "She's gone to lie down for an hour – come on, I'll show you your caravan."

I looked in appreciation around the inside.

"It's got all the modern conveniences apart from a washing machine," said Vera. "I can do that inside for you.

You can cook your own meals here on the gas cooker or you can eat in the house – we usually have a big crowd for dinner and it's a great communal event."

I decided in an instant that I was going to cook here, take responsibility for myself. Peeling more notes from my diminishing bundle, I paid Vera her rent.

"Thanks. I must introduce you to Gloria once you settle yourself in. She's in the caravan behind you. You'll like her. She's English – comes over from London every May and stays until October."

"Must love it here."

"Well, her husband did, but he died."

"That's sad."

"Happens a lot – we women get left alone. I'm glad to have Eunice here. She's really excited about going out painting with you, you know. But we'll need to fold her wheelchair into your car boot. She can't stay on her feet for any length of time."

"I hope it goes in," I muttered, suddenly feeling inadequate with my little Renault Clio.

"I'm sure it will no bother. Well, I'll leave you to get settled in."

I thanked her and then closed the door. I sat down on the sofa and looked at the place that was going to be my home for the next seven days, maybe more. For now, I needed to adjust myself to this new place in my life. There was something about it that seemed to comfort me. I looked out the window and was in awe of the vast canopy of sky that stretched out in front of me. I sat staring out at it. The sky was ever changing and magnificent. It held me captivated. Words of songs fluttered through my head – songs from the ballroom, country and western songs that I didn't really like.

It was like I had stored them up all my life to play on that day.

I spread the sheets out on the double bed.

I felt goose-bumps tickle my skin – this was somewhere new and it was a little scary. Best take it day by day, I reasoned. I'll need to go back to town later to stock up with some food.

Chapter Thirty-Eight

Deciding to introduce myself to my new neighbour, I went and called hello through the open door.

"Give me a minute!" her voice boomed out over the wind.

I withdrew a little distance, to respect her privacy.

She stepped down from the caravan.

I stood squinting in the sunlight, looking towards her as she walked deftly towards me, her long dangly earrings catching my eye. She smiled brightly at me, like she was trying to tell me that she didn't bite.

"I'm Hannah," I announced. "I've just moved in."

"Sorry, I didn't quite catch that."

The wind gushed from behind her, almost forcing her past me. In her sixties, I guessed, as I watched her silver hair blowing around her weather-beaten face. Her eyes were bright and kindly.

"I'm Hannah."

"Gloria. So you're looking to rent a mobile?"

"I already have done. I'm your neighbour for the next week at least."

"Well, I'd better invite you in for some tea then. We'll be blown away if we stay out here nattering."

Inside the caravan, I scoured the place with my eyes, looking for a place to sit. The clutter! Cups, plates and cutlery strewn all over the place – the sink, table, even the couch. Clothes everywhere. Musical instruments, a tin whistle, an oboe, Tarot cards. The only similarity between our caravans was the outside. I finally squeezed into a free space on the couch.

"If you're going to be touring the area, this is the perfect place to use as your base. Do you find it cold? I'll switch on this gas fire."

The kettle was building up slowly to a piercing whistle. Soon we were both sitting with hot mugs of tea and biscuits.

"Have you come to paint?" she asked.

"It's not what I came to do but meeting up again with Eunice has changed all that. I can't believe how well she is for her age. And you?"

Gloria laughed jovially. "I tell fortunes – as a pastime really. Right now things are quiet."

She looked the part with her voluminous skirts and bangles.

"I have a home in London and will go back at the beginning of November."

"I see you play some music, too."

"Oh, I have a go. I've played in the local traditional pubs and don't be surprised if you waken to my sounds in the middle of the night . . . insomnia. This is my third year here.

Peter and myself had retired from our jobs and were looking to buy something in Clifden. He was always talking about the place – he spent his childhood here. He was a talker, was Pete. Saturday night, or come to think of it any night, once he'd have a few pints, he'd remove himself to Connemara in his head, or his heart, more likely. It was his dream to come back here. We came on a trial run for the summer – I wasn't sure as we have a daughter and son in London. I fell in love with the place immediately. Then poor Pete goes and dies on me. He never got to reap the reward."

"I'm sorry."

"You'd think I should have seen it coming," she laughed mockingly. "I didn't. Anyway, I settle now for summers here and winters in London with my children and their children."

"I'm going into Clifden later to do some shopping," I said. "I have to get some art supplies for tomorrow. You might like to come if you need anything." Black clouds were massing in the sky – soon they would spill their contents.

Her face brightened. "Well, that's very kind of you, Hannah." She patted my arm. "It's nice to have someone around. But no, thanks, dear, I've got all I need. I'm doing a reading tonight – a group of young girls want me to go to their house to do it. They take it all so lightly – it's all for fun and I play along."

"Can you see bad things in the cards?"

"Of course I can." She paused and considered me for a moment. "But it's all how you interpret it."

"Yes, I suppose so." I put down my empty mug. "Well, thanks for the tea. I'll see you later." I stood up.

She got up and placed the mugs on the counter, then swung around, stirring up the tranquil air. "If there is anything you need – even just want to talk – I'm just across from you," she said.

It was as if she knew that I was a tortured soul, groping in the darkness.

Chapter Thirty-Nine

I had to flatten down the back seat of my Clio to get Eunice's wheelchair in. She was sitting in the front passenger seat, a small hamper on her knees. Vera had packed it, said painting up there on a windy day is hungry work.

"Did you sleep well?" Eunice asked as we set out.

"Yes, thanks."

"Now, did you get all the stuff?"

"Yeah, all packed in the back. I saw your painting back in the hotel."

Eunice did not reply for a moment, as if she was going down Memory Lane.

"Now, Hannah Duignan, I've told you the fundamentals that need to be in place so as to make a good artist. We need to do some revision this morning. Tell me what you learned."

I suppressed a giggle – she expected me to pick up on thirty years ago like it was yesterday. "You need a good eye for colours, to be able to appreciate them, understand the different stages of development that lead to change and evolution."

"Not bad at all. Any other essential?"

"Mmm . . . tell me?"

"Painting is always subjective – it's not about accuracy, it's about interpretation. You saw the painting of Ballynahinch Castle . . . That's how it looked four years ago: now it will have changed. Nature will have ensured that – the mountains, trees, lakes and rivers will have changed. No, you need to know and understand the history, the heritage, so as to take your viewer into the soul of the place. Take Ballynahinch for example. The ferocious O'Flahertys, Grace O'Malley the pirate. You need to capture the mood, the aura, and to do that you need to know the history." She tapped a fingernail on a small folder of books and pamphlets that no doubt I'd have to read later so as to capture the history bit.

"I'm getting the feeling that we're not going to be painting today," I said.

"You'd be right. No, we'll stop a while at each viewing point on the Sky Road. How many there are, I can't remember. You will jot down what you see at each point and we'll come back in the morning to start your painting. You need to be thinking about how you will source the best light, use your shadows effectively, create an atmosphere, a feeling of depth and distance. Tonight, though, you have to make your choice and tell me why first thing tomorrow. Thankfully, I've still got 20/20 vision," she finished with a conspiratorial wink.

So, at each viewing point, I observed and jotted furiously as Eunice just sat there absorbing it all, drinking it in.

Suddenly I could hear her voice all those thirty years ago. "Children, children, you don't need to be setting up rivalries. The person with the biggest list will most likely lose. They haven't stopped to appreciate the beauty, hear the birds, the squirrels . . ." I snapped my notebook shut.

"Eunice, we'll be doing this in the mornings. In the afternoons, I was hoping to look around, maybe Kylemore Abbey, the Aran Islands."

"I wouldn't be able for it, Hannah. I'm too old – I have to co-operate with God if I'm to hang on for the magic three figures and the letter from the President. You could join some of the excursions from the Tourist Office – personally I find the narrators tedious and commercial, trying to tell you what a place should mean to you. That's for the inner self to decide," she eyed me closely, "and it will be influenced by the past you bring with you."

Soon, I'll tell her about David and me, but not today.

"Will we set out our picnic?" I asked lightly.

Soon we were tucking into Vera's goodies: sandwiches of home-baked ham, salad and farmhouse cheese topped with chutney. Some rhubarb tart, still warm, and muffins. I poured more tea from the flask and was content to sit there on the edge of the world watching Eunice drift into a sleep.

* * *

"Thank you for today, Eunice, and thank Vera for the food. It was all lovely."

"And thank you. I enjoyed it immensely. Well, we'll meet

tomorrow again. Nine thirty."

I went on to the village, as the locals prefer to call it. I stocked up on the essentials and added in a few bottles of wine for good measure.

"You'll need a bottle-opener for them," said the middle-aged man, wearing a white shop coat. "I've taken to telling everyone that, saves them banging on my door in the middle of the night."

Back in the caravan, I reviewed my mobile phone. Fifteen missed calls, four new messages. A text from Timothy.

Mum, I'm finding it hard to hold out here. Dad, Gran, Cormac, they're all at me asking where you are. Ring Dad, let him know.

Messages from Mammy and Cormac. One from David. I stiffened as I heard his steely, controlled voice.

"Hannah, it's David. It's five thirty. If you haven't returned this call within two hours, I'll report you as a missing person to the Gardaí."

Not a mention about my calling card in the bedroom. Damn it, I'll have to ring him. David always keeps his promises when they're threats. I can imagine the news bulletins: *A nationwide Garda search has been called off after a forty-one-year-old woman was found safe and well in Clifden. Mrs Hannah Joyce, wife of well-known hotelier, David Joyce . . .*

Seven twenty. I go straight through to David's Message Minder. Alison showed me how to do it. Just put a five in front of it. Great when you want to be heard, but not to hear. No feedback or arguments.

"David, I got your calls. I have gone away for a while and do not want you to contact me further. There is no need to be contacting the Gardaí. I am safe and I do not want you to come

looking for me. There will be a record of me making this call so don't go ahead with your threat. You could be charged with wasting police time."

Immediately my mobile rang with David's number flashing. I sat there until it rang out. "Fuck you, David," I whispered.

*   *   *

"Hannah, are you in there?" Gloria called, sometime later. The day had darkened somewhat and the misty gloom that hung in the air seemed comforting. At that point I had become resigned to the fact that I was on my own. In fact, I resented Gloria interrupting me in my solitude. I opened my caravan door to her. She stepped in without being invited.

"How is it going?" she asked.

"Would you like a cup of tea?" I said. I suspected that she was lonely and just wanted a chat.

"Why not?"

"Make yourself at home."

She plonked herself down on the sofa. "How do you stand the quiet? Wouldn't you like a TV or something? I can lend you a radio if you like."

"No, it's fine. I like the quiet."

"Oh, are you a poet?" she asked as she nodded her head towards the notepad.

"No, nothing like that. Now, what would you like – tea, coffee or maybe a drink?"

"Oh, tea will be fine. My insomnia is bad enough. Coffee drives me bananas altogether."

"Go on, have a glass of wine with me – I could do with

one myself."

"Well, if you put it like that – yes, please."

"Good, it's nicer to share a drink with someone," I said. "Do it on your own and a bad mood can change to morbidity and depression quite easily."

"So where are you from?"

"Oh, the midlands," I said vaguely. I didn't want to talk about home.

She nodded at my wedding ring, which I had put back on. "Are you still married?"

"You're the fortune-teller, you tell me."

She raised her glass of wine and we clinked glasses. "Fortune-telling is about predicting the future. You need a shrink to deal with what's past. Cheers." She sipped some wine, her eyes settling on my flushed face. "You know, Hannah, I don't know what to do . . . I'm at a crossroads . . ." She raised herself off the sofa. "Do you have any cheese, crackers? I hate having a drink without something to nibble at."

"Well, you're in luck. I got some down in the village earlier. Hang on and I'll get some for you."

Returning with a plateful of crackers topped with cheese and an optional bottle of chutney, I prompted Gloria to resume. "You were saying you were at a crossroads, not knowing what to do?"

"Yeah, I love this place but I miss London. It's where my children are. I miss complaining about the traffic congestion and the noise, I miss my old friends. It was lonely here this summer. You're one of the few people who came here to O'Malleys' alone this year. Couples won't give you any time – they're engrossed in each other." She raised her face towards the ceiling. "He bloody well had to go and die on me, leave me here on my own!" She shook her head, wisps of white hair springing out from her head and making her look quite mad. She didn't seem to notice that I was in the room with her. She pulled open a locket around her neck and looked downward at what presumably was her husband's picture. "Just my bloody luck." She refilled her glass with wine. "I need to decide whether to book or not for next year soon. Vera is fine – she'd give me loads of space to make up my mind – but the caravans belong to her son. Two different worlds, here and London, and I love both places but for different reasons." She shook her head. "I'm looking for a sign, for someone or God to tell me what to do."

"I'm sure He will guide you . . ." I reflected on my own situation . . . I just didn't want to decide anything right now.

"Would you like me to tell your fortune?" she asked.

"Maybe some other time," I tentatively suggested.

"Nonsense, there's no time like the present."

"Okay . . . why not?"

She pulled my foldaway table out.

"Shuffle them up," she ordered as she gave me her pack of Tarot cards, which were very old and worn-looking.

The cards didn't tell me much about my future or perhaps they told me all I needed to know. Gloria couldn't see a dark-haired man coming to my rescue.

Eventually, she summed up. "There seems to be too much turbulence in your life right now: you seem to be running in a storm. You have big decisions to make, ones that will determine the pathway of your remaining years – but you are afraid of making them. I see a fork in the road and two pathways leading off it. You will resolve your inner conflicts by taking one of the pathways but something is holding you at that fork – an eternal purgatory, unless you decide. Does any of that make sense?"

"Some of it, Gloria, some of it . . . Gosh, it's half ten and I'm under orders from Eunice to have some preparatory work done before morning. Do you mind?"

"No, I really enjoyed myself. I'll see you tomorrow, then."

I looked out into the darkness as I watched her return to her place. The heady mixture of a euphoric, nostalgic day and the wine left me feeling carefree and with a sense of adventure. There was so much to see and do here and if poor Eunice couldn't go with me, I'd find someone else. Not Gloria, I reasoned – she probably had seen it all and she was a little too clingy anyway. I thumbed through my phone book A to Z and back again.

"Looks like you're my only hope, Murdoch!" I said, laughing somewhat manically. He might think . . . oh, what the hell . . .

I dialled his number.

"Murdoch, Hannah Joyce here."

"Hannah! Eh, thanks for returning my call."

I stopped for a moment, resisting the impulse to ask him what he's talking about. Let him continue, think he's doing the chasing.

"I was ringing the hotel to apologise most sincerely for bursting in on you in the leisure centre the other day. I was so embarrassed . . . I had no idea you were there."

"That makes two of us. At least you had something to cover your modesty." God bless alcohol and what it does to your inhibitions, I thought. "Anyway, the staff passed on your message and your apology is fully accepted. But I'm ringing you from my mobile as I've gone away for a few days to Connemara – Clifden, actually."

"My God, you're only a few miles from me . . . I'm down

here in Leenaun, beside Killary Harbour." A pause, then he tentatively said: "How did you manage to get David to down tools at the hotel and take off?"

"I didn't. He's not here. I've come to do some painting – it's a 'me' hobby, not an 'us' one, unfortunately. Landscapes are my favourite subject and there's no better place than Clifden to get stuck in. And my old art teacher, Eunice Jones, lives here."

"Eunice Jones? I think I've seen some of her work around."

"No doubt you have."

A brief silence followed.

"There's a few spots down Leenaun way that have come under the scrutiny of the artist's brush," he went on. "Killary Harbour and Maum Vallley, for example. You might try those some day. I don't suppose . . . no . . . maybe you'd like to come out for a bit of food tomorrow . . . . that's if you'd like."

"I could manage tomorrow evening. Can I ring you tomorrow?"

"Do. That's great."

"Okay then – till tomorrow."

* * *

I sat quietly alone in my caravan, sipping the last of my wine and marvelling at my audacity in ringing up Murdoch. I had often heard it said that Clifden hovered on the very edge of the western world, with nothing but a vast ocean between it and America, nigh three thousand miles away. I was convinced that I was hovering on the edge of the whole world, maybe *my* whole world, the edge of sanity, so powerful was the conflict between my free spirit and my conservative "self". I closed my eyes and visualised myself as referee in a boxing ring as the two adversaries wrestled for control of my soul. My free spirit landed the first telling blow.

"But, Hannah, it was the loss of self that took you on this journey – quit now and you will be damned to a life of what-might-have-beens, one lacking joy and fulfilment."

My conservative self recoiled and rebounded from the ropes.

"Charlatans weaving promises of unworldly joys not tangible! Fables! They do the devil's work. Come with us and restore thyself in the bosom of thy family and loved ones. It is there eternal peace awaits thee."

Chapter Forty

I awakened the following morning and checked my watch. Six thirty and it was bright. I had thumbed through my notes the previous night and skimmed through the book Eunice gave me. Eventually, I'd given way to the wine and fallen into a deep, peaceful sleep.

Nursing a cup of hot coffee, I reflected on my stroke of good fortune with Murdoch. It suited me perfectly that he thought I was returning his call and I had every intention of letting him continue to think that. Otherwise he'd think he had hit lucky, that I wanted to see him without his trunks, just to even things up. I winced as I visualised the macho bar-room stories he might concoct, strutting and holding court to a captive audience of bleary-eyed voyeurs: "*Saw me in the local gym in my shorts and followed me all the way to the Gaeltacht to see me without them!*" Before I left Castletown, I had him tagged as a possible escort for Lily, just to test

Vincent for jealousy and all that. It never got off the ground and here I was now, planning to set him up as an escort for myself. It couldn't have worked out better.

I reviewed my painting notes again and pondered my choices.

Clifden Castle . . . Coastal View . . . Clifden Harbour . . . the Fahy Tomb . . . Omey Island.

I decided that I had time to complete the Sky Road walk and firm up on my choice for the day. Impress Eunice too.

The morning was bright and fresh and I found my limbs loosening out as my endurance started to improve. It was obvious that this magnificently scenic route was well appreciated as, even at this time in the morning, I passed, met and was passed by walkers of varying ages and levels of fitness on the route. I decided that I would park my easel at the highest viewing point of the route when I came back later.

Back in the caravan I changed and ate a breakfast of scrambled eggs and toast and made my way out to collect Eunice. The obligatory hamper was loaded again and the wise old lady had brought a collapsible canopy to protect my painting in the event of rain.

"Okay, so you've decided on Clifden Harbour. We'll stop at Scardan then and set ourselves up for our day's work. We've agreed on oils, just to ease you back in. Errors with oils are not fatal – you can retrieve the situation, unlike watercolours where you get only one shot at getting it right. Now tell me what you've brought with you."

"Well, I have my wooden box easel . . . my colours . . . palette, including knife, three brushes, stretched canvas, oil sketching paper, alkyd gel."

"Very good, but you obviously don't believe in cleaning

up after you . . . I've brought some brush-cleaner, old rags and kitchen paper. I have some spare brushes too . . . three might not be enough."

Soon I was settled into my position overlooking Clifden Harbour. The "constants" in my painting would include skies, water, mountains, some trees, buildings, boats and grazing animals.

Eunice seemed to be reading my thoughts and interjected, "Then you'll have the variables, which distinguish the artist's 'feel' for the job. Understanding how hues change with light, the reflections, shadows . . . how to lead the viewer towards best appreciation by getting the perspective and angles right. Have a look at these old sketches – there's a farm track in Sierra Nevada, a spring thaw in Austria – who, apart from an artist, would understand that early evening sunlight would cause mountains to seem mauve or pale pink in colour?" She faltered momentarily. "God bless Ernest. His army pension gave me the opportunity to travel, see these places . . . to paint . . . I so wish we had more time together, but it was not to be."

I felt at a loss, inadequate suddenly – unable to comfort, provide solace to her in her memories.

"Ernest. It's sixty-four years today since he lost his life in the Second World War. I cope well most times but, on days like this, I want to see him again so much."

"You really loved him, didn't you?"

"Yes. I married him when I was twenty-two, seventy years ago. We would have loved to have children but it didn't happen. We had almost seven happy years, though, and I thank God for that."

"You were never tempted to marry again, were you, Eunice?"

"No, better to have loved and been truly loved once. I'm happy that I lived in my time – there is too much importance given to acquiring material things today – marriages and relationships are treated as disposable items."

I barely hesitated. "Eunice, what would you have done if you'd discovered that Ernest had a love-child from another relationship before he met you? And hadn't told you."

She gazed at me speculatively. "Oh, I don't know . . . It'd be hard for me to imagine . . . Ernest was so old-fashioned and strait-laced. Are you trying to tell me something, Hannah?"

I found myself telling her the whole story. She listened attentively while I retraced my relationship with David from the time we first met.

"I'm really not sure that I can ever go back to him," I said at last. "Things have changed so suddenly and dramatically."

Eunice stroked my hand comfortingly. "Well, you chose each other, just as I chose Ernest, but I'm not going to advise you whether to go back to him or not. But, Hannah, there is one thing I must say: I don't think that the sudden and dramatic change took place recently. I think it took place over twenty years ago."

"What do you mean? I don't understand . . ."

"Hannah, I don't want to speak ill of the dead but growing up in the shadow of Frank Duignan was not easy. He was a particularly brutal and nasty man, as your mother and Cormac would be well able to tell you."

My mind protested . . . then started drifting back to the noises from the kitchen . . . . Mammy screaming . . . Cormac trying to rescue her . . . Tears started streaming down my face . . .

"And you may well be punishing David for sins

committed against you long before you ever met him."

This was too much for me to take in.

Eunice continued. "But you triumphed in the face of all that, created a life and identity for yourself through your academic and sporting achievements and your painting. Then, all of a sudden you go and kill the real Hannah Duignan, bury her and create a new one, moulded to meet the expectations and needs of others. Right now, I think you're beginning to discover that you don't particularly like the new one – maybe you want the old one back. Now let's work and forget all that. Right now nothing matters but getting your painting done. And you'll need several days, including off-location work, to complete it."

*   *   *

I lay silently in my caravan bed staring at the ceiling and pondered over Eunice's observations. I needed to write, get active, stop brooding.

29/09/04
Clifden

Dear Journal ~
It's a few days since I shared my secrets with you and I'm so confused. It's an emotional roller-coaster and my need to look at the past is causing me great pain. Today, I've managed to bring up memories that I suppressed for many years and they're not nice at all. Seeing and acknowledging that evil was present in our home hurts.

I need to restore myself, build myself back up. I cannot go back home yet but I have been selfish about the secrecy. I must ring Mammy, Timothy, Sammi and Cormac, yes Cormac, and let them know I'm okay. They will be hurting. You will see I've left David off that list but I'm not ready to talk to him – I need to have my decisions made first. I've often scorned people who talked about "finding themselves", thought it was a silly little cliché, but that's what I'm doing right now – trying to ground myself and make the right decisions for Hannah.

I suppose Eunice was referring to my father when she suggested that I might be punishing David for sins committed against me before I hooked up with him. That idea is too enormous for me to cope with.

Bye for now,

Hannah

PS Update ~ I've spoken to Timothy and Mammy. All are happy that I'm okay. They want me home. They accept, well, at least Timothy does, that it won't happen for a few days yet.

"God, I promised to telephone Murdoch! It's three o' clock – he'll think I'm just a tease!" Murdoch answered immediately.

"Hannah, good to hear from you. What would you like to do?"

"I'm not sure, I've had a long day – I don't feel like eating out. What about I rustle up something light and we eat it at my caravan, then maybe go into Clifden for a drink?"

Armed with the necessary directions, Murdoch rang off.

I boiled some eggs and left them to cool in the fridge.

* * *

I jumped with fright when I heard a loud thud on my door. God, I've been sleeping . . . It's gone eight o clock . . . Murdoch . . .

"Are you in there, Hannah?" I heard Gloria shout.

"Yes," I said, going towards the door.

"I found this fella sneaking around the place and he said he's with you!"

I opened my door to see Murdoch standing there, his face flushed with embarrassment. Gloria had a tight grip on his arm.

"You can let me go," Murdoch said, his voice a thick whisper.

"Stupid idiot, snooping around!" Gloria said. She let go his arm and dramatically wiped her hands together. Then she pushed him into my mobile. "You look ready for bed," she remarked.

I was dressed in my pyjamas. "No, uh, I was about to have a shower, put these on for comfort. Started to read magazines. Next thing I know you pair are knocking on the door."

I had to stifle a giggle. Poor Murdoch. First he has to confront me in the altogether – next, and because of me, he is set upon by some primitive feral woman primed for battle if needs be. Then he's confronted with me in my pyjamas.

"Well, I'm off out," Gloria said and glared at Murdoch. "Next time use the paths."

"Yes, sorry about that – but you might consider cutting your nails before you go about digging into people's arms again!"

Another glare and Gloria departed.

"What exactly did you do wrong?" I asked curiously.

"I came up from the beach. I was just looking to see

which mobile home you were in. Ended up looking in a window at Winnie the Witch and she flew out at me."

The floor space was limited and we both stood awkwardly, each waiting for the other to say something more. God, I was thinking, how embarrassing! And after the nude episode.

Reading my thoughts, he added straight-faced: "Just continuing my career as a Peeping Tom."

I laughed. "Look, I'll go in and dress." I added apologetically, "Um, I was just going to prepare a salad."

I came out to a set table with plates of cheese, cold eggs, tomatoes, home-baked ham and various salads. A loaf of brown bread stood waiting to be cut and the kettle was whistling merrily away over the naked flame.

"God, you're a fast one, Murdoch . . ."

"Have to be. I've been living on my own since Mother died two years ago. She used to do everything, right down to polishing my shoes. I had to learn. I got better as I went along."

We set to hungrily.

Murdoch was wearing a soft brown sweater, off-white chinos and beige casual shoes. A blue denim shirt peeped out above the neck of his sweater. His six-five frame almost blocked out the rest of the caravan – it was hard to look elsewhere. His dark hair was beginning to show some grey at the temples – otherwise he was holding up well. A boyish forty-five, I guessed. Funny, I would have added five years to that when he came to the Castletown Arms in his dated suits and sober ties.

Murdoch cleared his throat. "I must say I was surprised first when I heard you were staying up here, what with all the fine hotels in the area. Now I'm not – it's really nice and peaceful here. You're unlikely to want to spend your holidays in a hotel, anyway."

"What brings you to stay in our hotel so often, Murdoch?"

"Well, it's central to a number of larger towns where I ply my trade. I just stopped off there one night a few years back, could have picked anywhere – then I stopped off again. It's reliable and consistent." He grinned. "Although, what with the *Evening Herald* story, my colleagues are up to all sorts of pranks – looking to change routes, get in on the action. It's hard to get home to Leenaun every evening – the scenery may be beautiful but the roads . . ."

Murdoch went on to tell me that he'd qualified in pharmacy in UCG and worked in several chemists in Dublin and Galway over the years. He had worked as a pharmaceutical representative for one of the multi-nationals for the past eight years. He stopped suddenly.

"Hey, this is not fair. If we're going to stick with a story-of-my-life-to-date theme, you'll have all the advantages. There's not much I can ask you about what you do – I've witnessed it all over the years."

"Well, not any more," I said suddenly. "I've been asking David to sell the hotel but he won't even consider it. I decided to come up here for a bit to cool off – things were going very badly between us. If you're staying in the Castletown Arms this week I'd prefer if you didn't say you saw me."

"I won't be staying there – I'm off for the rest of the week. Anyway, I won't be telling him anything, anytime. Now, will we go down to King's pub in the village?"

Minutes later, we were sitting in King's, nursing our drinks. A gin and tonic for me, a 7-UP for Murdoch. I felt a tinge of disappointment as I was hoping for a little fun – that he'd thaw out a little. Nice but too restrained, too reserved . . . maybe even formal.

"You don't drink and drive, Murdoch?" I said, making small talk to break the silence.

"I don't drink at all," said Murdoch, a little uncomfortably. "I'm a recovering alcoholic and recovering compulsive gambler. I ended up in jail because of it twelve years ago."

I felt myself flush. "Oh, I'm sorry, I wasn't meaning to pry . . . I had no idea . . ."

"I know that, but there's hardly a native in Connemara or the city that doesn't know about it. I had achieved my life's ambition of owning my own pharmacy in Galway. God, how proud my poor mother was! Anyway, the debts were mounting while I drank and gambled away merrily. My business was on the brink of repossession when I came up with a plan to burn it down, collect the insurance and pay off my debts. Went down with my can of petrol, drunk, and set it alight. Burnt to the ground. I was caught within twenty-four hours. I got two years for arson and served nine months."

"I'm sorry, Murdoch, you didn't need to tell me this . . . I feel my remarks triggered it . . ."

"Ah, no, I prefer to have it out in the open. I don't like having secrets, spending too much time in my head thinking they'll find out or already know. I was taken off to Mountjoy on the day I was due to be married. When I came out, the only person I could go to was my mother – everyone else shunned me. I think I made it up to her over the next ten years – she was my best friend."

"Listen, would you like to get out of here? I'm sure going

into pubs is not easy for you. We should have gone for that meal instead."

"Don't worry, Hannah. I don't feel any inclination towards it at all, thankfully. The gambling was always the biggie – there would be a hell of a lot of people who drink more than I ever did. I drank on my successes and losses at the bookies. The prisoner governor in Mountjoy at the time – he was very committed to rehabilitating the prisoners, preparing them to participate in society and all that. I did my time but I got great help in there – I didn't appreciate it all instantly though . . . I still had this vision that I could sit quietly with my few pints . . . No, I'm going to stay here for the music unless you really want to go. But maybe I've scared you off with my outpourings?"

I squeezed his hand briefly. "No, you haven't, Murdoch. I think you've suffered and are both brave and honest."

"Okay then – how about I teach you some Irish dancing when the music begins?"

"Murdoch Goodman, I doubt you had much of a step in you when I was winning rosettes at féile and feiseanna around the country – you might regret that."

* * *

Murdoch dropped me back at the caravan at twelve. "Thanks, Hannah, I really enjoyed myself."

"Me too."

"Thanks for listening too."

"I was glad to. Hey, I was hoping to go to the Aran Islands for a day before I go back. Would you like to come with me, seeing as you're not working?"

"I would. Could we do it Thursday?"

"Yeah, that would be good."

"I see the Wicked Witch is peering through the curtains at us."

I laughed, then impulsively I kissed him on the cheek. "I'll see you Thursday morning then."

* * *

Almost immediately Gloria came knocking on my door. "Are you in there?" she hollered, her voice high-pitched and demanding.

I resolved to make her visit as brief as possible, keep her interrogation to a minimum. I opened the door.

"I was thinking you were there," she said, pushing past me.

She seemed to fill the place, her skirts whirling around her, her bangles jangling on her wrists. I really didn't want this invasion but there was nothing I could do. We were neighbours after all.

A cool breeze swished through the place as she swirled and fell theatrically into the sofa. As usual, I thought.

"This insomnia will be the death of me. You couldn't get me to wake up when Pete was lying next to me. Can't get used to sleeping on my own."

I suppressed an urge to tell her that I didn't want to go down the insomnia route with her. Despite her gruff exterior, the loneliness was there for all to see – you didn't need to search for it. Gloria was just living out an existence, continuing in a limbo until the call came for her to join Pete. She would tell you she was fine, but her voice betrayed her

– it wasn't true.

I made some tea for her and we sat quietly together.

Eventually, she spoke. "How did you get on with the prowler?"

I looked at her, confused for a moment, and then started to laugh. Not at her but at my own secretiveness when she was around. Here I was, closing down on a past that was not so lurid and sensational for fear this harmless, aging woman would leak my whereabouts all the way back to Castletown. I contrasted my furtiveness with the openness of Murdoch as he confided his past to me with an easy resignation. Was it a lifetime with David that caused me to go white-knuckled at the thought of my privacy being intruded upon as a consequence of sharing life's trivial experiences with others?

"Why are you laughing?"

"Oh, nothing . . . it's just . . ." And I found myself filling her in on how I first met Murdoch and how it had gone from there. We rolled over laughing as I relived the leisure centre experience and by the time she stood up to leave, I felt unburdened and at peace.

"Gloria, I was thinking about going down to Kylemore Abbey tomorrow afternoon. My week is speeding on and I want to pick up some gifts for family and friends. I believe there's a nice gift shop down there. Would you like to come?"

"That would be great," said Gloria, her whole face lighting up. "I'd better let you get to bed then."

Chapter Forty-One

30/09/04

Dear Sinéad,

It's me, Hannah Joyce, writing to say how sorry I am for the pain I caused you. I've been wrestling with a guilty conscience since the day you came into my office and I'm hoping that saying sorry will relieve me of some of the shame that I feel. The mistake that I made was that I absorbed Lily's hurt and anger towards you, leading me to accept malicious gossip about you all too readily. Lily is, or at least was, my friend but I know now that I need to learn how to be supportive and understanding towards her without being prejudicial against others.

I really hope that my behaviour has not harmed your relationship with Vincent and you can take it that I won't be participating from now on when people tarnish you unfairly because of the love you share with him.

Again, I hope you accept that I am truly sorry.
Yours truly,
Hannah Joyce

I addressed an envelope and stamped it. I'd take it on my walk this morning. I felt a sense of comfort at my confession and apology – it was like my guilt had been somewhat purged. Previously, in circumstances like this, I would take refuge in food.

My morning passed quickly and peacefully with no major incidents. I smiled to myself as I reflected on the groove that I had fallen into – morning walks alone with my thoughts, painting with Eunice. This was better than any health farm – or diet for that matter. My jeans were fitting me comfortably now – even a little loose, I thought, as I caressed my flattening stomach.

"You're an attractive woman, Hannah Joyce," I said to the reflection in the oblong mirror.

"Indeed you are," came Gloria's voice from behind me. She looked different, all tidied up, her hair gathered up into a neat bun atop her head. "No need to blush now – if someone else won't say it for you, you might as well say it yourself." She looked closely at me, her eyes bright with enthusiasm. "Would you like to come over to my house and have some dinner with me this evening?"

"This evening . . ." My thoughts were racing as I tried to think of a suitable excuse. "I'm really not sure I can . . . I have things to do. We'll see how our shopping trip goes and we'll take it from there." I wanted to keep my options for the evening open.

"Well, if you change your mind you know where I am," she said, tilting her chin optimistically.

"Yes, yes. Thank you, Gloria. Would you like a cup of tea before we go? I'm afraid I've run out of milk."

"No, I'd prefer to get going."

The drive down to Kylemore Abbey passed quickly as I opened up more to Gloria. She listened without comment as I trawled over my life with David.

"I'm sure you'll come to the right decisions in the end, Hannah. Your two children are grown up so you're under no obligation to compromise your needs for anybody."

I got to know that Gloria worked for forty years with the National Health Service at the King's College Hospital in London. Peter was an aircraft technician at Heathrow.

"He was always keeping an eye out for cheap flights. He'd ring me at work on a Friday. One minute I'd be groaning to the girls in the office that I faced a weekend of ironing and cooking, next I'd be asking them if they wanted anything back from Rome, Berlin, Barcelona . . . I have some photos in my bag – I'll show you them when we stop at Kylemore."

* * *

"God, it's beautiful, isn't it?" Gloria said as we both stared up at the enormous statue of Christ with his arms outstretched on the mountain's upper slopes. "You'd almost think he was welcoming us."

"Maybe he is, Gloria, maybe he is. Can I meet you in the tearoom in, say, twenty minutes? There's something I want to do."

Soon, I was back with Gloria and she was eying me suspiciously, wondering where I went. She threw in the towel when she saw that I was keeping my lips sealed.

"So this is where the jet-set dump their daughters for their secondary school years. I don't care how beautiful or exclusive it is, the place where teenage girls should put their head down at night is the family home, not some dormitory run by Benedictine nuns out of touch with the ways of the world."

"Ah, they're not that bad, Gloria – but you're right. A child's place is at home."

An exasperated tour guide flopped into a chair at the table next to us. He was speaking quite audibly to a young female colleague. "I really can't take many more of these guided tours. In you go, your lines all rehearsed, only to discover you've got an 'expert' in your group, some sad man or woman who probably spent the night shining a torch on the entire history of the place. I've just had one like that, garish tracksuit, Australian, I think. Every spot I stopped at, every rehearsed commentary and she'd have an add-on at the end, the last word."

"Don't worry about it, Kenneth, ignore her. You'll be back at college next week, with her money nestling in your pocket. Oh-oh, I think someone matching that description is coming over this way right now."

The Australian woman stood at their table, talking in a loud voice. "Thank you so much, Kenneth, you were brilliant. So much knowledge, yet so young!" She turned her eyes to the girl, eying her name badge. "I say, Sandra, do you mind taking a photo of me and Kenneth?"

"That's no bother. Okay – ready? Great. Here we go. Cheese!"

"That's wonderful," said the Australian woman, taking back her camera. "I'm going to show this photo to my friends back at the hotel – tell them to look out for you,

Kenneth. You can take it that I'll be recommending you. A real gentleman, that's what you are."

"How about a tip instead?" muttered Kenneth as she disappeared from earshot. "Miserable cow!"

In the gift shop, I picked out some gifts for the people I left behind in Castletown. Am I telling myself something about going back, I asked myself? I chose three beautiful pottery mugs for the Coffee Triangle, a tin of specialty biscuits for Cormac and Louise. A leather handbag for Sammi, and Timothy . . . you'd run a mile from this stuff . . . I think I'll stop off at Hanley's Man's Shop in Galway on my way back.

I decided that I would give Mammy my painting when I finished it.

Gloria waited quietly in the background until I completed my retail therapy.

On the way back home, I suggested that we join Eunice, Vera and their guests for the evening meal.

"Oh, so you're avoiding my cooking?" she said with no little pique.

"It's nothing like that. I'd just like to join up with the crowd for a change. You should bring in your musical instruments – I'll bring in my wines."

She brightened up immediately. "We'll do that."

I looked at my watch. Five o'clock. "See you at seven thirty then?"

"Going for another walk?"

"Yes, I love walking."

"I've noticed."

"Would you like to come along?"

"Maybe the next time," she said, smiling at me.

"Yes," I replied, somewhat vaguely, knowing that it would never happen.

Clifden
30/09/05

Dear Journal ~
I went into the little Gothic Chapel at Kylemore today to look for guidance from God.
It was so peaceful ~ I asked his forgiveness for scorning Sinéad and for alarming my family with my selfish departure. I asked him to help them understand. I asked him to help David's son Jason, help him to find his father or to find a peace in not finding him. My resentment of David still burns bright – I'm just not ready to forgive, I suppose. I've grieved and mourned the loss of our marriage, but it's not the same as it is for Eunice, Gloria or even Vera, I suppose. It's so easy to hold on to your resentments when the 'other person' is alive ~ you live in the hope that they will change. Ernest and Pete can't do that now. There's me talking about loss, but I haven't decided yet, have I? He might not even want me back if I leave it too long. I'm going to the Aran Islands with Murdoch Goodman tomorrow. I'm looking forward to it ~ he's nice but . . .
Bye for now,
Hannah

I checked my missed calls and messages on my mobile. Nothing, apart from a message from Murdoch saying that he'd pick me up at nine thirty in the morning. And to pack a spare set of clothes. When the heavens spill around Aran, you can be converted to a drowned rat in a jiffy. Like standing under a waterfall and all that. I'd thought there'd be something from Lily or Alison and I felt disappointed. Nothing from David. His threat to call the Gardaí was merely him discharging his responsibility . . . My return call expunged his concern completely . . . did what you told me, he would say, left you alone.

A nice crowd were gathered in the dining room at Vera's house. It seated about twenty, I guessed. Gloria came stumbling in with her musical instruments in tow. Vera looked on in surprise and amusement. "God, Gloria, I'll have to consider a cover charge on our guests. We can't afford you," she said.

"Do you need any help in the kitchen, Vera?" I asked.

"Thanks, Hannah, I could do with a hand. Come in with me and I'll see what we can do. This will be the end of the summer rush, this week. I love the company but I can't say I'm sorry. I'll be seventy by the time next summer comes around and it's not getting any easier. Perhaps you could spoon out the starters from that pot for me and then carve up the roast lamb."

"What's this dish, Vera," I asked as I spooned out a peculiar-looking mixture into ramekin pots.

"It's an Italian dish – *cotechino*, that's boiled sausage in our language, with lentils. An Italian couple that come here during the summer brought it to me. They say that traditional Italians kick-start their New Year celebrations with this dish to remind them of their humble origins. It's served with crusty ciabatta bread – that's out on the tables. Imagine, coming all the way to Connemara to be served up Italian food! At least the lamb is from the area, free-range, organic and reared by my own son!"

"And I see you're finishing off with bread and butter pudding, my favourite! You can't get more Irish than that. Just as well I did the Sky Road twice today."

"Did Gloria tell you that this would most likely be her last summer to come over? She was in with me earlier on. It hasn't worked for her this year. She has been very depressed. Connemara is a beautiful place but you really need someone to share the beauty with – that is unless you're a writer or a poet or something. It's just so lonely for a person on their own like her."

During the meal, I mulled over Vera's remarks and felt old doubts and fears creeping in. I knew I would never be able to look at David in the same light again but I remembered Eunice's words: "*You chose each other, just as I chose Ernest.*" If I had been firmer with him, his naturally self-centred attitudes might not have solidified into irreversible character traits. Wasn't it Alison who had said something like that? That I had allowed David to become dominant, allowed myself to be overlooked?

I looked round the tables at Vera's guests. Setting Gloria and me aside, they were all couples and cosmopolitan at that. America, New Zealand, Germany, Austria and South Africa were all represented at the table, drawn together by the beauty of Ireland's west, Vera's wholesome cooking and a simple need to spend some quality time with each other.

Eunice had remained in bed for the evening. "She gets so tired these days," Vera explained.

The dishes were cleared and it wasn't long before Gloria was playing her tunes on her oboe and tin whistle to a captive audience: "The Lonesome Boatman", "The Belfast Child". Vera had made Irish coffees and a tipsy American man sang "Danny Boy" to polite but muted applause. Knows the words, I thought, but an Irish accent would come in handy.

My mobile rang suddenly. Murdoch.

"Hi, Hannah, just rang to ask you if we should go by boat or plane tomorrow? The boat trip is forty minutes – the plane gets there in under ten."

"Ah, I'd go for the boat – sure we've all day, haven't we?"

"Okay, see you tomorrow then."

Chapter Forty-Two

"Hello," said Gloria as I left my caravan. "Going for the morning walk?"

"Yes, I'm going away for the day and I want to get it out of the way."

"Come over and have a cuppa with me," she invited.

"Would you mind if I went for a walk first?"

She looked so disappointed. "I'll read your tea leaves," she said brightly.

I zipped up my rain jacket. "After my walk."

She waved a hand. "Very well, then," she said and shook her head in resignation.

The ache inside was growing – I too was lonely, just like Gloria. We should be spending this time together, I knew that. I followed the familiar trail. I knew it so well now. Quite suddenly, I turned back.

Gloria was still standing outside her caravan.

"Gloria, I'm sorry. I'll have that cup of tea. I can always walk some other time."

Her warm smile told me I had made the right decision.

Over tea she told me, "I've decided to go back to London tomorrow, Hannah. I haven't been well. I phoned my children last night and we agreed it was best I move on to the next stage. God is moving me on anyway . . . It's time to go."

"Oh, I'm sorry, Gloria, I didn't know . . . you're not . . ." A lump in my throat prevented the words from emerging.

She laughed. "No, I don't mean like that at all! I've been coming here for the past three years, living Pete's dream. It's not my dream, though, and it's time for me to go. I thought I could hold on to a part of him by coming here but the part I need is not coming back. Took me all this time to acknowledge it . . . I've been a fool."

"I wouldn't say you're a fool, Gloria."

"Oh, I am that, Hannah. The cards, the tea leaves, the alternative dress . . . all of that was a creation . . . felt I needed to invent some mystique . . . an aura in order to fit in, only to find that I need to go back to being me if I'm to have any chance."

"And you will, Gloria, you will," I said, hugging her closely so she couldn't see my tears. "Hey, listen, you promised to show me photos and you never got round to doing it. I'll boil up again and you get them out."

We spent the early morning looking over her albums – photos of family occasions, work, and holidays. Gloria had cast away her mask and I realised that the Gloria I knew until this moment was "in character" – just trying to belong somewhere. "London Gloria" was clearly one fashion-conscious woman, the high-pixel camera highlighting her designer outfits and use of cosmetics.

I overheard a car pulling up. That will be Murdoch, I thought.

"Thanks for coming back this morning, Hannah," said Gloria. "I needed that. I'm going up to Knock this evening to be in time for my flight early tomorrow morning. I'll be gone by the time you get back. Roy and Tina will be meeting me at the other end."

At the door, we hugged tightly again. "I'll leave my address under your door. You never know, you might get time some day. Oh, and tell your friend over there that I'm not really the Wicked Witch."

I looked at her quizzically. "How . . .?"

"The winds, Hannah, the winds. They tend to carry . . . Goodbye."

* * *

I smiled at Murdoch as the ferry made its way to Inis Mór. We had driven to Rossakeal in Murdoch's Peugeot 405 and boarded the ferry.

The seas were fairly angry this morning but it didn't matter. Inside I was calm and that's what counted. I felt really glad that I had gone back to Gloria. The boat rocked to and fro, and occasionally I silently congratulated Murdoch on his wisdom in suggesting a second set of clothes as sea-spray washed over us. We laughed as nature hurled us first together and then, just as our eyes met, apart. I laughed as I tried to balance myself upright, looking at Murdoch through damp, windswept hair.

"What now, Captain," I asked when we landed, as I gazed up enquiringly at this man-mountain. I'm a full foot smaller,

I thought, despite coming in at a respectable five foot five.

"Do you feel like eating something?"

"Absolutely, I'm famished. I wonder would you get seafood chowder at this early hour?"

"We can certainly try," said Murdoch, pointing towards Ostán Oileann Arainn, the Aran Islands Hotel.

Soon we were sitting at a cosy open fire with massive main-course bowls of fish stew and a variety of fresh baked breads. "You'll need it all where you're going," said the rotund barman, amused at my amazed look at the gigantic portions.

"And where's that?"

"Aren't you doing the Cill Rónáin walk – at least that's what Murdoch said. I bet you'll want to be fed again by the time you get back."

"I see the staff are familiar with you," I said teasingly when Murdoch came back. "Is this where you relax with your lady friends?"

"Oh – Muiris? There was a time he used to dread seeing me coming. The hotel wasn't there then, but Muiris was running a smaller place. I used to come out here and booze it up for days at a time – I was usually mourning a loss or avoiding paying my gambling debts – it wouldn't be a win for sure, as in that case, I'd be staying on the mainland to keep in touch with the bookies. Muiris once tried to get me barred off the ferry. That way he could avoid having to deal with me."

"Your fiancée, Murdoch . . . no, you don't have to tell me . . . I'm just nosey."

"Claudia. She was the daughter of Dutch people who came over here a long time ago. She had invested a considerable sum of money in the pharmacy too. She went

287

back to Holland. I've tried to contact her on occasion, primarily to pay her money back. Never got to, though . . ."

"Is that the only reason you want to see her, Murdoch?"

"Do you know, I honestly don't know. She drank too, and it sometimes comes back to Leenaun that she's still ploughing away at it. It wouldn't be wise for me but I would like to see her one more time, just to bring closure. We never said goodbye – too much anger floating around at the time."

"And – prison?" I asked haltingly.

"I didn't like being there. Not because of the place itself, but because of the stigma it carries outside. Some people can be so cruel. There's people who have been falling around drunk in Leenaun for the past forty years who still shout at me across the road: 'Are you coming in for a 7-UP, jailbird?' You learn to live with it, though."

Glowing warmly inside from my fish stew, I set off with Murdoch on the Cill Rónáin Walk. Twelve kilometres, he said, as if it was running out to the shop next door to buy a loaf. We walked in near silence, Murdoch pausing occasionally to point out churches and forts and answer my questions. I found it hard to keep pace with his giant strides and interlinked our arms to slow him down a bit.

Four hours later, we were back in Ostán Oileann Arainn, reading menus.

The ferry bobbled a little more gently over the waves on the way back and I looked out to the sea, wondering if life's pathway would bring me back this way again . . .

Climbing from the ferry onto the mainland, I became aware of the glowing sensations in my feet.

"God, Murdoch, my feet are red hot – I'll be in agony tomorrow."

"You don't need to be. There's no better place than

Connemara to get remedies, potions and lotions to wipe these pains away. We'll have to drop by at my house in Leenaun though."

"Anywhere to escape this pain."

"Have you seen the film *The Field*?" asked Murdoch as we approached the village.

"Yeah, Richard Harris . . . John Hurt. I liked it."

"It was shot mainly in Leenaun. If you look at it closely, you'll see me in it as an extra. It was back in 1989 and the pubs and restaurants cleaned up while it was on. I was thirty then and thought I'd always be thirty. After filming was over and the place quietened down, there was a hardcore of us who stayed in the pubs. Some of them are dead now. Well, here's my place. How are the feet?"

"Killing me," I said as I stepped gingerly from the car. "That's Killary Harbour over there . . . It's much nicer than the postcards . . . we must, oh, my poor feet!"

"We'll have you right in no time, don't worry."

Once inside, I removed my boots gingerly with Murdoch's help. He then went and brought a basin of hot water and some salts.

"Now, put your feet in there slowly . . . It will sting at first. I want to get some oils that'll help. I'll be back shortly. I'll just light up this fire before I go."

I winced as the salty water sent impulses into my feet but within minutes this changed to an occasional soothing tremor. The fire was glowing brightly by the time Murdoch came back with the oils.

"We'll give you a few more minutes with that," he said. "Then I can apply the oils. Would you like tea, coffee?"

"Coffee. Are you going to boil the water over the fire?"

"No, the electric kettle will have to do you for today.

That one is leaking."

My keen nose for fresh paint told me that the cottage had recently been repainted. All of the walls were a subdued white colour, in tune with the understated character of the cottage. The floors were a polished wood and were mostly covered by a deep-pile Persian rug that reached the fireplace.

"I'll take that water away now," Murdoch said. He removed the basin and then went down on his knees and started massaging my feet with oils. "Calming Balms" – that's what he called them and that's how they felt. His hands were strong, efficient and yet sensuous.

You shouldn't be here, Hannah Joyce, I mouthed silently to myself. Flashbacks to that sordid last night with David surfaced and my body ached to banish that terrible experience. I was so aware of this strong, powerful man in front of me, applying his gentle yet firm touch to my feet, and almost involuntarily my hands reached out to stroke his hair. I sensed him freeze for a moment and then our eyes met.

"Are you sure about this, Hannah?" he whispered softly.

"Yes, Murdoch, I am."

Taking me by the hands, he pulled me gently towards him until we were kissing, embracing. He moved as if to lift me up but I resisted.

"No, I want to do it beside the fire."

We slid down onto the fleecy rug. I felt his firm hands on my back, my breasts as he moved slowly downwards, unzipping my jeans as I fumbled awkwardly with his button-fly Levis. Eventually, with a little help, they lay discarded on the floor.

I whispered salaciously in his ear: "I now see what you

were hiding in the gym – can I call you Big Fella from here on?"

In the glow of the fire, Murdoch slowly slipped my panties over my hips and I wriggled out of them.

"You're driving me crazy," I whispered as he kissed my belly.

Murdoch was unhurried as he worked his hands all around my body while I yearned for that surge of manhood to enter me and banish the pain. Eventually the probing started, slowly, teasingly at first until I was wet with pleasure and anticipation. Suddenly, I was aware of the fullness inside me and I faced away from the fire and outwards to the night as Murdoch pushed powerfully from behind, grasping my breasts, my inner thighs, as my inhibitions dissolved under his rampant thrusts.

I exhaled coarsely aloud, "Yes, Murdoch, I am sure, absolutely sure, keep going . . . keep going . . ."

Afterwards we lay in embrace in front of the fire until its embers dimmed to a flicker. Wordlessly we proceeded to the bedroom and lay silently together in the dark until sleep took hold.

*　*　*

My nose started twitching as the smell of aromatic coffee beans wafted back and forward in front of my nose. Opening my eyes, I saw Murdoch in front of me, with two steaming mugs in his hands.

As we sipped away together, the silence was awkward until he spoke.

"Are your feet any better?"

"*All* of me feels better, Murdoch. It was nice."

"Only nice?" He looked apprehensive.

"Well, *very* nice . . . but I just feel a little embarrassed . . . I've never been with anyone else but David and I feel . . . oh, it's hard to put words on it, maybe shy, awkward . . ."

"Do you regret last night?" Now a faint note of tension had entered his voice.

"No, I don't regret it. I needed to *make love* again after my last experience with David . . . then there was no mutuality, no sharing . . . it was like he raped me. I *thought* it was mutual and shared . . . I *thought* it was love. But the sharing was only physical. There was no emotional sharing, no spiritual, no psychic sharing. I don't have any regrets about you but I'm just coming to terms with making love to a man outside of my marriage. I'm trying to find the right words to explain it to you . . ."

"Don't try for now, Hannah . . . We've shared a special day together and it's years since I've enjoyed myself so much . . . It's not just the sex."

"Deal . . . let's just both absorb what happened and see where it takes us."

Chapter Forty-Three

"Slow down," I said, gripping his arm fiercely.

"What is it?"

"That's Cormac's car up the road at the house, Murdoch – turn here, quick, and let me out. Jesus, what am I going to tell him?"

"I don't know . . . Your holdall is in the boot . . . I'll get it for you."

"No, don't you get out, I'll get it . . . I'll ring you, Christ, go . . ."

Sweating profusely, I opened the door of my caravan. Not here. That was his voice coming from the house. I went in to see him chatting with Eunice. He'd never have seen us from where he was sitting now.

Cormac looked up. "Well, if it isn't . . .?"

Eunice came to the rescue quite suddenly. "I'd love to make myself scarce right now, but I'm too old to go. Off you both go to the caravan now, where you can talk in private."

Once in the caravan, he embraced me in a warm hug.

"Great to see you, sis. We are all very worried about you."

"How did you find me, Cormac?"

"Well, I noticed that Timothy seemed far too carefree about it all. I kept working on him until he spilled it out. Don't blame him. I think he wants to see the thing sorted out anyway."

"I guess you think it's stupid?"

"Hey, it really doesn't matter what I think."

"No, it doesn't," I said, in agreement.

"What's happened to you?" he asked in interrogation mode.

I didn't respond. I would only be wasting my energy on him.

"David said you left a hostile message on his mobile telling him not to call you. What's going on between you two? Mammy, myself, your friends – nobody saw this coming." He paused for a moment, waiting for a reply.

I fidgeted nervously as I tried desperately to think up a plausible excuse. I just couldn't tell him about Jason and I was no longer convinced myself that Jason was the real reason for my leaving.

"Hannah, you can talk to me, I'm your brother."

I nodded. "I'm just tired of the hotel business."

Cormac looked at me in bewilderment. "So, do something about it," he suggested.

"I tried to *do* something about it," I retorted, "but David turned me down flat. Wouldn't even consider it."

He lolled back on my sofa. Dressed in a dark brown leather jacket and cords, hair gelled. He looked so well preserved I thought it was a shame he didn't age a little. He still had a boyish look about him. And those boyish good looks could only get him into more trouble. I couldn't say the same for Louise. Worry lines were etched in the corners of her eyes. As for Jasmine, sometimes I thought she acted like the adult in that house. Yet, there he was sitting on my sofa in this rented accommodation, preaching to me. This was what it had come to.

"Give up the job, do something else or do nothing," he said impassively.

"Exactly, but you're not listening. David won't buy into it, says he's not selling up and that's all there is to it."

Cormac sighed. "I think I'm getting the waters muddied here. I'm talking about *you* doing what *you* want. David loves the hotel, you know David. Take him away from the place and he's like a fish out of water. He'll never leave it."

"What makes you so sure that he wouldn't sell up . . . sometime?"

"Not a snowball's chance. I went to him last week about selling my share. He's been chasing me ever since, even in the middle of this crisis. No, you'd stand a better chance of getting him out of there in a wooden box, just like Frank Duignan."

I was reflecting on my brother's presence in Clifden. Cormac had never followed me anywhere – wouldn't even help search for me when I ran away from home for two days during my teenage years.

"Why did you do that, Cormac? Decide to sell your share?"

"I'm not sure. Perhaps I'm beginning to realise that I don't want to live in the shadow of the Castletown Arms any longer."

"It could be that . . . but I think it's more got to do with

Nadia Constantine and the *Evening Herald* story. You've come a long way to see me, Cormac – you're away from the prying eyes of the Criminal Assets Bureau and Superintendent Matthew Kennedy. Would you like to talk about Nadia and her friends?"

Cormac chuckled. "Talk? About what?"

"Oh, I don't know, like what happened to them for a start?"

"How would I know? I don't even know them. You've been reading too much of the nonsense, Hannah, and believing it."

"That's possible, but I think it might be something else. You see, the Cormac Duignan I know loves being a sleeping partner in the Castletown Arms – guaranteed income, investment growing all the time. Gets to swan round the bar, introduce himself as part-owner – enjoys the kick of getting up David Joyce's nose. And, then, suddenly he wants to throw it all away. Why did you come to see me, Cormac?"

I noticed his face beginning to redden, the shroud of nonchalant indifference beginning to fall away. He got up and started to pace up and down, scratching his head vigorously.

"Listen, maybe it's not a good idea that I came here. I should go. Everyone back in Castletown is worried about you. I just took on the responsibility for finding you and getting you back home."

"It's all so noble and chivalrous of you, Cormac, but you really don't give a toss whether I come back home or not, do you? You're here for something else and you really don't want to go, do you?"

"You're talking in riddles, Hannah – it must be the air up here or something. You should know that I was tailed here by the Gardaí, so they'll know that you're here too. They've been watching me ever since the *Evening Herald* article – you know David has inside contacts in the force. They'll have him tipped off in next to no time."

"Makes sense, but I don't care who knows I'm here any longer. I'll come back when I'm ready – or not, as the case may be. In the meantime, I want you to leave. Now get out, Cormac."

He clenched his fists tightly, the colour draining from his face completely. He slammed the door of the caravan on the way out. From the window, I saw him kicking the tyres of his car, the gravel on the road. He sat down on the cut-stone walls of Vera's extended cottage, head in hands. Eventually he was back at the caravan door.

"Okay, you win, I'll level with you."

"That's good. You'll feel better after clearing the air. Only thing, I always do my walk around now. Will you wait until I get back?" I was really prolonging his agony. Serves you right, brother, I thought.

He hesitated for a minute. "I'll join you . . . could be a better idea . . . these walls may have ears."

* * *

Afterwards in the caravan, we sat down to tea and leftover lamb sandwiches, courtesy of Vera. Cormac ate quietly for a while before turning to face me.

"You do know that Mammy is worried sick about you?"

"I hope you've been going to visit her."

Cormac made a face and left down an untouched cup of tea. "Yes, I take Jasmine along – she shields me from

Mammy's sharp tongue. You know I can never do anything right for Mammy. 'Your father' this and 'your father' that – she should start a petition to get the bastard canonised. One day when we were coming away Jasmine said to me that she thought Granny didn't like me much. Imagine my own daughter saying that!"

I sipped some tea and decided to say nothing. As always, he ended up talking about himself.

I was reflecting on what he had told me during our walk. A thought then occurred to me.

"I forgot to ask you, Cormac – just one thing that doesn't fit – what prompted Nadia to go to the newspapers?"

The silence that greeted this alerted me. I put my mug down. "Cormac. Out with it. Stick to the truth."

He had the grace not to make eye contact as he told me. "Revenge . . . on me. Nadia and I were sleeping together for the last twelve months. She wanted to quit the prostitution game, us to go away somewhere together. She even talked about starting a family with me. That was never going to happen."

I bit back a sarcastic reply. Cormac had already fallen a long way. I didn't need to add to his distress.

Then there was silence and I found myself staring out the window, watching the sun settle contentedly. It was drawing its breath, streaking the sky in hues of red. If only I could capture that.

"You have to come home with me, Hannah," he said, breaking into my thoughts.

"I don't want to go back – not right now anyway, Cormac. I'm here until next Monday at least. We'll have to see then."

Chapter Forty-Four

Clifden
Friday
02/10/04

Dear Journal ~
Me again. My week in Clifden is coming to an end. By Monday, I will be packing my bags, to face what future I'm not sure. So much has happened to me this week and I'm no nearer making any decisions, but that doesn't matter right now. What I have learned is that they will be my decisions and that I am free to make them whenever I want. I don't feel guilty about me and Murdoch at all right now ~ it seems uncomplicated ~ he wanted me and I wanted him, it was natural and it rescued me from regression towards my teenage fears and phobias. Murdoch, you wouldn't know what I'm talking about, but you passed the Alan Ladd test with honours. Thank you.

I feel all-powerful right now. This would definitely be a gold-star day for me, and you. Don't know where my stickers are gone, though.

Think, I know more about Nadia than Matthew Kennedy and his cronies and it's their job to know more than me. Cormac and I did the Sky Road walk and I got to hear the full story. I never mentioned that Declan Burke our solicitor rang me, tipped me off that Cormac was trying to close the sale of his share to David and the essential missing ingredient to it all was my signature. Take your time, Cormac, I told him. I'd love to get a feel for this Nadia, particularly after seeing her in the hotel lobby.

I can see now that the Herald *reporter did a very good job only to have his credibility scuppered by Nadia's disappearance. Without her, it became the invisible crime, no witnesses. It's a relief to hear that David paid Nadia off, better than bumped her off or involved our Timothy in it. The grip that the hotel has on him ~ even paying off a hooker so as to keep the negative spotlight away. Anyway, I'm glad it's David that's in the grip of it ~ not me, not any longer.*

I'm not angry with Cormac any more. It's true that he's locked in self-pity and justifies the Nadia escapade by pointing to the denial of his rightful inheritance. The childhood beatings, though ~ I knew they went on, but not that bad. I also know that what Cormac says about David is right: I'll always be second best to the business and I'm going to have to accept it and deal with it. There you go now, the Relate counsellor might say. Two big conflicts resolved by the inner self. Only way it works.

I'm going to do some more work on my painting with Eunice in the afternoon. Murdoch said he'd ring later. I wonder if ~ but we'll have to wait and see ~

Bye for now,

Hannah

Eunice was not able to come with me to the Sky Road that day.

"Chest infection," Vera explained. "I don't know how many times we've thought she was at the end over the past few years – but she keeps bouncing back. She has no fear of moving on. Sometimes she talks of her work being done – time to go and join Ernest, she says."

"I'll go in and see her for a minute, if you don't mind."

I sat in Eunice's dimly lit bedroom, watching her chest rise and fall under the blankets. Her eyes were closed and I swept strands of her white hair away from her eyes. I looked at the lines of her wizened face and tried to read what she might be thinking. I picked up a photo of Ernest and her on their wedding day, black and white – a stark contrast to the kaleidoscope of colours that rested in her soul, ready to emerge into reality once she sat with brush in hand. Her rosary beads, dangling loosely between her gnarled fingers, depicted her unquestioning trust in God. I was unaware of my own tears until her hand reached out from the bed to caress my cheek.

"No need for that, dear – I'm just a little weary right now. How did things go with Cormac?"

"We walked the Sky Road together, Eunice. We talked a lot. He's a complete rogue but I think I got to love him all over again – just like when we were children."

"I can remember that, and he loved you too." Her face broke into a smile. "I remember you both went missing one day . . . He was about six, I think, and he went off with you in the pram. Everybody was out looking for you until he appeared from nowhere carrying you in his arms. He was crying badly and couldn't explain what became of the pram. It was found nearly two miles away, all mangled like a car had hit it. He must have carried you all the way back."

"Eunice, I never knew . . . you've never told me that one before."

"Maybe there was never a right time, until now that is."

* * *

"Murdoch," I said, switching my brush to my left hand while using my shoulder to jam the mobile against my ear, "I'm trying to make progress on my painting. I'm hoping to give it to Mammy when I get back on Monday night."

"You really should have started on Killary Harbour, down here, Hannah – less detail, more beauty – well, I would be likely to say that, wouldn't I?" His voice dropped then a little, sort of subdued. "So, I hear you saying that you're going back home on Monday . . . back to the daily grind . . . and all that goes with it."

"Murdoch, it's not that I've decided anything, I haven't actually – but I want to get this right. There's twenty-one years involved." I giggled artificially, desperately trying to introduce a flippancy, a sort of devil-may-care tone, to counteract the emotions and butterflies heaving in my stomach. "It's only a short time ago when I had a near heart-attack at this stranger who got to see me in the nip . . . I'm glad I got to see you back, but I'm afraid of complicating it all, Murdoch – it's not about you, it's just me."

His voice became more urgent. "Come down and stay with me, Hannah, for the weekend – just these few days. I know you'll most likely go back to your family – but I mean, you'll be on your own up there, with Gloria gone."

"I'll drive down later on this evening – no promises,

though. I'm worried where this will all lead to. I don't want anybody getting hurt, especially me – that might be selfish but I need to look after me. "

The rains came quite suddenly, pelting hard like small hailstones on my face. Hurriedly, I packed up my stuff and made my way back. Vera was talking to a man at the gate – he was packing a small case into his car. I noticed her wiping her eyes with her handkerchief.

"It's Eunice, dear, she's fading – this is Doctor Moore. She won't go into hospital, though. Doctor Moore has given her some painkillers to help her through . . . All we can do is wait. Maybe she'll come up again like the last time."

I bit my lip hard, wondering if the days atop the Sky Road had been too harsh for her, sped things up, sort of.

Vera saw me looking despairingly at my still-wet oil painting on the car's back seat. "Don't you go thinking like that now. Poor Eunice would be long gone if trips round Connemara were bad for her. It's what kept her alive."

"You ring me, Vera, the minute you need any help. I don't want to intrude but I'm here to help – you just call me, you hear?"

* * *

"Murdoch, it's me, Hannah. Look, would it be alright if I came down now?"

"But of course . . . is everything okay? I'll come up and collect you – if you want, that is."

"No, I'll come down – I just don't want to be alone."

Chapter Forty-Five

I rested my head on Murdoch's bare torso as night descended over Killary Harbour. I'd brought my painting equipment with me – perhaps I would get a chance to test his bias towards his little piece of heaven. Maybe I'd do this one for Lily, a sort of peace offering – a reaffirmation of our friendship. For now, though, I was sharing his bed – my ears somewhat tickled by the fine downy hair of his chest. The embers of the fire spread a dim glowing light across the room.

"It's so much more personal than central heating, isn't it? It's just like the fireplace in the bedroom of my gran's old cottage in Tarmon. Shall I put more wood on, Murdoch?"

"Only if you plan on staying here for the rest of the night. What brought on the sudden change of heart?"

"I just didn't want to be alone this evening. I guess I wanted someone to take care of me. The little girl in Hannah is to the forefront at the minute."

"It can get very lonely here in the winter. The amount of bachelors you get retiring to the pubs once darkness sets in – I suppose you saw the difference with Gloria gone."

"I'd hardly have been likely to end up in bed with Gloria, though."

Suddenly, it had felt just right to retreat into Murdoch's lair, perhaps for the weekend. I didn't want to intrude too much on Eunice in her final days . . . She needed peace right now, to let Ernest know she was coming – give him time to get the place ready, she would say.

Murdoch accepted my presence without question although he knew there were no guarantees. He listened attentively as I went over my life with David, not interrupting or offering any advice as to what I should do come Monday or afterwards. I was gratified by the fulfilling yet unobtrusive way we were bonding. It seemed to me that we both understood that we shouldn't spoil our time by tainting these idyllic nights with vices like jealousy and possessiveness – only occasionally did my self-conscious side take over, warning me that I was merely in the company of a lecherous predator who pounced on the opportunity of "no strings" sexual trysts. But my conscious self felt Murdoch didn't fit that bill.

Slowly, the weekend evolved into daytime drives around Connemara with Murdoch and I got to discover his passion for photography.

"Best camera on the market," he boasted proudly, holding up a miniscule little gadget in the air. "Highest definition you can get right now – still cheaper than a wager on the three thirty at Leopardstown."

Over that Saturday and Sunday we near covered all the

mainland beauty spots of Connemara that repeatedly draw the tourists from home and abroad. Murdoch took several photographs at each place and I took notes as we went along. We let hunger dictate where we would eat, agreeing to stop where we saw the next sign once the pangs came. I was glad that he shared, or at least for this weekend pretended to share, my love of walking – I felt less guilty over the generous helpings of soups, steaks, fish platters and apple-pie that we consumed. Murdoch went away for a while on the Sunday evening and returned with all his photographs developed. Together we built a multi-pocketed folder of prints and notes.

"There you go now – you'll while away many a dark winter's evening painting from this gallery of notes and snapshots."

"Thank you, Murdoch. I'm not sure Eunice would approve but I have to compromise on the ideals. I'd say places like the Hill of Doon and Mannin Bay will be fairly grim come the depths of winter. My memories and these will hold me in good stead." I added jokingly: "I'll mention you in the acknowledgements at my next exhibition."

Murdoch lit both open fires in the house on that Sunday night and I sipped at Irish coffees while he made cups of cocoa.

"Don't you mind people drinking alcohol around you?" I asked.

"No, not at all. Like I said, it's not so much the drink that was the problem in the past but a few brandies invariably brought me to the bookie's door. No, I'm better off without them both."

I awoke later that night to find that Murdoch was not in the bed. Peering out through the window, I could see his giant shadow as he stood silently in the dark, staring out towards the harbour.

I went outside.

"What is it, Murdoch?" I asked, linking my arms around his waist. I'd wrapped an old tweed coat around my flimsy nightdress but the chill western winds still found their way through, tingling my skin, firming my breasts up until I felt a dull ache.

"Tomorrow, that's what, Hannah – nothing more than that. I've kept reminding myself that you don't belong to me, but it's been hard. I've pretty much kept to myself since I came out of prison and I thought it was going to continue that way. Come to think of it, that's the way it *is* continuing – you'll be off tomorrow and I'll be back to my normal routine."

I stood quietly in the face of the Atlantic breeze, not able to find any words that would reassure or encourage him. I felt frozen with fear at the thought of going home and at *not* going home. Almost involuntarily, I undid the belt of my coat and pressed myself in to Murdoch so he could feel my heartbeat, the stiff anticipation of my nipples in the penetrating wind.

"Come back to bed, Murdoch," I whispered. "We won't solve it out here. I want you beside me tonight – don't quit on me now."

Chapter Forty-Six

I had kept in touch with Vera over the weekend and now here I was back in her cottage, sitting opposite Eunice propped up in her armchair beside the range. "A bloody marvel, a complete miracle," was all that Vera could say. Most of the spark was back in Eunice's eyes as she told us of a dream she had last night.

"I was trying to work out why God wouldn't let me past the gates, wouldn't let me in to join Ernest. Then he told me that Ernest had found another woman . . ."

"You're joking us, lady, we're not that easily fooled," Vera interrupted. "Well, I'm off down to the village to get some essentials. You two will most likely have some catching up to do. It was great having you, Hannah – make sure you come back this way soon, best of luck."

It was time to say my goodbyes to Eunice and we hugged in silence. I let her go once I was sure there were no further tears that her keen eyes would spot.

"Thanks for everything, Eunice – the paintings, the company – I don't know what to say. I feel revitalised, still hurting but restored and optimistic, nonetheless. I would be a long way back were it not for you."

"You had to do it yourself, Hannah – don't go all modest on me now. How is your painting?"

"I've Clifden Harbour nearly complete, just needs touching up. I'm giving that one to Mammy. I've started on Killary Harbour – I'm hoping to complete that for Lily, a friend of mine at home."

"You're forgetting that I know Lily – she's the gardener, isn't she? I had her daughter Erin on my last summer school – I think she did a painting of her mother's garden."

She's moved on a little since then, I thought sardonically. I wonder if Timothy is still paying her attention or more than that? I must get him to put some direction and focus on his life when I get back.

My conscience suddenly whispered in my ear: "*Ever the preaching mother, Hannah! Cast not the first stone!*"

Eunice wafted in on my thoughts. "And what's the future for Hannah Duignan – I've tried not to ask but you're near going now. What's it to be?"

"I'm going back to talk to David: see can we salvage our marriage. I accept now that I played a big part in him taking me for granted. I married too young – that's not to say that I shouldn't have married David – there is a difference. With a little more experience, I would have seen it's a case of *one* love but *two* people – I saw us as one and let David become *the one*. I'm going to change myself, make decisions about *me* and the hotel not *us* and the hotel. I know now I'll never get him to sell the Castletown Arms – he lives and breathes the hotel business. Even his outside interests were all linked to pulling in more business for the hotel. The golf club, the restoration of the castle . . . you name it."

"And his first son – Jason, wasn't it – how will you cope with knowing about him?"

"Funny, I don't think about it as coping any more. There are parts of it that I don't like, the secrecy associated with the payments for Jason, but I can see why he might not want to tell me. I took some letters and things of David's when I was leaving and only got round to looking at them this morning. David *has* met with Jason. There were photos of them together. Not marked, of course – even if I had come across them he could have passed them off as photos of someone in the hotel trade or some young colleague he had met at a conference. But the likeness was unmistakeable to me."

"And you don't mind?"

"No, the opposite, actually. It showed that he cared enough to contact him. Until I saw the pictures, I had David firmly labelled as a man without a heart."

We hugged one last time and I promised Eunice that I would phone regularly, keep in touch, so to speak.

"Just you keep up your painting, Hannah Duignan. It will make bad days good and good days very good. Beats visits to the doctor any day."

* * *

I packed the last of my belongings into the Clio and left a thank-you note for Vera pinned to the fridge door.

I knew once I opened the caravan door she had left her

calling card – the smell of fresh baking assailed my nostrils. A warm batch of scones and a luscious sponge sandwich lay on the counter. I was tempted to call a meeting of the Coffee Triangle for the evening . . . but there were family matters to be sorted first and a painting to finish off for Lily.

My mobile rang just as I prepared to exit Vera's cottage driveway. Mammy – better take it, I thought, I've put her through enough.

"Hannah, dear, is that you? I've been worried about you. Cormac said you might be coming home today – I'm hoping that's true –"

"It's true all right, Mammy – I'm coming home today. I'm sorry for being so selfish but I was at the end of my tether. I feel so much better now – I'm coming home with a different outlook, looking forward, not backwards."

"You sound very good, dear. We're all looking forward to seeing you. You get on home, now. I won't delay you."

"Mammy, it could be Tuesday morning by the time I get around to see you. I need to talk with David and it will be evening by the time I get back anyway."

"That's fine, Hannah – only yesterday I didn't know when I'd get to see you again. Just one last thing – Jasmine sends her love. She took your going very badly, cried more than anyone – she keeps talking about an evening you took her to Athlone."

No reproach or recriminations from Mammy. Things were looking up already.

Chapter Forty-Seven

Castletown
Monday
05/10/04

Dear Journal ~
Well, here I am, right back where I started. I needed to come in here to the Coffee Dock to plant my feet firmly on the ground. You see, as soon as I came within ten minutes of Castletown, the panic attacks began ~ I almost turned back for Clifden, even Leenaun. I really feel bad about Murdoch ~ maybe some day he will understand that it's too hard for me to call time on my marriage. David is the father of my only child ~ I just cannot bring myself to turn my back on him and Timothy. Sammi too, although her life has moved on.

I stopped off in Galway to get something in Hanley's Man's Shop for my two men. I've rehearsed what I'll say to David over

and over – it's almost like I'm going on my first date all over
again. I'll tell him that I no longer want him to sell up the hotel
but I have a list for him that I want practised from here on.

I want: to be free to make my own choices for myself;
complete honesty between us; no secrets any more.
Bye for now,
Hannah

I sipped at my espresso. I was tempted to include a
demand that he love me but dismissed it as an absurd
impulse. It's also a matter for David if he wants to visit his
father more often or make his peace with Bessie Maloney. I
had whittled my list down from ten to two but I didn't
mind. It helped me see the difference between things I'd like
and things I was entitled to insist on.

Rhonda was hovering apologetically in the background.
"Hannah, can I get you anything else? We're about to shut
up."

I looked at my watch. Quarter past six. "God, I'm sorry,
Rhonda, you should be gone fifteen minutes back. I just lost
track of time – I'm on my way right now."

* * *

The foyer of the Castletown Arms was buzzing that
Monday evening as a tour bus of middle-aged to elderly
people checked in at reception. A Golden Oldies tour, I
presumed. David had opted, with a number of hotels, for
providing special packages for the off-peak days during the
autumn and winter months. They were advertised for the
"over fifty-fives" but nobody was checking – you weren't

asked to bring your birth certificate.

I smiled to myself as a memory of a new receptionist summoning David to reception surfaced.

Mr David Joyce to reception, please. Mr David Joyce to reception . . . That lady was doing it by the book – she wanted Joyce the Decision-Maker – something big was taking place and nobody else would do.

"What is it, Majella? I'm in the middle of a meeting – this had better be important."

"Don't look immediately now, Mr Joyce, he's looking this way – but the man in the biker's jacket over there – he came to reception with the booking form for the Golden Oldies offer completed. But there's no way he's a *day* over forty. The same goes for his partner – she's gone to the loo."

David had looked as if he was about to explode but harnessed himself into steely, controlled mode. "Yes, I can see you have a problem. I want you to get that torch beneath the counter and shine it on his hair. If you locate a grey one, let him in – God bless us, did anyone ever hear of the term 'your own initiative' around here? And have you forgotten the *reason* the Golden Oldies package exists? To *increase business.*"

I was grinning at this memory when I saw Timothy emerging from the dining room. I took a step backwards in surprise. This was a very different Timothy to the one I had left less than ten days back. Suited, with shirt and tie in place – hair cut short. I needed to watch this for a minute, I thought – I had texted him that I'd be calling in at seven subject to his dad not being there. A "coast is clear" message had come back immediately – Dad had taken some paperwork home.

Giselle spoke over the paging system: "*Could all those*

who are part of the Sussex 'Active Age' Group please go to the bar-room next to reception, please – Mr Timothy Joyce, hotel management, will be giving you a talk on what is in store for you during your next few days on our special promotion. Congratulations on your choice of the Castletown Arms for your holiday – we hope you enjoy your stay."

Timothy, now seated in a corner of the bar, was joined by Juliet Barnes, resplendent in a black suit and dazzlingly white blouse. I'd like to see that one beside Marguerite, my hairdresser, I thought – she might even shade her for height.

"Can I have your attention, please, ladies and gentlemen?" said Juliet. "We want to commence our welcoming reception – your voucher for a complementary drink is with your welcome pack. Mr Joyce will be giving you details of your tour itinerary."

A surge of motherly pride went through me as I watched Timothy win over the attention of his audience with his smooth but engaging approach. He's building an instant rapport with them, I thought. Nice one that, having Giles our master-chef at hand and the managers of the golf club, the castle, Jarlath who is a walking anthology of anything that's worth seeing and your Customer Liaison Officer, Giselle. Smart lady, that one – has adapted very quickly.

Suddenly, I was tapped on the shoulder from behind. It was Laura.

"Laura," I whispered, "what's going on here – I've not seen this done before – and Timothy taking the lead?"

Laura looks flustered, impatient. "Can we talk, Hannah? Maybe go to your office?"

"Okay, you go in there – I'll follow you immediately."

I took a quick detour into David's office and replaced the little bundle I took from his safe all those days back. Not the money of course . . . just the letters, the photos . . . it would be interesting to see if he mentioned meeting up with Jason . . . a test on one of my two conditions, so to speak.

"Now, Laura, fill me in on what's going on. Don't leave anything out."

"You can be sure I won't! Hannah, I've been here for eleven years through thick and thin and your husband goes and gives a promotion to Giselle, invents a new title for her. She's only been here six weeks – it's not fair!" She was blinking back the tears.

Here we go again, I thought – I've only just crossed the hotel threshold and I'm sucked right back into the politics all over again. Haven't even got to see my husband yet.

"Could you start at the beginning, Laura? I'm finding all of this hard to follow."

Laura wiped her eyes with a tissue. "David, Mr Joyce, called a staff meeting last Monday. The gist of it was that he wanted change at the hotel, improvement. We were going to bounce back from the recent bad publicity and he was putting together a new structure to make it happen. Your son, Timothy, Juliet 'Giraffe' Barnes and Giselle – 'who has won this promotion in record time, owing to her exceptional communications skills' – those were his words. I feel so humiliated, in front of the staff and all."

I bit my lip on giving Laura any commitment that I would take up the battle on her behalf. Here I was, back five minutes and already at risk of breaking my own rule – don't get involved again, Hannah, give it a wide berth.

Laura departed for home and I sat back in my chair to digest events. David only got to know of my disappearance on Sunday evening and he had "life goes on" arrangements in place by the following day. Hannah airbrushed into the hotel's history. No hall-of-fame award to go with it, though – only the future mattered to David Joyce. I heard muffled voices in the adjoining office. The sharp voice of Juliet Barnes.

"We need to get rid of Laura Jennings, Timothy. Get it done without risking action against the hotel – make it impossible for her, force her to resign. She's a bad influence – we can't afford to have customers seeing her pouting, hostile face first thing when they come in the door."

"You're right – do you think we might send her on the customer services course? She wouldn't have got it. Dad only put it in place here a few years ago."

"She's got to go – she's got the wrong attitude. I wouldn't waste money on her."

"But would that not leave us open to accusations of discrimination? I mean, if we're giving this training to new staff?"

"We'd pass that one easily, Timothy. Laura was treated the same as her fellow employees when she started working here – none of them got formal training then. Our hotel management course addressed that. Experience should have brought her to at least the same competence level as Giselle. We've got to let her go."

"Okay . . . Mum is coming in later on . . . I'll talk to her about it. Laura and her go back a long way."

"Your mother is no longer involved, Timothy. Didn't your father tell us that? She can console her over tea and biscuits out at your house, if she wants. You need to become a decision-maker and fast if David's idea of us being the future of the hotel is to work. Now, I'm off for the evening – you'll be collecting me at eight for basketball training."

"Mum!" Timothy exclaimed, seeing me at the office

door. "Eh, come in, have you met Juliet, she's our new –"

"I know who Juliet is, Timothy, but we haven't met," I said as she matched my frosty stare. Unswerving eyes, I noticed, as she stood beside Timothy facing me. I looked down towards her feet – flat shoes, slightly taller than my boy. Would have made a fortune as a model . . . if it weren't for *that* nose.

"I'm pleased to meet you, Mrs Joyce." Her eyes never wavered – not the slightest bit of blushing even though she surely knew I'd overheard her remarks. This lady combined her height and eyes to convey an aura that she came from a superior gene pool, raw intimidation oozing from every pore. Could it be insecurity, a defence mechanism to combat a phobia about her towering elevation?

"Could I speak alone with my son, please, Miss Barnes."

"Of course, I'll meet up with you later, Timothy." She walked past, brushing nonchalantly against my son as she left. She turned at the door. "Oh, Mrs Joyce, I've moved into the house behind the hotel. There was some stuff belonging to you there. Clothes mainly. I've sent them out in boxes to your house with Dennis the porter. Some of them looked quite dated, fashion-wise. Like they'd been hanging in the wardrobe for years. I was tempted to throw them out but I felt I should consult with you first."

"Thank you, Miss Barnes," I replied stiffly, recalling my father's wisdom: *If there's anything worse than an auld bitch, it's a young bitch.*

"I'm not letting you go just yet," I whispered, clutching Timothy tight to my chest then holding him backwards at a tilt. "Look at you, I go away for a week and you reinvent yourself completely. Are you reading the *Financial Times* to go along with this new look?"

"Stop your slagging, Mum – I'll still let you wash my jeans and T-shirts – let me fill you in on all the changes . . ."

I waved a hand. "No need, Laura has done all that. I want to know how you feel about all of it. I can't get over you looking like this."

"Excited, maybe even elated by it all. Juliet hit on Dad once he'd put the new arrangements in place. He handed her over two grand without a word of protest. She took me up – well, I took her up in Dad's Mercedes to Galvin's in Tullamore. Spent the lot on suits, shirts and ties for me. She's a real dominatrix for sure."

Suddenly, the thought of Timothy and Erin together became appealing. Maybe even Lily would take to him with his new image. The thought of this dominatrix casting her giant shadow over my home, my life, would surely test my new credo of "live and let live". The only person I could think of that could look downwards at her was Murdoch and not by much.

"Are you seeing Erin at all these days?"

"No, you were right about her, Mum – she's not doing anything with her life. Working in a sandwich bar in Dublin."

"Don't lose the run of yourself, Timothy, with all this new power. You were unemployed, didn't even have a job a very short time ago. Oh, I brought you something from Galway – had I known that you'd undergone a style transformation, I might have got you something different. Here."

"They're lovely, Mum. Thirty-four leg – spot on – no alterations needed. Ralph Lauren and all and a polo shirt to go with it. I'll put them on now. I'm going into Athlone to play basketball tonight. Thank you."

We hugged and I departed for home to meet my husband.

Chapter Forty-Eight

I turned the key in the house door. Back at Cedar Woods – my journey come full circle. Looks like someone is putting an effort in, I thought, noting the fresh flowers and the background music. David was in the kitchen, the table set. My Neff oven was obviously in full flow, a fusion of aromas wafting across the kitchen.

Our eyes met and soon we were locked in a tight embrace.

David kissed my forehead lightly. "Welcome home, Hannah – I've missed you. I've run a bath for you – food will be ready when you come down."

"How did you know that I was coming, even down to the minute?"

"I was being kept in touch over the last day or so. Timothy rang on – said you were on your way out." His hand glanced across my cheek as I walked past.

I was glad that he'd suggested the bath. This was building up to a romantic situation and I needed to ease out the aches of a four-hour journey back home. Plus, I'd said my goodbyes to Murdoch earlier that morning. I switched on the whirlpool option and let the hot soapy water go to work on cleansing body and soul – the memories would have to wait a little longer to fade until they became less significant, perhaps put into perspective by the renewal of faith and spirit that I craved so intensely.

I sat down at the table and looked agape at my starter. Tiger prawns with chilli sauce. David was smiling conspiratorially. "I thought I'd start by trying to repair the damage done the last night we spent together. When I mentioned, by accident of course, to Giles what I was cooking for you, he remarked on our similar tastes . . . then went all quiet, said I'd heard him wrong."

I laughed heartily. "You can't get away with anything, can you?"

"No, you can't, Hannah – not in the long run, anyway. I don't know where to begin . . . Sorry seems hypocritical . . . It was a small lie to begin with but it grew and grew until I felt trapped – I was damned if I confessed and damned if I didn't."

"I'm not here to fight with you, David, I'm here to listen and talk. It was *never* a small lie – it was a big one – a denial of your son. You both have missed out on so much. It didn't have much to do with me to begin with but the deceit, the payments . . ."

David appeared to be struggling, at sea with his feelings. "It wasn't the money, though, it was Claire . . . She was my first love, I couldn't –"

"And you were *my* first love," I interrupted, my anger

beginning to rise.

"I couldn't, I just couldn't . . . risk . . . the car crash . . ." Tears started to fall on his face – he suddenly looked older, hunched by the weight of exposing his secrets, his frailties.

I was beside him now. "And I know, David, I know . . . but you decided, made choices. There are so many people hurt – Jason, Frances, Timothy and Sammi – me too – I need time to trust you all over again. I'm just not sure of what you thought you were risking by telling me. I had accepted Sammi without question and that wasn't easy – I was only twenty-one."

"I haven't told Timothy or Sammi yet, Hannah. I just don't know how to do it. I was afraid Timothy might get to know – I rushed through the new arrangements at the hotel, partly to let him see that he was my *real* first son. I just hope he'll see it that way."

"He doesn't need to know right now – he's not even twenty yet. It might add to the pressure of his new responsibilities, could set him trying too hard to measure up. You need to tell him sometime but maybe not right now."

We lapsed into silence for a while, fiddling with our food. He served the main course – Beef Wellington, of course – but his attempt at reliving the mood of that other evening was already doomed. Yet I felt a strange glow, a waft of certainty that if we pushed through the pain we'd come out better on the other side.

David resumed. "I met Jason and his two children, my grandchildren, earlier this year in Dublin. It wasn't easy. We've spoken on the phone a few times since – I'm trying to reach a peace with him, but it's an uneasy one." David faltered and swallowed before continuing. "He talked about Frances – she went on to have two more children by different men – being broken by her experience with me. I tried to say sorry for ruining her life – 'Don't worry, Dad,' he said, 'you just *shaped* out the outline for her, she did the rest.'"

I was beginning to discover a new Hannah, that my time walking the Sky Road, alone with my thoughts, had not been wasted. I was not going to let David feel sorry at *his* pain because he hurt people – he needed to see *their* pain. I broke in to tell David about my visit to Bessie Maloney and how callous he had been to her.

"Don't you see, David, that you have been keeping people at a distance your whole life? Even Sammi has to tiptoe around you, forced to lie to you – cannot visit her grandmother openly. Take your Dad – he's not near as bad as you make out. I went to see him. You could see his feelings, his hurt, and I bet the few times you go, you walk in and out of there without noticing. How do you think he feels watching you with your back to him, unable to put into words what he's feeling? Go down to see him, David – look into his eyes for once and then come back and tell me that you saw nothing. You won't be able to do it."

A further silence ensued. I cleared away our dinner plates and poured some coffee. I sat beside him again holding his hand, witnessing the fear, the vulnerability emerging. He looked vacantly at our hands for a while – then stirred himself again. "You know this Nadia Constantine thing? You remember you were asking me where I went that night. Well, I went to see her – one of Matthew Kennedy's men tipped me off where she was. I paid her off, got her out of the country. I wasn't involved with the rest of it – I had nightmares for days afterwards. All for the sake of the reputation of the good old Castletown Arms. I could've given myself a heart attack."

You've been hooked on the "poor boy made good cycle" for too long, David, I thought silently. Look at him now, the audience would chorus, spent all these years doing well for himself only to discover he has no self.

"Let's go to bed, David, I'm tired. It's been a long day."

Chapter Forty-Nine

I'd felt almost an electric tension between me and David in the kitchen that night. It wasn't that it was sexual – it was near violent, as if my anger was ready to explode at this man I had loved for so long, father to my only child and, warts and all, still the honey-pot that my affections were glued to. It was as if this sudden exposure of his fragility was feeding a powerful force within me, calling me to take charge, banish the demons that clouded our lives. I felt that I *needed* to take charge: this was not a night for soft lights and sentimentality – it was a time to exorcise my tensions and all of David's deceits and expunge the violent impulses coursing through my brain.

David stood wordlessly in our room as I pulled my top, my bra above my head and dropped my pants to the floor. I pushed him vigorously down on our bed, pulling roughly at his trouser flies until we were both naked, his manhood the subject of my mouth's and tongue's attention. I was in complete charge now, his hands pinned back as I adjusted our positions and thrust my womanhood down on his enlarged penis, both of us quickly bathed in intense sweat by the sheer physical nature of my approach. It was over quite quickly. David could not delay his release any longer as his most erogenous zones were subjected to a demented energy that needed to be sated.

I was glad that he could not see my tears in the enveloping darkness. This was the second man to ejaculate within me that day and a fierce urge drove me towards believing that taking my husband's fluids inwards would banish all other intrusions that had occurred. A state of monogamy restored – closure to the promiscuous career of Hannah Joyce.

"Tell me a little more about your *dream-team* at the hotel," I murmured in his ear. "Is this a sign of you handing over . . . maybe listening to what Hannah says?"

"Maybe. I don't want to quit, Hannah. I'll probably never be able to do that but I do need to make changes. I really don't need to know about every slice of toast that gets burned down there. You know that there was a group interested in building a super hotel complex, holiday homes and all overlooking the golf course . . . Well, I was thinking of putting in my proposal . . ."

"I don't think I want to hear this, David Joyce – you're taking your insatiable thirst off to another location . . ."

"No, hear me out. I wouldn't want anything that size – it's not needed and it would take trade from the Castletown. No, I'm talking about a smaller effort, say twenty bedrooms. It'd keep me ticking over, get to play a few rounds of golf – maybe we'd even get to take in these cities that you're always talking about – Barcelona, Biarritz . . ."

"And what would you do with the hotel?"

"Haven't we a new management team in there right now? Let's see how they get on over the coming months, years maybe. It could take at least two years to get the golf course thing up and running."

"Yeah, but what if Timothy finds a partner, gets married – that will leave *Miss Barnes* on the outside."

"What if *Miss Barnes* became *Mrs Joyce*," said David, mimicking my voice.

I sat up in the bed. "You're crazy – I'm beginning to think I'm in bed with my father – you've taken up matchmaking."

"I'm only joking – but I get the feeling they're casting glances each other's way already. When the stampede of affections start to grow, get out of the way, I'd say."

"But look at her, David! My Timothy, our Timothy wouldn't . . . she's . . ."

"Six foot two," David finished my sentence. "That's what she says. She looks more."

"But she's not Timothy's type . . . She's not even good looking . . . the nose!"

"Ah, but the legs, Hannah, what about the legs . . . if I was younger . . . ouch!"

"David . . . why did you keep the teddy bear . . . and the gun?"

"Eh, I don't know, really. I didn't have many friends growing up. I never looked for them and they never came looking for me. I kept my special toys as compensation, maybe, I don't know. The longer I kept them the harder it was to get rid of them. Do you not see Bugsy on your bedside locker? He's been waiting for you to come home."

I looked for his face in the darkness of our bedroom.

328

"That was some Pandora's Box, that case. Was that all of your secrets, David?"

"The lot, Hannah, it was all in there."

Chapter Fifty

Castletown
Tuesday
12/11/04

Dear Journal ~
I hope you'll forgive me for ignoring you lately. It's been several weeks since I came home and it's been hectic. I've had to remind my family and friends not to spoil me too much ~ I haven't been kept hostage for years like Brian Keenan, you know.

I completed the paintings for Mammy and Lily. They now hang proudly in their homes and I'm glad, proud of myself maybe.

Things are much better between David and me ~ would you believe he went with Sammi to see Bessie Maloney last week? He's making slow progress with Jason. He regrets going to

Dublin in the Mercedes to meet him ~ it got them off to a bad start ~ it was a goad to Jason who saw the contrast with his mother's impoverished life. He's completed the purchase of Cormac's share of the hotel. For now, we're all terribly civil to each other ~ it's as if something good has come out of it for everybody.

Cormac has put in a bid for a small pub in Athlone, just a stone's throw from the Garda Station. Trust him to rub it in right under the noses of Matthew Kennedy and his boys. He'll come a cropper some day, my brother.

Timothy, my only child, seems to be growing into his managerial role at the hotel. He's talking of buying his own car to go with the new clothes and all the responsibility. Beats seeing him with that statuesque giant, Juliet, in her car. Looks like they might be building up towards being "an item". Nothing I can do about it, so I'm not going to try. Does most of her office work in " the dungeon" these days, she does. Hasn't dared yet to remove my name from the door. If she does ~ I shouldn't care, should I? I'll let on I do, though ~ she needs keeping in check, does Ms Barnes.

Alan is due back from the States tomorrow – that should perk up Sammi a bit. She's gone a bit cool on me all over again ~ my fault for leaving her poor dad in the lurch, I suppose ~ she'll get over it.

Mammy is just Mammy ~ nothing much has changed for her, as stoic as ever. We all got together for family lunch at Cormac's last Sunday. Louise really put us all to shame ~ she cooked a fantastic meal and she has no Giles hidden in her closet.

Coffee Triangle is back in full swing ~ Lily is giving classes in gardening and flower arranging at the vocational school, says she's amazed at the number of men who are getting involved.

Maybe in time she'll get to walk some new man up the streets of Castletown.

Murdoch has stopped coming to the hotel. He's rung me a couple of times, not pleading or anything, but I know he's hurting alright. It's hard for him ~ I really hope he doesn't relapse but I had to move on, make decisions.

David has stepped up the pace on his attempt to build a small "exclusive hotel", as he calls it, at the golf course. He has Eddie and Vincent on board, as builder and architect ~ Vincent secretly, of course. The Guinness Triangle they are now named ~ that's my retaliation for David labelling our little housewives' club. All I can do is warn David about his association with Vincent ~ like Cormac he likes to live a little on the edge ~ in a different way, though.

Hannah is looking after herself pretty well these days, too. I've booked us ~ David and me, in case you were wondering – on a city-hopping trip at the end of the month. Five days, taking in Prague, Vienna and Budapest. I've managed to fade into the background at the hotel and I've set up a meeting, sort of interview, with the school principal at St Emer's about going back ~ that's not the right word ~ starting my teaching career. This morning at eleven I'm seeing her, so I'd better wrap up on our little chat. All the wasted time I've spent trying to get people around me to change ~ you get much better job satisfaction looking after yourself.

Bye for now,

Hannah

PS I haven't mentioned Alison ~ that's because I'm seeing her for coffee later.

Alison waved at me from her vantage point in the Coffee Dock. Her two-fingered salute to Rhonda yielded two frothing cappuccinos in no time.

"God, look at the style here," she remarks, surveying my new black blazer and beige trousers. "Are you trying to embarrass me, or what?"

"No, I had my interview with the new school principal this morning. Gosh, she's so young, twenty-five tops, I'd say. So many young career women around these days . . ." I pause to reflect on Juliet Barnes . . . I'll have to sit down with Timothy and ask him straight out. She needs no help in casting a giant physical shadow around the place . . . I'll have to let go of it, if that's what he wants.

"Tell me about you, Hannah. I didn't come here to hear about young women and their high-powered jobs."

I told her all about the interview.

"She's sending me on a course. 'Teacher Refresher Training' she called it – she was a little put off when she heard the length of time since I graduated from St Pat's. My results offset her concerns, though." I paused to sip on my cappuccino. "She reckons that she could have near full-time temporary work covering for absences and that. Asked me was I interested in working with special needs children. Have to complete the course first, though. Then we'll see."

"That's great. You're really getting yourself organised these days. You going away that time really made people sit up and take notice. It helped you take back control again, too."

"Indeed. Look, I can't delay too long. I'm going in to see Doctor Breslin this morning. I was in with him last week – he did some tests. I've been suffering from fatigue, no energy. Likely to be a reaction to recent events."

Alison waved a hand. "Off you go then, see you soon."

* * *

I sat silently facing Doctor Breslin in his surgery. His face faded into a blur before my eyes, re-emerged and then faded. There was, however, no fading to the chilling resonance of his words: it was as if they hung on a banner above his head.

"You're pregnant, Hannah."

I was about to suggest there must be a mistake but it seemed the wrong thing to say. After sixteen years, discounting the years I was on the pill after Timothy's birth. No congratulations to go with his announcement . . . must sense that it wouldn't be the right thing to say.

"Thank you, doctor," I mumbled, taking some notes from my purse.

* * *

I sat quietly towards the rear of the near deserted church in Castletown. An old lady rustled her way down the aisle, stuffing her rosary beads into her pocket. There was only one thing for it, I decided suddenly. God might give you the inspiration, but you needed to take the first big step alone.

"Hello, Mrs Joyce." Giselle's melodic voice wafted out over the phone. "David . . . I think he went up to the golf club . . . Let me ask somebody else here . . . Yes, that's where he is."

I arrived just in time to see David shaking hands with a short, obese man and then waving him off down the club driveway.

"Hannah, what brings you up? I was showing off our

plans for the new hotel. He seemed impressed. I left them in the committee room, need to bundle them up. There's a kettle in there. I'll boil up."

In the room, David returned his papers to a zipped leather folder. "Now, are you going to tell me what you came up here for? Must be something out of the ordinary – we don't get you up this way very often."

I could feel my whole body shaking, my lips quivering as I tried to form the words. You need to spit it out, Hannah, go on.

"We're expecting a baby, David – I'm pregnant."

Silence. David's mobile phone rang. He looked at me vacantly as if lost in some distant thought, eventually croaking hoarsely: "I need to take this call – I'll be back in a minute."

Ten minutes . . . fifteen maybe . . . I looked at my watch. Where have you gone, David? Hurry on back.

Suddenly, he was back in the room.

"Well, what do you think?" I said shakily. "After all these years, we're expecting a baby."

I found myself locked in his steely stare, the one he gave when he was about to vent his disapproval. "Come on, David, say something – I know it's a big shock but don't hold out on me . . ."

"It's not me that's holding out, Hannah – the baby you're carrying is not mine."

His words hit me like a jackhammer. "What? Who the fuck do you think is the father, David? Have you lost your marbles altogether?"

"I don't know who the father is but I know it's not me. It's not possible – I had a vasectomy fourteen years ago, after you came off the pill."

There seemed so little else to say – there was no arguing with fact. The icebox that was David Joyce had reincarnated itself with chilling immediacy. I could think of just one thing.

"But you said you had no more secrets . . ."

"I told you the truth. That all my secrets were in the case in the attic. You'll find the bill for the 'job' in the suitcase, that's if you want to go up to the attic again."

The cold, clinical logic of it!

"Now, Hannah, are you going to tell me what's going on?"

"You've been like this for all that time while I was hoping, hoping . . ."

Chapter Fifty-One

Castletown
Saturday
31/12/05

Dear Journal ~
  It's that time again, the end of the year when we look back together over the past twelve months, see how we got on. I was checking back on the early days recently, in your archives. Do you know, I wrote twelve pages on the day Timothy was born. Thought I needed to write down every detail then. I can't dally so long right now. Sorcha is sleeping but it won't last that long – she'll be bawling out her demands fairly soon. Sorcha is the big story of 2005. She's over six months old now. I know it's last year's stuff but you won't mind me repeating it ~ walking away from David on the golf course was the lowest point and I thought I'd seen it all. Look at me now, beautiful daughter in

tow, new house in town and my family come round to accepting things as they are ~ mainly down to Louise that is: she tore strips off anyone who dared slur my name. It's strange how Louise emerged as the "dark horse" of last year and is now one of my closest friends. She understood everything immediately, having fought so hard to unlock the barriers that delayed Jasmine's arrival on the scene. "Think of it," she said. "Me going to Dublin for all these treatments and that bastard leading you up the garden path all these years! We went to Cheaper by the Dozen II a few weeks back with Jasmine ~ think of it, you'd most likely be in the same boat as Steve Martin's wife with your hit record, only you had that bollocks firing blanks all these years!" She doesn't seem to mind that Cormac is working all hours in his new pub. "Let him at it," she said.

Sadly, the coming of little Sorcha in 2005 also saw Eunice's eventual passing. I got to see her six weeks before she passed away ~ she'll never know how much she helped me, or maybe she does. Timothy and Juliet came along with a present for Sorcha – she's okay really. I mean, there's every chance that Sorcha might reach her lofty height, what with her dad's genes and all that and I wouldn't want anyone laughing at her, would I?

David and I have not tied up all the loose ends yet but we have drafted up an agreement that will see me well off financially. Likes to pass himself off as generous ~ he had no option really unless he wanted to put all of his secrets into the public domain. Sammi has cooled a bit but it was always a seesaw situation with her. She could learn a little from Jasmine ~ she's eleven now and she spends all her free time wheeling "her little sister" around Castletown.

Looking back, I should have kept going the time I first walked out on David. Poor old Eunice was right, God rest her, it wasn't really about Jason. It was that brutal night back in Castletown when the fading lights of Bunbeg and Mauritius were finally extinguished. But all that's forgotten now and despair has converted to joy and new hopes.

Sorcha, Murdoch and me. A new flame burning.

Bye for now,

Hannah

PS I forgot to describe my daughter Sorcha. So I'm pasting in a photo of her on this page. Take good care of her.

Bye again,

Hannah

The End

Published by Poolbeg.com

It Started with a Wish

Kathy Rodgers

*'I AM CERTAIN SOMEBODY IS
TRYING TO CAUSE ME HARM'*

Sophia Jordan was a young woman with a future. She
lived in an upmarket apartment with the love of her life
Matt and enjoyed a sucessful career. Her life should have
been blissful, but then a series of sinister and unexplained
events led her to abandon career, love and home.

Foolishly believing that this relocation will protect her
from the ghosts of her past, she settles into her new life
and succumbs to the charms of a handsome stranger to
whom she can never belong.

Marianne Taylor is a woman with a past. This past
includes memories, photos, hatreds and obsessions. Her
days are absorbed in a review of this past and each revisit
strengthens her conviction that somebody needs to pay.

That 'somebody' is Sophia Jordan.

ISBN 1-84223-190-1

Published by Poolbeg.com

Afterglow

KATHY RODGERS

"I have to find her ... you've got to help me."

Once the cottage has been sold Ella thinks another unhappy chapter in her life has been closed. But she is wrong again.

Hidden in the attic, a dusty cardboard box containing a doll, a teddy and some old photographs poses new questions. And Ella has to find the answers. How could her mother, Betty, have lied to her? For years, her slurred words and unfinished sentences fuelled by alcohol had hinted that there were questions unanswered and secrets sealed away, never to be revealed...

But the little girl in the faded photograph has to be Ella's sister and that man has to be her real father.

Ella feels anger well up inside her. How could Betty have hidden the existence of her other daughter, Nina? Had Nina got on with her life and forgotten about them?

Ella cannot trust Betty. If she is to make sense of her life she will have to find her sister.

ISBN 1-84223-135-9

Published by Poolbeg.com

Misbehaving

KATHY RODGERS

"His voice opened up the past, making my heart race. A part of me longed to reach out and touch him, to see if he was real..."

Michelle's life is busy, ordinary busy. She has a job, a baby boy Jack and a husband Gary.

Five years ago, heartbroken, she fled from Sydney and her boyfriend Damien did nothing to stop her. Rescued from misery by Gary, she fell willingly into his reliable arms.

Now Damien has come back and expects to take up where he left off. As she looks into his devilish eyes, dormant feelings begin to resurface – a sense of excitement and danger fills her with new energy. Would a little *misbehaving* really ruin everything?

Only if she gets caught!

ISBN 1-84223-115-4

Direct to your home!

If you enjoyed this book why not visit our website:

www.poolbeg.com

and get another book delivered straight to your home or to a friend's home!

www.poolbeg.com

All orders are despatched within 24 hours.